W. G. Collingwood

The Life and Work of John Ruskin

W. G. Collingwood

The Life and Work of John Ruskin

ISBN/EAN: 9783337095406

Printed in Europe, USA, Canada, Australia, Japan

Cover: Foto ©Raphael Reischuk / pixelio.de

More available books at **www.hansebooks.com**

Ruskin

THE LIFE AND WORK OF JOHN RUSKIN BY W. G. COLLINGWOOD M.A. EDITOR OF "THE POEMS OF JOHN RUSKIN" ETC. WITH PORTRAITS AND OTHER ILLUSTRATIONS IN TWO VOLUMES VOL. I

Methuen & Co.
18 BURY STREET W.C.
LONDON
1893

TO

MRS. ARTHUR SEVERN,

WITH GRATITUDE FOR THE HELP

WHICH HAS BROUGHT THEM TO COMPLETION,

THESE MEMOIRS OF HER DISTINGUISHED COUSIN,

ARE INSCRIBED BY

THE AUTHOR.

PREFACE.

NO reader, I hope, will expect in this instance the usual apologies for writing a book on one who is yet among us. Mr. Ruskin has been public property, so to say, for more than half a century ; his thoughts have been common subjects of discussion, and his actions of criticism ; so that there need be no indiscretion in relating the true story of his life and work.

If excuse were wanted, I could point to his own confessions, and take shelter under the permission he has often accorded his friends, myself included, to print his letters and to pry into the details of his past. Already quite a literature has grown up about him, inviting the reader's interest, and then disappointing it with slightness of treatment. Few, even among the warmest admirers of his genius, seem to be fully aware of the circumstances of his development, the extent of his studies and occupations, and the breadth of his outlook upon the world. His autobiography has indeed given us a charming picture of his boyhood, in all its most intimate details ; but the readers of *Præterita* cannot help wishing to hear the sequel of

the story so untimely ended ; to trace the fortunes of that
precocious child throughout a career which they all know
to have been brilliant, though, from want of a connected
account, they cannot follow it, as they: would, from dawn
to meridian, and from noonday to evening light.

When it was proposed to me to write such an account,
I believed that previous study would make the task an
easy one. I had the privilege of long acquaintance with
Mr. Ruskin, and the advantage of having worked under
him, in different capacities, at different times, during some
twenty years, on most of the subjects which have occupied his attention since his call to Oxford. I had already
collected material enough for a volume, in order to write a
biographical outline published in 1889 under the editorship
of Mr. John Waugh of Bradford. I was compiling from
Mr. Ruskin's works an attempt at a review of his art-
philosophy, and retracing with care, in the manuscript
poems and other remains of his youth, the history he has
indicated, from his own point of view, in *Præterita.*

But to complete a biography much fuller information
was needed. All the materials at Brantwood were kindly
placed in my hands. Papers put aside for the continuation
of *Præterita* and *Dilecta* I did not think right to include,
in the hope that one day he might be able to finish his
own work. Of private letters I have made a sparing use,
for Mr. Ruskin has been an extraordinarily fertile correspondent ; there are already several collections of his letters
in print, and no doubt more will ultimately appear. A
" Life and Letters " worthy of the title would be altogether

too voluminous and one-sided,—quite a different kind of
work from that which is here attempted ; though a number
of samples of his style in correspondence, many of them
new, are given, with permission from his publisher, Mr.
George Allen. Of letters received by Mr. Ruskin, a few
specimens by Carlyle and Browning, with a distinct
biographical interest, are inserted.

To the information gained from these papers much has
been added from many sources. Among the older friends
of Mr. Ruskin who have contributed their reminiscences,
I would especially mention Miss Prout, the great artist's
daughter, whose recollections reach back to the early days
of Denmark Hill ; for later years, Mr. and Mrs. Arthur
Severn are the chief authorities, and they have given every
kind of assistance. Mrs. Arthur Severn took the trouble
to read the whole work in proof, correcting and adding
many points of importance. Mr. Arthur Severn kindly
sketched Mr. Ruskin's three homes purposely for this
work, choosing the most characteristic points of view. The
drawings by Mr. Ruskin, illustrating the development of
his artistic style, have been lent, with one exception, by
Mrs. Severn. The frontispiece is from a sketch by Mr.
Ruskin in her possession, of unique value and interest:
the original is a good likeness of a face whose most noteworthy expressions no artist or photographer has quite
succeeded in catching, and the plate is a triumph of
chromolithograph facsimile. To the same friend I owe
the four blocks of portraits by Northcote and Richmond, which have appeared in the *Magazine of Art* to

illustrate a notice of the " Portraits of John Ruskin," by
Mr. M. H. Spielmann.   Another portrait has been lent
by Mr. H. Jowett, Editor of *Hazell's Magazine*, from the
photograph which Mr. Ruskin has considered the best
likeness of himself.

The framework of chronology into which all the details
so discovered had to be fitted, and which is given in brief
abstract in the Appendices, was mainly compiled, with
infinite labour and wide research, by Mr. Sydney C.
Cockerell.   To his care and generosity I am indebted for
the confidence with which I have been able to treat the
course of the story ; and, while tacitly correcting errors
of date in previous publications, to assure the reader
that, whatever be the shortcomings of this work, its main
statements of fact are founded on the fullest attainable
evidence, most carefully sifted and weighed.

Together with all students of Ruskin, I must express
great obligations to my former collaborateur, the Editor
of *Arrows of the Chace, On the Old Road, Ruskiniana,*
etc., whose valuable work has paved the way to systematic
study of Mr. Ruskin's life and writings.   Another important source has been the great Bibliography now
in progress ; to its editors, Mr. T. J. Wise and Mr.
James P. Smart, jun., I owe not only private help, but
permission to abstract from their exhaustive work the
condensed bibliography which will be found in the
Appendices.

In the compilation of the Catalogue of Mr. Ruskin's
dated drawings, which is also a mere abridgment of fuller

information, I have again to acknowledge great help from
Mr. S. C. Cockerell, as well as the kindness of Lady Simon,
Mrs. Talbot, Mrs. W. H. Churchill, Miss and Mr. F.
Hilliard, Prof. C. H. Moore and Mr. Richard Norton of
Cambridge, U.S.A., Mr. A. Macdonald of Oxford, and
many others.

Lastly, I ought to apologise to some, whose names I
have taken the liberty of mentioning in connection with
Mr. .Ruskin's, without asking their leave.   Perhaps, however, the apology is due rather to those whose friendship
and services have been left unnoticed.   But they are begged
to remember that this book was not to be " The Life and
Friends of John Ruskin," nor his " Life and Times."   Its
limits are expressed by the title.   It is intended neither
as an apology nor as a criticism ; it records—too inadequately, too inefficiently, I know—but with warm regard
for its hero and earnest respect for truth, the story of
a noble life, and the main issues of a great man's work.

W. G. C.

LANEHEAD, CONISTON,
    October 21st, 1892.

CONTENTS OF VOL. I.

BOOK I.

THE BOY POET (1819—1842).

BOOK II.

THE ART CRITIC (1842—1860).

APPENDIX.

LIST OF ILLUSTRATIONS

VOL. I.

BOOK I.

THE BOY POET.

(1819—1842.)

> " Eat fern-seed
> And peer beside us, and report indeed
> If (your word) 'genius' dawned with throes and stings
> And the whole fiery catalogue, while springs,
> Summers and winters quietly came and went."
> *Sordello.*

VOL. I.

CHAPTER I.

THE RUSKIN FAMILY.

(1780—1819.)

"And still within our valleys here
  We hold the kindred-title dear,
  Even when, perchance, its far-fetched claim
To Southern ear sounds empty name ;
  For course of blood, our proverbs deem,
  Is warmer than the mountain-stream."
                                    Scott.

IF origin, if early training and habits of life, if tastes, and character, and associations, fix a man's nationality, then John Ruskin is a Scotsman. He was born in London, but his family was from Scotland. He was brought up in Surrey, but the friends and teachers, the standards and influences of his early life, were chiefly Scottish. The writers who directed him into the main lines of his thought and work, not so much because he chose them as leaders, as because he was naturally brought under the spell of their inspiration, were Scotsmen—from Sir W. Scott and Lord Lindsay and Principal Forbes to the master of his later studies of men and the means of life, Thomas Carlyle. The religious instinct so conspicuous in him is a heritage from Scotland ; so is his conscience and code of morality, part emotional, part logical, and often unlike an Englishman's in the points that satisfy it or shock it. The

combination of shrewd common sense and romantic sentiment ; the oscillation between levity and dignity, from
caustic jest to tender earnest ; the restlessness, the fervour,
the impetuosity,—all these are characteristics of a Scotsman
of parts, and highly developed in Ruskin.

There are many points on which his judgments are
totally different from any which we English should anticipate ; no doubt because he represents a racial character
which, to many of us, is practically alien. We who are
not his kinsfolk find ourselves studying him almost as we
would study a foreigner, the more interesting from his
unfamiliarity. And as no man is a prophet in his own
country, though he may find a few disciples there, it is
from Scotland that he has met with the severest opposition, the deepest disappointments of his life ; as well as
the best help and most devoted hero-worship.

The English world owes much to Scotland, in conduct of
war, and in enterprise of commerce and industry ; but still
more in literature. And above the rest, four names stand
preëminent : Burns and Scott ; Carlyle and Ruskin.

But there are Scots and Scots. Ruskin is not only
Scottish, but Jacobite. Although one of his great-grand-
fathers represented a Covenanting stock, the tradition of
loyalty to the Stuarts ran in his other kindred ; and a
tradition which meant so much, during a hundred years
of struggle and strife, could not fail to leave an impress on
the family character. It comes out in his tastes in literature, in his ideals of politics and society. That strange
Tory revolutionism of *Fors Clavigera*, at once monarchical
and democratic, loyal and radical, holding so close to established usage and yet so ideal in its aims ; the romanticism,
the altruistic self-abandonment, the readiness to rush in on

the weaker side with a passionate cry for poetical justice ;—
these mark him as inheriting a character uncommon among
us English, who like fair play, indeed, but leave the disputants to fight it out ; whose conservatism is law-abiding,
and whose reforms are nothing if not immediately practical.
It must be an old Scottish trait that comes out, too, in his
devotion to France and the French, in spite of a free
criticism of them ; an Englishman with his tastes would
have been more at home among the ancient Greeks, or the
modern Italians ; a Scot of the other party, like Carlyle,
loved the Germans.

There is not only the Scot and the Jacobite, but something of the Highland Celt, in Ruskin.

The origin of the family name is unknown. It was
commonly supposed to be simply a vulgar nickname—
Roughskin ; but every one who has looked into such affairs
knows how little the popular derivations are to be trusted ;
they are usually no more than blundering explanations of
things that have been forgotten. And in this case, if
Ruskin be Roughskin, how comes it that there is a family
of Rusken, with an "e," of earlier origin apparently, of
greater worldly standing and expansion ? to whom the
Ruskins claimed some kind of affinity ; whose arms, with a
difference, they assumed.

The question is trifling, except to those who are curious
about the race from which an interesting man has sprung.
It is certain that there once was a family of Rusking, the
patronymic for some Teutonic hero Rusk (or whatever the
form was) ; and they were Angles, for a branch of them left
their mark in the settlement in Lincolnshire with the
Anglian ending " ton,"—Ruskington. As the Angles also
colonised the Lowlands of Scotland, another line may have

preserved the name, curtailed by dropping the "g"; and with that genealogy, if it could be proved, Mr. Ruskin might be claimed by the admirers of the Anglo-Saxon genius as a Teuton. But this explanation, also, hardly gives the variant Rusken.

Both names are unusual; they do not figure in history; the family is not one of the great clans. The name seems to start up in the eighteenth century, as far as we are concerned, with a solitary Ruskin in Edinburgh, as if he were some immigrant known by the name of his place of origin : one of the many who drifted to the towns in that period seeking safety, or a field for labour; with clan-name either concealed through prudence, or too common to identify him. We find a kirk of Roskeen, near Invergordon, on the firth of Cromarty; a Gaelic name which, variously transliterated into the Sassenach, might give Rusken to an earlier immigrant, Ruskin to the later. About this dimly-seen person we only know that his son was famous for his handsome looks, and handed on to his children the deep-eyed earnestness and poetical countenance of the typical Highlander; and that his great-grandson has exemplified, like any chieftain or bard of romance, the distinguishing spirit of the Gael. For the ideals of John Ruskin are surely Celtic. Whether he comes from the clans of Ross, or from some obscurer and less traceable stock, he stands as the central figure among those artists and poets, writers and orators, whose inspiration we refer to survivals of Ossianic nature-worship, Fingalian heroism and Columban piety; he exemplifies the "recrudescence of the Celt."

But the exponent of a national ideal is rarely pure-bred; if for no other reason than this : to expound an ideal, one must be in touch with the actual; to introduce one party to another you must hold the hands of each. It is commonly remarked that notable men are of mixed race. And in this case the Celtic fire was fed with some west-country piety and tempered with an infusion of coolness from a sailor of the North Sea.

Ruskin of Edinburgh, the second known of the name, married, about 1780, Catherine Tweddale, daughter of the minister of Glenluce* in Wigtownshire, and born in the old abbey of St. Ninian. Her miniature shows a bright and animated brunette, run away with, at sixteen, by the handsome young husband. He was in the wine-trade in Edinburgh, and lived in the Old Town at the head of George Wynd, then a respectable neighbourhood. They belonged to the upper middle class, with cultivated tastes and comfortable surroundings, highly connected, and entertaining among others such a man as Dr. Thomas Brown, the professor of philosophy, a great light in his own day, and still conspicuous in the constellation of Scotch metaphysicians.

Their son, John James Ruskin (born May 10th, 1785), was sent to the famous High School of Edinburgh, under Dr. Adam, the most renowned of Scottish headmasters; and there he received the sound old-fashioned classical education. Before he was sixteen his sister Jessie was

* To a Catherine Tweddale, aunt or great-aunt of this man, the original " Solemn League and Covenant" had been delivered by Baillie of Jarviswood before his execution, about 1685. The document was sold at the sale of this Mr. Tweddale's library, at his death, when his children were yet young. His brother-in-law was the Dr. Adair who is seen in Benjamin West's picture, supporting General Wolfe at Quebec, and trying to stanch his blood. Robin Adair of the song was, they say, an ancestor. The Adairs of Gennoch, Rosses of Balsarrach, and Agnews of Lochnaw, from whom Mr. Ruskin is descended, were among the noblest families of the south. His detailed pedigree is thick with names of distinction in the army, navy and learned professions.

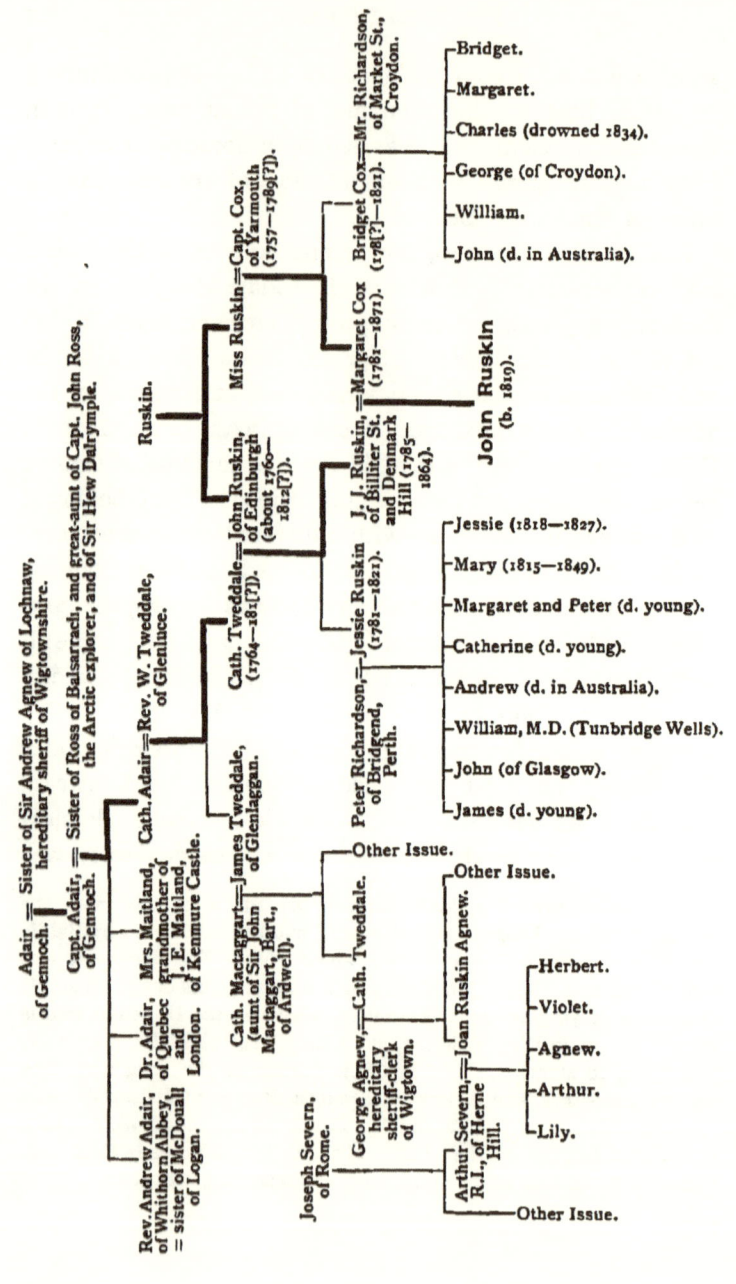

already married at Perth to Peter Richardson, a tanner, living at Bridge End by the Tay. And so his cousin Margaret Cox was sent for, to fill the vacant place.

She was a daughter of old Mr. Ruskin's sister, who had married a Captain Cox, sailing from Yarmouth for the herring fishery. He had died in 1789, or thereabouts, from the results of an accident while riding homewards to his family after one of his voyages; and his widow, with Scottish energy, maintained herself in comfort by keeping the old King's Head Inn at Croydon market-place, and brought up her two daughters with the best available education. The younger one married another Mr. Richardson, a baker at Croydon; so that by an odd coincidence there were two families of Richardsons, unconnected with one another except through their relationship to the Ruskins.

Margaret, the elder daughter, who came to keep house for her uncle in Edinburgh, was then nearly twenty years of age. She had been the model pupil at her Croydon day-school; tall and handsome, pious and practical, she was just the girl to become the confidante and adviser of her dark-eyed, active and romantic young cousin,—his guardian angel.

Some time before the beginning of 1807, John James, having finished his education at the High School, went out to seek his fortune in London. He was followed by a kind letter from Dr. Thomas Brown, who advised him to keep up his Latin and to study Political Economy; for the Professor looked upon him as a young man of unusual promise and power. During some two years he worked as a clerk in the house of Gordon, Murphy & Co., where he made friends and laid the foundation of his prosperity. For along with him at the office there was a Mr. Peter

Domecq, owner of the Spanish vineyards of Macharnudo, learning the commercial part of his business in London, the headquarters of the sherry trade.   He admired his fellow-clerk's capacity so much that, on setting up for himself, he offered the management of his London branch to John James Ruskin ; and not only that, but practically the headship of the firm, since the London agency was naturally the most important part of the concern.   And so they entered into partnership, about 1809, as Ruskin, Telford & Domecq ; Domecq contributing the sherry, Mr. Henry Telford the capital, and Ruskin the brains.

He returned home to Edinburgh on a visit, and arranged marriage with his cousin Margaret if she would wait for him until he was safely established ; and then he set to work at the responsibilities of creating a new business. It was a severer task than he had anticipated ; for in course of time his father's health and affairs both went wrong : he left Edinburgh and settled at Bower's Well, Perth ; ended unhappily, and left a load of debt behind him, which the son, sensitive to the family honour, undertook to pay before laying by a penny for himself.   It took nine years of assiduous labour and economy.   He worked the business entirely by himself.   The various departments that most men entrust to others he filled in person.   He managed the correspondence, he travelled for orders, he arranged the importation, he directed the growers out in Spain, and gradually built up a great business, paid off his father's creditors, and secured his own competence.

This was not done without sacrifice of health, which he never recovered ; nor without forming habits of over-anxiety and toilsome minuteness which lasted his life long. But his business cares were relieved by cultured tastes.

He loved art, and drew well in water-colours in the old style. He loved literature, and read aloud finely all the old standard authors, though he was not too old-fashioned to admire " Pickwick " and the " Noctes Ambrosianæ " when they appeared. He loved the scenery and archi-tecture among which he had travelled in Scotland and Spain ; but he could find interest in almost any place and any subject,—an alert man, in whom practical judgment was joined to a romantic temperament, strong feelings and opinions to extended sympathies. His portraits by Copley and Northcote give the idea of an expressive face, sensitive, refined, every feature a gentleman's.

So, after those nine years of work and waiting, he went to Perth to claim his cousin's hand. She was for further delay ; but with the minister's help he persuaded her one evening into a prompt marriage in the Scotch fashion, drove off with her next morning to Edinburgh, and on to the house he had prepared in London at 54, Hunter Street, Brunswick Square.

The heroine of this little drama was no ordinary bride. At Edinburgh she had found herself—though well brought up, for Croydon—inferior to the society of the Modern Athens. As the affianced of a man of ability she felt it her duty to make herself his match in mental culture, as she was already in her own department of practical matters. Under Dr. Brown's direction and stimulated by his notice, she soon became—not a blue-stocking—but well-read, well-informed above the average. She was one of those persons, too rarely met with, who set themselves a very high standard in every way, and resolve to drag both themselves and their neighbours up to it. But, as the process is difficult, so it is disappointing. People became rather shy of Mrs. Ruskin, and she of them, so that her life was solitary and her household quiet. It was not from any narrow Puritanism that she made so few friends ; her morality and her piety, strict as they were within their own lines, permitted her the enjoyments and amusements of life ; still less was there any cynicism or misanthropy. But she devoted herself to her husband and son : she was too proud to court those above her in worldly rank, and she was not easily approached except by people fully equal to her in strength of character, of whom there could never be many. And so the ordinary acquaintances got an unkindly view of her ; by the young especially she was, in her later years, feared rather than loved. But to the few who made their way to her friendship she was a true and valuable friend.

It is worth while thus briefly studying the parents, the sort of people from whom John Ruskin sprang : for it was not only in the unconscious heredity of race that they contributed to his character. No man was ever more carefully formed by deliberate training and prearranged education ; and few men have more conscientiously and effectually carried out their parents' plan. Most of our talented young people revolt from the parental regimen, and owe, or fancy they owe, everything to themselves. They set up to be intellectual Melchisedeks, " without father, without mother, without descent." They boast in being mentally " self-made " men and women, as if such spontaneous generation of genius were possible. The rest of mankind, the vast majority of virtuous respectabilities, accept the family tradition and walk in it, without either inquiry or restiveness : what was good enough for their parents is good enough for them. But in John Ruskin we see a son who accepted the parental direction—luckily for him, worthy of acceptance; he never came into violent collision with his Lares and Penates. Of course he always had his own view of things, his own character and individuality, from the first; undisguised interests and occupations beyond and beside the prescribed rule of home life; and naturally, in course of time, this graft of his own personality grew, and spread, and blossomed into a new variety of the species; but always on the parent stock. He built him the "more stately mansion" that the poet tells of, but without first dismantling the ancestral home.

And yet the gradual enlargement of his ideas and sphere of thought involved a gradual estrangement from his parents; much more painful than any sudden revolt, because then they would have known, so to speak, the worst, and some sort of reconciliation on a new basis would have been possible. As it was, they saw—or thought they saw, for they could not tell how it would end—their work being gradually undone, their cherished hopes frustrated, their intentions unfulfilled. And all their pride in his fame, and their confidence in his dutiful affection, could not hide the fact that, once launched on his life's true career, he had drifted away from their track, out of their sight, voyaging through strange seas of thought, alone.

CHAPTER II.

THE FATHER OF THE MAN.

(1819—1825.)

> " While yet a child, and long before his time,
>   Had he perceived the presence and the power
>   Of greatness."
>
> *Wordsworth.*

INTO this family John Ruskin was born, on the 8th of February, 1819.

It might be, if we had fuller information about the personages of history, that we could trace in all of them the influences of heredity and early training as distinctly and as completely as in his case. But the birth and breeding of most writers and artists are, in essential points, comparatively undetailed. We have anecdotes about them; we hear of their sudden appearance, their struggles, their adventures; but we cannot trace the development, step by step, of their genius. We see the result; but the process is like the growth of a Jonah's gourd, something that seems to have sprung up in the darkness, whence, or how, we can only surmise. And so, not the least interesting fact about this life is the circumstantiality with which its early part is known. We have not only the autobiography, but the recollections of friends, and, most important of all, the actual relics of the very time, in old letters and notebooks

14

and documents, by which the child's mental growth can be traced, year by year,—almost, in many periods, day by day.

We see what he owed to his parents. But there are three sources of any man's personality,—heredity, and training, and that private and particular individual character which, however explained, is present in him from the beginning and remains with him to the end, binding his days "each to each in natural piety." In John Ruskin this individuality was seen at an earlier stage than in most children, because it was more definite and influential; and it goes on rapidly but steadily developing, recurring continually to old lines, haunting accustomed scenes, asserting itself in one department after another of study and work; so that the story of his life cannot rightly be given in a set of *tableaux vivants*, a few strong situations; the whole interest of it lies in the gradual unfolding of a notable character, and in tracing from its germ a mind which, however we rate it, has assuredly been one of the great motive forces of the modern world.

We can chronicle no comet for his birth, as they do for some—not greater—men; but this year 1819 was prolific in characters of interest. We may remark that it was the year of our Queen Victoria; and among literary men three notables—Charles Kingsley, James Russell Lowell, and Walt Whitman. Mr. Ruskin, who has his mood of playing with the occult, believing at times, like so many, that "there is something in it," declares that Saturn presided at his birth: another way of saying that an unfortunate influence seems to have predominated over his life. Weak health, especially, has to be set off against a fair share of wealth; a certain ill luck in little things and personal aims against the supreme gift of genius. The violent reaction of a too sensitive nervous system discounts his keen capacity for enjoyment; and renown, public notice, has been much more trouble to him than it was ever worth.

But while his "line of luck"—so a student of palmistry declares—is broken, both at the head and at the heart, it is straight for his early years. His character showed itself fixed from an early age, but his destiny at first seemed to be a happy one. Few notable men have opened their career so fortunately, so brilliantly.

His mother "devoted him to God," and herself to him. There were no other children to create division of interests; there were no petty cares or sordid struggles for life and social standing-place. The whole of her was at his disposal; and the very strength and sincerity of her nature taught her to guard her own affection with a show of serene severity, which to gossips appeared almost too Spartan. There is a story told as against her, that when her baby cried to handle the bright tea-kettle, she forced the nurse to let him touch it; and dismissed him screaming. It seems that she did not consider her child as a toy, but as a trust; to be taught by experience, or when that failed, to be punished into obedience and into something like her own self-control. When he tumbled downstairs she whipped him that he might learn to be careful; and he certainly acquired an adroitness and presence of mind which have often surprised his companions in mountain-climbing. When he came in to dessert or played among the fruit-trees, she drew the line at one currant; and there are few men of his artistic and poetical sort who are less tempted to self-indulgence in anything. When an affectionate aunt sent him a gaudy Punch and Judy they were

JOHN RUSKIN, AT THE AGE OF THREE.

By James Northcote, R.A.—1822.

[Vol. I., p. 17.]

put away, and he was thrown on his own resources for amusement. Another child would have wept, perhaps, or screamed, to attract attention; but he invented games with his bunch of keys, his cart, and ball, and bricks; he discovered how interesting things are if you look at them enough—patterns on carpets, watercarts filling at the plug, any view from any window, at which he would stare till, as they put it, the eyes seemed coming out of his head. From this training came a habit of investigation, so that he could not pass a scene or a picture as most of us do, lightly and carelessly; he must always be studying it, brooding over it and thinking about its plan and purpose; which when written turned out to be the imaginative description we wonder at, the eloquence which we put vaguely down as a gift or a style, the analytic mind of Ruskin.

Though he was born in the thick of London he was not city bred. His love for landscape was not the result of a late discovery of it, and of an enthusiastic contrast of wild nature with streets and squares, as it has been in some cases. He was always acquainted with country life, and even mountains were familiar to his childhood. His first three summers were spent in lodgings in what was then rustic Hampstead or Dulwich; so early as his fourth summer he was taken to Scotland by sea to stay with his aunt Jessie, Mrs. Richardson of Perth. There he found cousins to play with, especially one little Jessie of nearly his own age; he found a river with deep swirling pools, that impressed him more than the sea; and he found the mountains. Coming home in the autumn he sat for his full-length portrait to James Northcote; and being asked what he would choose for background he replied, "Blue hills."

4ᵇ

Northcote had painted Mr. and Mrs. Ruskin, and, as they were fond of artistic company, remained their friend. A certain friendship, too, was struck up between the old Academician, then in his seventy-seventh year, the acknowledged cynic and satirist, and the little wise boy who asked shrewd questions and could sit still to be painted; who, moreover, had a face worth painting, not unlike the model from whom Northcote's master, the great Sir Joshua, had painted his famous cherubs. The painter asked him to come again and sit as the hero of a fancy picture, bought at the Academy by the flattered parents; relegated since to the outhouse at Brantwood. There is a grove; a flock of toy sheep; drapery in the grand style; a mahogany Satyr taking a thorn out of the little pink foot of a conventional nudity, poor caricatures of the Titianesque. But the head is an obvious portrait, and a happy one; far more like the real boy, so tradition says, than the generalised chubbiness of the commissioned picture.

In the next year (1823) they quitted the town for a suburban home. The spot they chose was in rural Dulwich; on Herne Hill, a long offshoot of the Surrey downs; low, and yet commanding green fields and trees and scattered houses in the foreground, with rich undulating country to the south, and looking across London toward Windsor and Harrow. It is all built up now; but their house (the present No. 28) must have been as secluded as any in a country village—the suburbs *were*, of course, once country villages—and as pleasant in its old-fashioned comfort. There are ample gardens front and rear, well stocked with fruit and flowers; quite an Eden for a little boy, and all the more that the fruit of it was forbidden. It was here that all his years of youth were spent. Here, under his

THE THORN IN THE FOOT.

By James Northcote, R.A.

[Vol. I., p. 18.]

parents' roof, he wrote his earlier works, as far as vol. i. of *Modern Painters.* To this house, as his own separate home, he returned for a period of his middle life; and in the same place, handed over to his adopted daughter, he still finds his own rooms ready when he cares to visit London.

So he was brought up almost as a country boy, though near enough to town to get the benefit of it, and far enough from the more exciting scenes of landscape nature to find them ever fresh when, summer after summer, he revisited the river scenery of the west or the mountains of the north. For by a neat arrangement, and one fortunate for the boy's education, his summer tours were continued yearly. Mr. John James Ruskin still travelled for the business, then greatly extending; Mr. Telford, the capitalist partner, meanwhile taking the vacant chair at the office and amiably lending his carriage for the journeys. There was room for two; so Mrs. Ruskin accompanied her husband, whose indifferent health would have given her constant anxiety during long separations. And the boy could easily be packed in, sitting on his little portmanteau and playing horses with his father's knees; the nurse riding on the dicky behind. They started usually after the great family anniversary, the father's birthday on May 10th, and journeyed by easy stages through the south of England, working up the west to the north, and then home by the east-central route, zigzagging from one provincial town to another, calling at the great country-seats, to leave no customer or possible customer unvisited; and in the intervais of business seeing all the sights of the places they passed through: colleges and churches, galleries and parks, ruins, castles, caves, lakes and mountains; and seeing them all, not listlessly, but with keen interest ; noting everything, inquiring for local information, looking up books of refer- ence, setting down the results, as if they had been meaning to write a guide-book and gazetteer of Great Britain : *they*, I say, did all this, for as soon as the boy could write he was only imitating his father in keeping his little journal of the tours ; so that all he learned stayed by him, and the habit of descriptive writing was formed.

We could follow out the tourists in detail, if it were worth while : in the chronology at the end of this work will be found enough to identify their whereabouts at different dates, which is sometimes useful in verifying letters and drawings.   But it must suffice here to notice the points of interest which influenced and impressed the boy's mind, and left a mark upon his work.

In 1823 they seem to have travelled only through the south and south-west : in 1824 they pushed north to the lakes ; stayed awhile at Keswick ; and while the father went about his business, the child was rambling with his nurse on Friar's Crag, among the steep rock and gnarled roots, which suggested, even at that age, the feelings ex- pressed in one of the notable passages in *Modern Painters.* Thence they went on to Scotland and revisited their rela- tives at Perth.   In 1825 they took a more extended tour, and spent a few weeks in Paris, partly for the festivities after the coronation of Charles X., partly, no doubt, for business conferences with Mr. Domecq, who had just been appointed wine-merchant to the King of Spain.   Thence they went to Brussels and the field of Waterloo, of greater interest than the sights of Paris to six-year-old John, who often during his boyhood celebrated the battle, and the heroes of the battle, in verse.

These excitements of travel alternated with the quietest homekeeping, employed in uneventful study, not stimulated by competition, nor sweetened by any of those educational sugarplums with which the modern child's path is so thickly strewn. And yet his lessons were followed with both steadiness and interest, for he had already begun his life's work, in the sense that his later writing and teaching are demonstrably continuous with his earliest interests and efforts. He has been laughed at for seeing in a copy of verses written at seven the germ of his Political Economy, and what not. But it is true that the expressions there used are expressions of the very same feeling and the same habits of thought that gradually developed into the theories he laid before the world ; they are the initial segments of lines which, drawn boldly out, are recognised as his own lines ; and even from these early indications we now, looking back, can see the man.

Before he was quite three he climbed up into a chair —the chair that all his friends have seen him sitting in of evenings—and preached. There is nothing so uncommon in that. Of Robert Browning, his neighbour and seven years older contemporary, the same tale is told. But while the incident that marks the baby Browning is the aside, *à propos* of a whimpering sister—" Pew-opener, remove that child," the baby Ruskin is seen in his sermon : " People, be dood. If you are dood, Dod will love you. If you are not dood, Dod will not love you. People, be dood." That was all ; but it shows that he never was exactly an Evangelical.

At the age of four he had begun to read and write, refusing to be taught in the orthodox way—this is so

accurately characteristic—by syllabic spelling and copy-
book pothooks. He preferred to find a method out for
himself, as he always did ; and he found out how to read
whole words at a time by the look of them, and to write
in vertical characters like bookprint, just as the latest
improved theories of education suggest. When once he
could read, thenceforward his mother gave him regular
morning lessons, in Bible-reading and in reciting the
Scotch paraphrases of the Psalms and other verse, which
for his good memory was an easy task. He made rhymes
before he could write them, of course.

At five he was a bookworm, and the books he read at
once fixed him in certain grooves of thought ; or rather,
say they were chosen as favourites from an especial interest
in their subjects, an interest which arose from his character
of mind, and displayed it. But with all this precocity he
was no milksop nor weakling. He was a bright, active
lad, full of fun and pranks, not without occasional companions, though solitary then at home, and kept precisely,
guarded from every danger. He was so little afraid of
animals—a great test of a child's nerves—that about this
time he must needs meddle with their fierce Newfoundland
dog, Lion, which bit him in the mouth and spoiled his
looks. Another time he showed some address in extri-
cating himself from the water-butt, a common child-trap.
He was not afraid of ghosts or thunder ; instead of that,
his early-developed landscape feeling showed itself in
dread of foxglove dells, and dark pools of water, as in
the popular Italian dream-presage ; in coiling roots of
trees—things that to the average fancy have no significance
whatever.

At six, he began to imitate the books he was reading,

to write books himself. He had found out how to *print*, as children do ; and it was his ambition to make real books, with title-pages and illustrations ; not only books, indeed, but series of volumes, a complete library of his whole works. About these there are two prophetic circumstances, the one pointing to his habit of bringing out a work not all at once, but in successive parts, at intervals perhaps of "olympiads," as he once said ; and the other, to his unfortunate tendency to find himself unable to complete his enterprises, to let one subject be crowded out by others, and to drop it in the forlorn hope of resuming it at the more convenient season which is so long in coming ; so that there is hardly a title of his which stands before a properly finished work. The *Seven Lamps* and *Stones of Venice* are indeed complete in themselves ; but *Modern Painters* was concluded in a hurry, quite inadequately ; *Fors* is a bundle of letters ; and so is *Time and Tide* ; other works are only collections of lectures or detached essays : of hardly any can it be said that it is carried out according to a studied programme.

The first of these sets was imitated in style from Miss Edgeworth : *Harry and Lucy Concluded, or Early Lessons,*—didactic he was from the beginning. It was to be in four volumes, uniform in red leather, with proper title, frontispiece and "copperplates"—"printed and composed by a little boy and also drawn." It was begun in 1826 and continued at intervals until 1829. It was all done laboriously in imitation of print ; and, to complete the illusion, contained a page of errata—a capital touch of infantile realism. This great work was of course never completed, though he laboured through three volumes ; but when he tired of it, he would turn his book upside down and begin at the other end with other matters ; so that the red books contain all sorts of notes on his minerals and travels, reports of sermons and miscellaneous information, besides their professed contents ; in this respect also being very like his later works.

The fact that much of his childish writing consisted of accounts of summer tours gave him practice in description, which is commonly thought to be his strong point. His drawings at first were made to illustrate his books ; and as a rule in after times when he sketched it was usually with the same object in view ; hence, not only his own style, but a tendency in all his criticism to look at pictures as illustrations—a tendency which was shaken off only in his later period.

For his travels he sometimes planned a skeleton journal beforehand, and noted in advance the chief sights, that nothing might be missed. After the journey he filled in his impressions : architecture, scenery, minerals and products, engineering and economy. His *Harry and Lucy* is mainly a dramatised account of tours ; himself being Harry, with an imaginary sister, studied from Jessie of Perth or Bridget of Croydon, for he had nobody then to act permanently in that capacity, as his cousin Mary did afterwards. The moralising mamma and literary papa represent his parents to the life. Beside the tours we read of white rabbits and silkworms, air-pumps and fireworks ; the scrapes of a savant in pinafores in quest of general information, from hydraulics, pneumatics, acoustics, electricity, astronomy, mineralogy, to boat-building, engineering and riddles. Much, of course, is ideal : as where Harry— anticipating, shall we say ? a later enterprise at Coniston, constructs a great mud globe, " and when his mamma and papa saw this, whenever they were at a loss for the situation of any country, they went to Harry's globe for satisfaction !"—or when he experimented with a well-appointed laboratory for the astonishment of Lucy.   But the description of a week at Hastings in the spring of 1826 is probably a bit of history, and told with lively artlessness.

There you have our author ready made, with his ever fresh interest in everything, and all-attempting eagerness. Out of which the first thing that crystallises into any definite shape is the verse-writing.

CHAPTER III.

PERFERVIDUM INGENIUM.

(1826—1830.)

"Après, en tel train d'estude le mist qu'il ne perdoit heures quelconques du jour : ainsi tout son temps consommoit en lettres."

Gargantua.

THE first dated "poem" was written a month before little John Ruskin reached the age of seven. It is a tale of a mouse, in seven octosyllabic couplets, "The Needless Alarm," remarkable only for an unexpected correctness in rhyme, rhythm, and reason.

His early verse, like his early prose, owes much to the summer tours ; it was from the practice they gave that he became a descriptive writer. The journey to Scotland of 1826 suggested two poems, of which one is really interesting for its sustained sequence of thought—the last thing you ask from a child. And the final stanza has a ring of wild imagery of the infinite, like Blake's best touches :—

> "The pole-star guides thee on thy way,
> When in dark nights thou art lost ;
> Therefore look up at the starry day,
> Look at the stars about thee tost."

But these are only the more complete bits among a quantity of fragments. These summer tours were prolific

26

in notes ; everything was observed and turned into verse. And the habit lasted ; and grew into the poetical journals of Ruskin's boyhood, and the ample diaries and notebooks of later years, which supplied the materials for his great works.

The other inspiring source during this period of versification was his father—the household deity of both wife and child, whose chief delight was in his daily return from the city, and in his reading to them in the drawing-room at Herne Hill. John was packed into a recess, where he was out of the way and the draught ; he was barricaded by a little table that held his own materials for amusement ; and if he liked to listen to the reading, he had the chance of hearing good literature ; the chance sometimes of hearing passages from Byron and Christopher North and Cervantes, rather beyond his comprehension ; for his parents were not of the shockable sort : with all their religion and strict Scotch morality they could laugh at a broad jest, as old-fashioned people could. And it did the child less harm to hear an occasional coarse expression among the sound judgments and great thoughts of fine literature, than it would have done to have been accustomed from the first to the namby-pamby and the shallow twaddle of the modern schoolroom shelf.

So he associated his father and his father's readings with the poetry of reflection, as he associated the regular summer round with the poetry of description ; the two manners were like two rivulets of verse flowing through his life ; occasionally intermingling, but in their main channels and directions kept distinct. As every summer brought its crop of description, so against the New Year (for being Scotch, they did not then keep our Christmas) and against his father's birthday in May, he used always to prepare some little drama or story or "address" of a reflective nature. The first of these, on "Time," written for New Year's Day, 1827, has perhaps received more notice than was needed.

In 1827 they were again at Perth; and on their way home, some early morning frost suggested the not ungraceful verses on the icicles at Glenfarg. By a childish misconception the little boy seems to have confused the real valley that interested him so, with Scott's ideal Glendearg; and, partly for that reason, to have taken a greater pleasure in "The Monastery"; which he thereupon undertook to paraphrase in verse. There remain some hundreds of doggrel rhymes; but his affection for that particular novel survived the fatal facility of his octosyllabics, and reappears time after time in his later writings. It is a little curious that Scott's immediate critics thought "The Monastery" a failure, while Ruskin, who has done more than any one to perpetuate the worship of Sir Walter, counts it his most characteristic work.

Next year, 1828, their tour was stopped at Plymouth by the unwelcome news of the death of his aunt Jessie, to whom they were on their way. It was hardly a year since the bright little cousin Jessie of Perth had died, of water on the brain. She had been John's especial pet and playfellow, clever like him, and precocious; and her death must have come to his parents as a warning, if they needed it, to keep their own child's brain from over-pressure. It is evident that they did their best to "keep him back"; they did not send him to school for fear of the excitement of competitive study. His mother put him through the Latin grammar herself, using the old Adam's manual which

his father had used at Edinburgh high school. She had
the secret of engaging his interest in her lessons, without
using any of those adventitious means which teachers nowadays recommend.   Even this old grammar became a sort
of sacred book to him ; and when at last he went to school,
and his English master threw the book back to him saying " That's a Scotch thing," the boy was shocked and
affronted, as which of us would be at a criticism on *our* first
instrument of torture ?   He remembered the incident all
his life, and pilloried the want of tact—it was no more—
with acerbity in his reminiscences.

They could keep him from school, but they did not keep
him from study. The year 1828 saw the beginning of
another great work—" Eudosia, a Poem on the Universe " ;
it was " printed " with even greater neatness and labour :
but this too, after being toiled at during the winter months,
was dropped in the middle of its second " book."   It was
not idleness that made him break off such plans, but just
the reverse—a too great activity of brain.   His parents
seem to have thought that there was no harm in this
desultory and apparently quiet reading and writing.   They
were extremely energetic themselves, and hated idleness.
They seem to have held a theory that their little boy
was all right as long as he was not obviously excited, and
to have thought that the proper way of giving children
pocket-money was to let them earn it.   So they used to
pay him for his literary labours,—" Homer " was 1*s.* a page,
" Composition " 1*d.* for 20 lines ; " Mineralogy " 1*d.* an
article.   And the result of it all is described in a chapter of
Harry and Lucy, written at the end of 1828.

" After Harry had learned his lessons he went to a poem
that he was composing for his father on New Year's Day,

as he always presented his father with a poem at that
period. The subject of it was a battle between the Pre-
tender, or "Chevalier" as Harry would have him called,
and the forces, or part of the forces, of George II. All
the poems that he had hitherto presented to his father
were printed in what Harry called *single letters*, thus—
n or m ; but Harry printed this *double print*, in this
manner—m ; and it was most beautifully done, you may be
sure. It was irregular measure.

"Harry, when he had done what he thought a moderate
allowance of his poem, went to his map. But scarcely had
the pen touched the paper when in came dinner. However, that hindrance was soon over, and Harry returned
to his map. Harry to-day nearly finished it ; and, after
having had some 'Don Quixote,' he went to bed.

"But as, whenever the world was left 'to darkness and
to me,' a bright thought came into Harry's mind, he
thought that if he could contrive to make a Punch's show,
or rather Fantoccini, out of paper, he could exhibit it when
he presented his poem, and please his father a little more.
So he fell to work to invent or plan one. First, he settled
the size, which was to be about five inches long, two broad,
and two sideways. The top, where the figures were to act,
was to be two inches square.

"This settled, Harry began to think how he should
make it. This was rather difficult. Harry first thought
what shape the piece of paper must be, before it was put
together so as to form the show. [Follows a description
with diagrams, elaborate and correct, of a marionette-
theatre, reduced to lowest terms, with pasteboard figures
worked from below with sticks.]

"Harry, being now quite satisfied with his plan, fell

asleep. . . . And in the morning . . . alas! he was, to use
his own words, in a hugeous hurry! Four days, and he
would be entering upon another year! How was he to get
a poem finished consisting of eighty-nine lines,—finished in
that style of printing,—with the show? It was altogether
impossible. So Harry put off the show till his father's
birthday."

This was the end of that long-continued episode; for
he had now found a real Lucy, and the ideal vanished.
The death of his aunt Jessie left a large family of boys
and one girl to the care of their widowed father; and the
Ruskins felt it their duty to help. They fetched Mary
Richardson away, and brought her up as a sister to their
solitary son. She was not so beloved as Jessie had been,
but a good girl and a nice girl, four years older than John,
and able to be a companion to him in his lessons and
travels. There was no sentimentality about his attachment
to her, but a steady fraternal relationship; he, of course,
being the little lord and master, but she was not without
spirit which enabled her to hold her own, and perseverance
which sometimes helped her to eclipse, for the moment, his
brilliancy. They learnt together, wrote their journals
together, and shared alike with the scrupulous fairness
which Mrs. Ruskin's sensible nature felt called on to show.
And so she remained his sister, and not quite his sister,
until she married, and after a very short married life died.

Another accession to the family took place in the same
year (1828): the Croydon aunt, too, had died, and left a dear
dog, Dash, a brown and white spaniel, which at first refused
to leave her coffin, but was coaxed away, and found a
happy home at Herne Hill, and frequent celebration in his
young master's verses. So the family was now complete;

papa and mamma, Mary and John, and Dash.   One other
figure must not be forgotten,—nurse Anne, who had come
from the Edinburgh home, and remained always with them,
John's nurse and then Mrs. Ruskin's attendant, as devoted
and as censorious as any old-style Scotch servant in a
story-book.

The year 1829 marked an advance in poetical composition.   For his father's birthday he did something better
than the "show," a book more elaborate than any ; sixteen
pages in a red cover, with a title-page quite like print :
" Battle of Waterloo | a play | in two acts | with other small
| Poems | dedicated to his father | by John Ruskin | 1829
| Hernhill (sic) | Dulwich."   The play, modelled on a
Shakspere history, shows Wellington with his generals,
and Bonaparte with his guards, mouthing " prave 'orts "
like Prince Harry and Pistol.   There is a Shaksperian
chorus, bidding you imagine the fight ; and in the next act
the arrival of Blucher is dramatised, and Louis XVIII.
with the Duchess of Angoulême praying for the issue.
Then we have Bonaparte soliloquising on the deck of the
Bellerophon ; with the chorus at the end describing. the
triumphal procession in London.

To this are appended, among other pieces, fair copies of
the May, and Skiddaw, and Derwentwater, printed in his
collected Poems from a previous copy.   There is something very Ruskinian in the thought—when comparing
Skiddaw with the Pyramids—

> " All that art can do
> Is nothing beside thee.   The touch of man
> Raised pigmy mountains, but gigantic tombs.
> The touch of nature raised the mountain's brow,
> But made no tombs at all."

Right or wrong, that has always been his leading motive, the normal beneficence of Nature ; and no wonder, for Nature, as he knew her, was very kind to him in those glorious early years of home love and summer excursions into wonderland.

An illness of his postponed their tour for 1829 until it was too late for more than a little journey in Kent. Mr. Ruskin has referred his earliest sketching to this occasion, but it seems likely that the drawings attributed to this year were done in 1831. He was, however, busy writing poetry ; at Tunbridge, for example, he wrote that fragment "On Happiness" which catches so cleverly the tones of Young— a writer whose orthodox moralising suited with the creed in which John Ruskin was brought up—alternately, be it remembered, with *Don Quixote.*

Coming home, he began a new edition of his verses, on a more pretentious scale than the old red books ; in a fine, really bound volume, exquisitely " printed," with the poems dated. The fair copying seems to have been quite as important to him as the composition ; and it laid the foundation of his interest in calligraphy generally, and missals in particular.

An enormous quantity of verse follows here, of which only samples have seen the light. The "poems" are curious from their great variety of style and subject, grave and gay ; but—as might hardly be suspected—the violent-heroic predominates. There was a strong touch of Celtic bravura in little John's character ; he liked to be dressed as a soldier, and lived in imagination much among warriors. And down to his later years, though nobody has so ener-getically denounced the waste and the cruelty and the folly of war, yet nobody has dwelt so lovingly on the virtues that war brings out in noble natures, and on the dignities of a knight's faith. " 'Tis vice," he says in one of the poems of this time, " 'tis vice, not war, that is the curse of man."

He was now growing out of his mother's tutorship; and in this last autumn he was put under the care of Dr. Andrews for his Latin. He relates the introduction in *Prœterita*, and more circumstantially in a letter of the time to Mrs. Monro, the mother of his charming Mrs. Richard Gray, the indulgent neighbour who used to pamper the little gourmand with delicacies unknown in severe Mrs. Ruskin's dining-room. He says in the letter—this is at ten years old :—" Well, papa seeing how fond I was of the Doctor, and knowing him to be an excellent Latin scholar, got him for me as a tutor; and every lesson I get I like him better and better, for he makes me laugh 'almost, if not quite,' to use one of his own expressions, the whole time. He is so funny, comparing Neptune's lifting up the wrecked ships of Æneas with his trident to my lifting up a potato with a fork, or taking a piece of bread out of a bowl of milk with a spoon ! And as he is always saying [things] of that kind, or relating some droll anecdote, or explaining the part of Virgil (the book which I am in) very nicely, I am always delighted when Mondays, Wednesdays and Fridays are come."

Prœterita hardly does justice to the "dear Doctor," who was not only "an excellent Latin scholar" and a genial teacher, but distinguished as a humanity student in his university of Glasgow. But, alas for school distinctions and honours by examination ! In the perspective of history such accidents, by some law of evanescence, disappear; and the personality of the man alone remains, emphasised and explained by the relationship in which he stands to a pair of charming figures. Mrs. Ruskin, who let none but pretty girls come to her house, welcomed the Doctor's daughters ; one, who wrote verses in John's notebook, and sang " Tambourgi," still lives in Bedford Park ; the other lives in Mr. Coventry Patmore's *Angel in the House.* When Mr. Ruskin, thirty years later, wrote of that doubtfully-received poem that it was " the sweetest analysis we possess of quiet modern domestic feeling," few of his readers could have known all the grounds of his appreciation, or suspected the weight of meaning in the words.

Dr. Andrews' lessons did not interfere with the private book writing and mineralogy, during this winter of 1829-30. Perhaps it was the influence of the " long roll " of the Virgilian hexameter that infused a greater sonority into the verses of this period, and gave a greater rhetorical roundness to their lines. For mere literary study there is sound work in this kind of thing :—

> " Meantime, the mourning victors bore
> Their Nelson to his native shore ;
> And a whole weeping nation gave
> Funereal honours to the brave " ;

and everywhere in the MS. of 1830 we see the same new impulse towards alliteration and far-sought phrasing—two tricks of Virgil's that Ruskin has never unlearnt. A little pedantry is natural in a boy who liked his schooling ; but you can hardly call the lad a " prig." A prig has been happily defined as *an animal overfed for its size.* John Ruskin was just the opposite. He was starved, intellectually, or at all events kept on short diet, for fear of the results of mental surfeit. His omnivorous appetite was like that of a young Gargantua, not like the fairy change-lings who eat and eat and never grow. His "good digestion turned all to health," and he soon became an *enfant terrible* on the hands of his pastors and masters, something much bigger than they had meant to breed, and ready like a fairy-tale hero for the roughest exchange of hugs and buffets in the wrestling ring of the literary world.

CHAPTER IV.

MOUNTAIN-WORSHIP.

(1830—1835.)

"The North and Nature taught me to adore
Your scenes sublime, from those beloved before."

Byron.

CRITICS who are least disposed to give Mr. Ruskin credit for his artistic doctrines or economical theories unite in allowing that he has taught us to look at Nature; and especially at the sublime in Nature, at storms and sunrises, and the forests and snows of the Alps. Not that such things were unknown to others, but that he has most impressively united the merely poetical sentiment of their grandeur with something of a scientific curiosity as to their details and conditions; he has brought us to linger among the mountains, and to love them. And as a man rarely convinces unless he is convinced, so Ruskin's mission of mountain-worship has been the outcome of a passion beside which the other interests and occupations of his youth were only toys. He could take up his mineralogy and his moralising, and lay them down; but the love of mountain scenery was something beyond his control. We have seen him leave his heart in the Highlands at three years old : we have now to follow his passionate pilgrimages to Skiddaw and Snowdon, to the Jungfrau and Mont Blanc.

The summer tour of 1830 is important as the first of which he has left his impressions completely recorded. Earlier than that there are rhapsodic fragments about Ben Lomond and the hill of Kinnoul, about the Lakes and North Wales; but now he began to treat the scenery as a subject of art, and to develop his journals consciously into poems.

They had planned a great tour through the Lakes and the North two years before; but were stopped at Plymouth by the news of Mrs. Richardson's death. This time the same plan was carried out. A prose diary was written alternately by John and Mary, one carrying it on when the other tired, with rather curious effect of unequally-yoked collaboration. We read how they "set off from London at seven o'clock on Tuesday morning, the 18th of May," and thenceforward we are spared no detail: the furniture of the inns, the bills of fare; when they got out of the carriage and walked; how they lost their luggage; what they thought of colleges and chapels, music and May races at Oxford, of Shakespeare's tomb, and the pin-factory at Birmingham; we have a complete guide-book to Blenheim and Warwick Castle, to Haddon and Chatsworth, and the full itinerary of Derbyshire. "Matlock Bath," we read, "is a most delightful place"; but after an enthusiastic description of High Tor, John reacts into bathos with a minute description of how they wetted their shoes in a puddle. The cavern with a Bengal light was fairyland to him, and among the minerals he was quite at home.

Everything was interesting on these journeys, everything was noteworthy: and the excitement was certainly kept up

at a high pitch. Sightseeing by day was not enough:
John must get out his book after supper in the evening at
the hotel, and write poems; when he had written up his
journal he went on with some subject totally unconnected
with his travels or the place he was in. For instance, after
seeing Haddon, that very night he finished a gruesome
account of the Day of Judgment! This power of detaching himself from surroundings and fixing his mind on any
business in hand has always been one of his most curious
and most enviable gifts. How few writers could correct
proofs at Sestri and write political economy at Chamouni!
After spending the morning in drawing early Gothic, and
the afternoon driving to some historic site, with a sketch
of sunset perhaps, he could settle down in his hotel bedroom
and write a preface to an old work; and next morning
be up before the sun, busy at a chapter of *Fors* or
Præterita. It is this "ohne Hast, ohne Rast' that has
enabled him to do so much and so varied work; the
power is the result of a habit, and the habit was formed
from the beginning.

To resume the tour. "Manchester is a most disagreeable
town," but at Liverpool they were delighted with the river,
assisted at a trifling collision, and got caught in the old
dockgates; on which adventure John bursts into ballad
rhyme. Then they hurried north to Windermere. Once
at Lowwood, the excitement thickens, with storms and
rainbows, mountains and waterfalls, boats on the lake
and coaching on the steep roads. This journey through
Lakeland is described in the galloping anapæsts of the
"Iteriad," which was simply the prose journal versified
on his return: one of the few enterprises of the sort which
were really completed.

To readers who know the country it is interesting as giving a detailed account of it sixty years ago, in the days of the old régime, when this "nook of English ground" was "secure from rash assault." One learns that, even then, there were jarring sights at Bowness Bay and along Derwentwater shore, elements unkind and bills exorbitant; Coniston especially was dreary with rain, and its inn extravagantly dear; "*but*," says John, with his eye for mineral specimens, "it contains several rich copper-mines." An interesting touch is the hero-worship with which they went reverently to peep at Southey and Wordsworth in church; too humble to dream of an introduction, and too polite to besiege the poets in their homes, but independent enough to form their own opinions on the personality of the heroes. They did not like the look of Wordsworth, at all.

The dominant note of the tour is, however, an ecstatic delight in the mountain scenery; on Skiddaw and Helvellyn all the gamut of admiration is lavished. Reluctantly leaving the wilder country, they returned to Derbyshire; and meeting a friend to whom it was new, they revisited everything with revived pleasure. They did not seem to know what it was to be bored. The whole tour was a triumphal progress, or a march of conquest.

On returning home, John began Greek under Dr. Andrews, and was soon versifying Anacreon in his note-books. He began to read Byron for himself, with what result we shall see before long. But the most important new departure was the attempt to copy Cruikshank's etchings to Grimm's Fairy-tales, his real beginning at art. From this practice he learnt the value of the line, the pure, clean line that expresses form. It is a good

instance of the authority of these early years over Mr.
Ruskin's whole life and teaching, that in his " Elements
of Drawing " he advises young artists to begin with
Cruikshank, as he began ; and wrote appreciatively both
of the stories and the etchings so many decades afterwards
in the preface to a reprint by Messrs. Chatto & Windus.

His cousin-sister Mary had been sent to a day-school,
when Mrs. Ruskin's lessons were superseded by Dr.
Andrews ; and she had learnt enough drawing to attempt
a view of the hotel at Matlock—a thing which John could
not do. So, now that he too showed some power of neat
draughtsmanship, it was felt that he ought to have her
advantages. They got Mr. Runciman, the drawing master,
to give him lessons, in the early part of 1831. His
teaching was of the kind which preceded the Hardingesque :
it aimed at a bold use of the soft pencil, with a certain
roundness of composition and richness of texture, a conventional " right way " of drawing anything. This was not
what John wanted ; but, not to be beaten, he facsimiled
the master's freehand by a sort of engraver's stipple, which
his habitual neatness helped him to do to perfection. Mr.
Runciman soon put a stop to that, and took pains with
a pupil who took such pains with himself ; taught him, at
any rate, the principles of perspective, and remained his
only drawing-master for many years.

Now he could rival Mary when they went for their
summer excursion. He set to work at once at Sevenoaks
to draw cottages ; at Dover and Battle he attempted
castles. It may be that these first sketches are of the
pre-Runciman period ; but the Ruskins made the round of
Kent in 1831, and though the drawings are by no means
in the master's style, they show some practice in using

the pencil. From the first John Ruskin cared more to carry away a true record of his subject than to produce a pleasing picture ; he is even diagrammatic in this early stage, lettering his architecture with references to enlarged detail, and finishing parts with a characteristic disregard for the unity of his composition.

The journey was extended by the old route, conditioned by business as before : round the south coast to the west of England, and then into Wales. There, his powers of drawing failed him ; moonlight on Snowdon was too vague a subject for the black lead pencil, but a hint of it could be conveyed in rhyme :—

> " Folding, like an airy vest,
>   The very clouds had sunk to rest ;
>   Light gilds the rugged mountain's breast,
>   Calmly as they lay below ;
>   Every hill seemed topped with snow,
>   As the flowing tide of light
>   Broke the slumbers of the night."

Harlech Castle was too sublime for a sketch ; but it was painted with the pen :—

> " So mighty, so majestic, and so lone ;
>   And all thy music, now, the ocean's murmuring."

And the enthusiasm of mountain-glory, a sort of Bacchic ecstasy of uncontrollable passion, struggles for articulate deliverance in the climbing-song, " I love ye, ye eternal hills."

It was hard to come back to the daily round, the common task, especially when, in this autumn of 1831, to Dr. Andrews' Latin and Greek, the French grammar and Euclid were added, under Mr. Rowbotham. And the new tutor had no funny stories to tell; he was not so engaging a man as the "dear Doctor," and his memory was not sweet to his wayward pupil. But the parents had chosen the best man for the work: one who was favourably known by his manuals, and capable of interesting even a budding poet in the mathematics. For our author tells that a little later he spent all his available time in trying to trisect an angle, and that at Oxford, and ever after, he knew his Euclid without the figures; in French, too, he progressed enough to be able to find his way alone in Paris two years later. And however the saucy boy may have satirised his tutor in the droll verses on "Bed-time," Mr. Rowbotham always remembered him with affection, and spoke of him with respect. John Ruskin, boy and man, has had a terrible power of winning hearts.

In spite of these tedious tutorships, he managed to scribble energetically all this winter: attempts at Waverley novels which never got beyond the first chapter, and imitations of *Childe Harold* and *Don Juan*; scraps in the style of everybody in turn, necessarily imitative because immature. He was curiously versatile; one time he would be pedantic, or stiff with the buckram and plume of romance; again, gossipy and naïf and humorous; then sarcastic and satirical, sparing no one; then carried away with a frenzy of excitement, which struggles to express itself, convulsively, and dies away in nonsense. No wonder his mother sent him to bed at nine, punctually; and kept him from school, in vain efforts to quiet his brain. The lack of companions was made up to him in the friendship of Richard Fall, son of a neighbour on "the Hill," a boy without affectation or morbidity of disposition, whose complementary character suited him well. An affectionate comradeship sprang up between the two lads, and lasted until in middle life they drifted apart, not quarrelling, but each going on his own course to his own destiny.

John Ruskin made some real advance this winter (1831-32) with his Shelleyan " Sonnet to a Cloud " and his imitations of Byron's *Hebrew Melodies*, from which he learnt how to concentrate expression, and to use rich vowel-sounds and liquid consonants with rolling effect. A deeper and more serious turn of thought, that gradually usurps the place of the first boyish effervescence, is traced by him to the influence of Byron, in whom, while others see nothing more than wit and passion, Mr. Ruskin sees an earnest mind and a sound judgment.

But the most sincere poem, if sincerity be marked by unstudied phrase and neglected rhyme,—the most genuine " lyrical cry " of this period,—is that song in which our boy-poet poured forth his longing for the " blue hills " he had loved as a baby, and for those Coniston crags over which, when he became old and sorely stricken, he was still to see the morning break. When he wrote these verses he was nearly fourteen, or just past his birthday ; it had been eighteen months since he had been in Wales, and all the weary while he had seen no mountains ; but in his regrets he goes back a year farther still, to fix upon the Lakeland hills, less majestic than Snowdon, but more endeared ; and he describes his sensations on approaching the beloved objects in the very terms that Dante uses for his first sight of Beatrice :

> "I weary for the fountain foaming,
>   For shady holm and hill ;
> My mind is on the mountain roaming,
>   My spirit's voice is still.

"I weary for the woodland brook
    That wanders through the vale ;
I weary for the heights that look
    Adown upon the dale.

"The crags are lone on Coniston
    And Glaramara's dell ; *
And dreary on the mighty one,
    The cloud-enwreathed Sca-fell.

"Oh ! what although the crags be stern
    Their mighty peaks that sever,—
Fresh flies the breeze on mountain-fern,
    And free on mountain heather. . . .

"*There is a thrill of strange delight
    That passes quivering o'er me,
When blue hills rise upon the sight,
    Like summer clouds before me.*"

Judge, then, of the delight with which he turned over
the pages of a new book, given him this birthday by the
kind Mr. Telford, in whose carriage he had first seen these
blue hills,—a book in which all his mountain-ideals, and
more, were caught and kept enshrined,—visions still, and
of mightier peaks and ampler valleys,—romantically " tost "
and sublimely "lost," as he had so often written in his
favourite rhymes. In the vignettes to Rogers' *Italy*,
Turner had touched the chord for which John Ruskin had
been feeling all these years : no wonder that he took
Turner for his leader and master, and fondly tried to copy
the wonderful " Alps at daybreak " to begin with, and then
to imitate this new-found magic art with his own subjects,
—and finally to come boldly before the world in passionate
defence of a man who had done such great things for him.

This mountain-worship was not inherited from his father,

* So in the MS. ; changed afterwards to " Loweswater's dell."

however it may have been an inheritance, as some think, from remote ancestry. Mr. J. J. Ruskin never was enthusiastic about peaks and clouds and glaciers, though he was interested in all travelling in a general way. So that it was not Rogers' *Italy* that sent the family off to the Alps that summer; but, fortunately for John, his father's eye was caught by the romantic architecture of Prout's *Sketches in Flanders and Germany* when it came out in April 1833; and his mother proposed to make both of them happy in a tour on the Continent. The business-round was abandoned, but they could see Mr. Domecq on their way back through Paris, and not wholly lose the time.

They waited to keep papa's birthday on May 10th, and early next morning drove off; father and mother, John and Mary, nurse Anne and the courier Salvador. They crossed to Calais, and posted, as people did in the old times, slowly from point to point; starting betimes; halting at the roadside inns, where John tried to snatch a sketch; reaching their destination early enough to investigate the cathedral or the citadel, monuments of antiquity or achievements of modern civilisation, with impartial eagerness; and before bedtime John would write up his journal and work up his sketches, just as if he were at home. Once or twice he found time to sit down and make a Proutesque study of some great building, probably to please his father; but his mind was set on his Turner vignettes.

So they worked through Flanders and Germany, following Prout's lead by the castles of the Rhine: but at last, at Schaffhausen one Sunday evening — " suddenly—behold —beyond ! "—they had seen the Alps. Thenceforward Turner was their guide, as they crossed the Splügen, sailed the Italian lakes, wondered at Milan Cathedral and the Mediterranean at Genoa, and then—whether because it was too hot to go southward, or because John having tasted the Alps importuned for more—roamed through the Oberland and back to Chamouni. All this while a great plan shaped itself in the boy's head : no less than to make a Rogers' *Italy* for himself, just as once he had tried to make a *Harry and Lucy* or a *Dictionary of Minerals*. On every place they passed he would write verses and prose sketches, to give respectively the romance and the reality— or ridicule, for he saw the comic side of it all, keenly ; and he would illustrate the series with Turneresque vignettes, drawn with the finest crowquill pen, to imitate the delicate engravings. That was his plan ; and if he never quite carried it out, he got good practice in two things which went to the making of *Modern Painters*—in descriptive writing, and in getting at the mind and method of Turner, by following him on his own sketching-ground and carrying out his subjects in his own way. This is just what Turner had done with Vandevelde and Claude ; and it is the way to learn a landscape painter's business : there is no other, for simple copying neglects the relation of art to Nature,— it is like trying to learn a language without a dictionary ; and unguided experiments are not education at all. By this imitation of Turner and Prout, John Ruskin learnt more drawing in two or three years than most amateur students do in seven : he had hit upon the right method, and worked hard. For the first year he has the " Watch-tower of Andernach " and the " Jungfrau from Interlaken " to show, with others of similar style ; and thenceforward alternates between Turner and Prout, until he settles into something different from either.

But Turner and Prout were not the only artists he knew :

at Paris he found his way into the Louvre, and got leave
from the directors, though he was under the age required,
to copy. It is curious that the picture he chose was a
Rembrandt; it shows, what the casual reader of his works
on art might miss, that he is naturally a chiaroscurist, and
that his praise of the pre-Raphaelite colour and draughtsmanship is not prompted by his taste and native feeling so
much as by intellectual judgment.

Between this foreign tour and the next, John Ruskin's
chief work was to draw these vignettes and to write the
poems suggested by the scenes he had visited: that was
what he did *con amore*; his studies in classics and mathematics were mere routine. He had outgrown the evening
lessons with Dr. Andrews, and as he was fifteen it was
time to think more seriously of preparing him for Oxford,
where his name was put down at Christ Church. His
father hoped he would go into the Church, and eventually
turn out a combination of a Byron and a bishop: something like Dean Milman, only better. For this, college
was a necessary preliminary; for college, some little
schooling. So they picked the best day-school in the
neighbourhood, that of the Rev. Thomas Dale, in Grove
Lane, Peckham, the author of various learned and theological works—as it appears from second-hand catalogues—
and afterwards Canon of St. Paul's. His first start with
the new boy was unfortunate, and he never regained the
confidence he had lost when he called Adam's Grammar
" that Scotch thing." John Ruskin worked with him
rather less than two years. In 1835 he was taken from
school in consequence of an attack of pleurisy, and never
returned; though he attended Mr. Dale's lectures at King's
College, London, in 1836.

More interesting to him than school was the British Museum collection of minerals, where he worked occasionally with his Jameson's Dictionary. By this time he had a fair student's collection of his own, and he increased it by picking up specimens at Matlock or Clifton or in the Alps, wherever he went ; for he was not short of pocket-money : he earned enough by scribbling even if his father were not always ready to indulge his fancy. He took the greatest pains over his catalogues, and wrote elaborate accounts of the various minerals in a shorthand he invented out of Greek letters and crystal forms.

Grafted on this mineralogy, and stimulated by the Swiss tour, was a new interest in physical geology ; which his father so far approved as to give him Saussure's *Voyages dans les Alpes* for his birthday in 1834. In this book he found the complement of Turner's vignettes, something like a key to the "reason why" of all the wonderful forms and marvellous mountain-architecture of the Alps.

In our hills of the north these things do not so obviously call for explanation ; but no intelligent boy could look long and intently at the crags of Lauterbrunnen and the peaks of Savoy without feeling that their twisted strata present a problem which arouses all his curiosity. And this boy was by no means content with a superficial sentiment of grandeur. He tried to understand the causes of it, to get at the secrets of the structure ; and found poetry in that mystery of the mountains, no less than in their storms and sunrises. He soon wrote a short essay on the subject, and had the pleasure of seeing it in print, in Loudon's *Magazine of Natural History* for March 1834, along with another bit of his writing, asking for information on the cause of the colour of the Rhine-water. It was rather characteristic that he began his literary career by asking questions that got no answer ; and that his next appearance in print was to demolish a correspondent to the same magazine, whose account of rats eating leaden pipes was discredited by the extraordinary dimensions which he assigned.   The analytic John Ruskin was already an *enfant terrible.*

He had already made some acquaintance with Mr. J. C. Loudon, F.L.S., H.S., etc., and he was on the staff of that versatile editor not long afterwards, and took a lion's share of the writing in the *Magazine of Architecture.* Meanwhile he had been introduced to another editor, and to the publishers with whom he did business for many a year to come.   The acquaintance was made in a curious, accidental manner.   His Croydon cousin, Charles, had come to town as clerk in the publishing house of Messrs. Smith, Elder & Co., and had the opportunity of mentioning the young poet's name to Mr. Thomas Pringle, who edited their well-known annual *Friendship's Offering.*   Mr. Pringle came out to Herne Hill, and was hospitably entertained as a brother Scot, as not only an editor, but a poet himself,—not only a poet, but a man of respectability and piety, who had been a missionary in South Africa.   In return for this hospitality he gave a good report of John's verses, and after getting him to re-write two of the best passages in the last Tour, carried them off for insertion in his forthcoming number.   He did more : he carried John to see the actual Mr. Samuel Rogers whose verses had been adorned by the great Turner's vignettes ; but it seems that the boy was not courtier enough—homebred as he had been—to compliment the poet as poets love to be complimented ; and the great man, dilettante

THE SCALA MONUMENT, VERONA.

By John Ruskin.—1835.

[Vol. I., p. 51.]

as he was, had not the knowledge of art to be honestly delighted with the boy's enthusiasm for the wonderful drawings which had given his book the best part of its value.

After the pleurisy of April 1835, his parents took him abroad again, and he made great preparations to use the opportunity to the utmost. He would study geology in the field, and took Saussure in his trunk ; he would note meteorology, the colour whether of Rhine-water or of Alpine skies, and invented a cyanometer—a scale of blue to measure the depth of tone. He would sketch ; by now he had abandoned the desire to make MS. albums, after seeing himself in print ; and so chose rather to imitate the imitable, and to follow Prout, this time, with careful outlines on the spot, than to idealise his notes in mimic Turnerism. And he meant to keep his journal in verse, warned by the labour and the failures involved in re-writing everything on his return. But even that poetical journal was dropped after he had carried it through France, across the Jura, and to Chamouni. The drawing crowded it out, and for the first time he found himself over the *pons asinorum* of art, and as ready with his pencil as he had been with his pen.

His route is marked by the drawings of that year, from Chamouni to the St. Bernard and Aosta, back to the Oberland and up the St. Gothard ; then back again to Lucerne and round by the Stelvio to Venice and Verona ; and finally through the Tyrol and Germany homewards. The ascent of the St. Bernard was told in a dramatic sketch of great humour and power of characterisation ; and a letter to Richard Fall records the night on the Rigi when he saw the splendid sequence of storm, sunset,

moonlight and daybreak which forms the subject of one
of the most impressive passages of *Modern Painters*.

It happened that Mr. Pringle had a plate of Salzburg
which he wanted to print in order to make up the volume
of *Friendship's Offering* for the next Christmas. He
seems to have asked John Ruskin to furnish a copy of
verses for the picture ; and at Salzburg, accordingly, a
bit of rhymed description was written, and re-written, and
sent home to the editor. Early in December the Ruskins
returned ; and at Christmas there came to Herne Hill
a gorgeous gilt morocco volume " To John Ruskin, from
the Publishers." On opening it, there were his " Andernach" and " St. Goar," and his "Salzburg," opposite
a beautifully engraved plate, all hills and towers and
boats and picturesquely-moving figures under the sunset,
in Turner's manner more or less,—really by Turner's
engraver. It was almost like being Mr. Rogers himself.

CHAPTER V.

A LOVE-STORY.

(1836-39.)

" I think there is no unreturned love—the pay is certain, one way or another.
I loved a certain person ardently, and my love was not returned,
Yet out' of that, I have written these songs."

Leaves of Grass.

WHENEVER a new biography comes, be it of poet or statesman, engineer or philanthropist, I confess to turning the pages in hope of a love-story. Other readers, it seems, do likewise ; and not unreasonably. There is so much to be learnt from the behaviour of a man under those trying circumstances ; one gets the character unveiled in moments of passion. If he is an egoist, he shows it then, perhaps, after keeping it dark for years. If he is coarse or selfish by nature, with only a veneer of culture, in his love-affair the true man comes out. *In vino veritas*, they used to say ; meaning that when a man is quite off his guard, he tells his secret. And so it is in love. Note him then, and you have the truth about him. That is perhaps why we lay stress on the domestic relations of our leaders : we cannot trust a man who has deceived the woman he chose ; we cannot believe in the ideals of a man who has falsified them in the critical

53

opportunity of his life. On the other hand, we forgive much to one who loves much : we admire a man who forbears much ; and we augur well of the youth whose first romance has left him nothing that he need be ashamed of.

In the quiet household on Herne Hill, the ordinary temptations of youth were unknown. *Don Juan* and *Don Quixote*, with all their supposed evil example, coarse expression and suggestion, ran like water from a duck's back : to the pure all things are pure. The ideal Harry of our young hero's early days, who mirrored him in everything, took little interest in his reading unless he had "seen something like it" outside of books ; and there was nothing to be seen like Julia or Maritornes in his immediate surroundings. Not that it was a monastery : there was plenty of liveliness ; there were pretty playmates and charming neighbours ; but the blight of unwatched schoolboyhood never touched him. If it had, there would surely be some indication of it in his work ; but there is no trace of even ordinary interest in womankind in the mass of notes and scribbles of all these early days. Rather, if anything, an antagonism to girls ; for they teased him about his rhymes as not being sentimental enough.

So, when love came, it was a surprise. There had been no foretaste of it, no vulgarisation of it ; nothing to take the bloom off, to discount the impetuosity of a first passion. And it is no wonder if, looking back, he was amused at himself, and wrote jestingly in *Præterita* of the affair, to cover the annoyance with which one regards the absurdities of one's youth. But it was a quite serious affair, on his side ; and led to serious consequences.

The Ruskins had reached home early in December 1835, and found cold cheer in England after their travelling. The father especially felt it hard to settle down to work in his dingy office after the excitements of Italy. In a clever scene in which John dramatised a typical family talk at breakfast, satirising his parents with a freedom which shows that any severity recorded of them was only superficial, the father is made to describe the tedium of business-talk and the annoyances of the warehouse in very lively terms ; while his good wife " flytes " him, as in duty bound.

But they were not to be left long without excitement. A few weeks later, Mr. Domecq came over from Paris on business, and brought his four younger daughters—the eldest having been lately married to a Count Maison, heir to a peer of France. It was an unaccustomed invasion of the house, and something new to have a bevy of young ladies to take about and entertain, while their father was busy with partners and customers.

There were four of them : the " first really well-bred and well-dressed girls " John had met ; all charming and clever and pretty. His mother might have known that he was bound to fall in love with one or other ; but she argued that he was safe in his studies ; and then the girls were foreigners and convent-bred Catholics, which seemed to put a great gulf between them and a true-blue Briton and Protestant. As to Mr. Domecq—— When one has four daughters, and a first-rate business-partner with a clever son, what may not one think right to do ?

Any of the sisters would have charmed him, but the eldest of the four, Adèle Clotilde, bewitched him at once with her graceful figure and that oval face which was so admired in those times. She was fair, too ; another recommendation. He was on the brink of seventeen, at the ripe moment ; and he fell passionately in love with her. She was only fifteen, and did not understand this adoration, unspoken, and unexpressed except by intensified shyness. For he was a very shy boy with strangers, brought up as he was without any regular experience of drawing-room manners and social affability. If he had been taught a little to dance, it was only enough to discover that quadrilles were invented by Stupidity itself ; and now, what would he not have given for a share of that despised man-of-the-worldliness and assurance of address ? In company he sat uneasy ; when he got the chance of separate conversation, a jibbing Pegasus plunged him into perverse and inconsiderate behaviour. His uneasiness bred an appearance of antagonism ; in fit upon fit of shyness he disputed, prosed, sulked, did everything that could alienate a bright girl—from Paris, too ; whose notions of British morgue and phlegm were only too justified by his want of style and his obvious awkwardness.

And yet he had advantages, if he had known how to use them. He was tall and active, light and lithe in gesture, not a clumsy hobbledehoy. He had the face that caught the eye, in Rome a few years later, of Keats' Severn, no mean judge surely of faces, and poets' faces. He was undeniably clever, he knew all about minerals and mountains, he was quite an artist ; and a printed poet ! But these things weigh little with a girl of fifteen who wants to be amused ; and so she only laughed at John.

He tried to amuse her, but he tried too seriously. He wrote a story to read her—" Leoni, a Legend of Italy " ; for of course she understood enough English to be read to, no doubt to be wooed in, seeing her mother was English. The story was of brigands and true lovers, the thing that was popular in the romantic period, when Eastlake's Banditti were admired in the Royal Academy, and Schiller's *Robbers* had not lost its effect. The costumery and mannerisms of the little romance are out of date now, and seem ridiculous as an old-fashioned dress does; though Mr. Pringle and the public were pleased with it then, when it was printed in *Friendship's Offering*. But the note of passion was too real for the girl of fifteen, and she only laughed the more.

When they left, he was alone with his poetry again. But now he had no interest in his tour-book; even the mountains, for the time, had lost their power; and all his plans of great works were dropped for a new style of verse, the love poems of 1836. In reading these one is struck by something artificial: they are too closely modelled on well-known forms; for the poet was not mature in his art; and it means great accomplishment when the height of passion is united with absolute freshness in diction; the *celare artem* of the consummate writer. The best love poems have been written to imaginary loves; and real-life love-letters are generally but poor literature, a cento of common-places. So that the derivative nature of these verses does not preclude the genuineness of the passion that inspired them.

This formality appears more strongly in those pieces which were afterwards revised for publication; for the extraordinary thing is that this passion and poesy were no secret. His father, from whom he kept nothing, approved the verses, and did not disapprove his views on the young lady. A marriage could hardly have been a mésalliance on either side from a worldly point of view, for the Ruskins were now well off, and business is business: perhaps the bishopric in view would have been lost sight of. But to Mrs. Ruskin, with her religious feelings, it was intolerable, unbelievable, that the son whom she had brought up in the nurture and admonition of the strictest Protestantism should fix his heart on an alien in race and creed. The wonder is that their relations were not more strained: there are few young men who would have kept their full allegiance to a mother whose sympathy failed them at such a crisis. As it was, this marks the first step towards the withdrawal—not of affection—but of completely reposed confidence.

To end the story we must anticipate a little. There are so many strands in this complex life that they cannot be followed all at once. When we have traced this one out, we can resume the history of John Ruskin as student and poet and youthful savant.

As the year went on his passion seemed to grow, in the absence of the beloved object. His only plan of winning her was to win his spurs first: but as what? Clearly, his *forte*, it seemed, was in writing. If he could be a successful writer of romances, of songs, of plays, surely she would not refuse him. And so he began another romantic story, *Velasquez, the Novice*—opening with the monks of St. Bernard, among whom had been, so the tale ran, a mysterious member whose papers, when discovered, made him out the hero of adventures in Venice. He began a play which was to be another great work, *Marcolini*, to which he has alluded in terms which leave one in doubt whether its author has re-read it since it was written under the mulberry tree in Herne Hill garden, that summer of 1836.

Partly Shakspearian, but more Byronic in form, it does not depend merely on description, but shows a dramatic power of character and dialogue indicated by many earlier attempts at stories and scenes, which justifies the remark of Mrs. Thackeray Ritchie; "Ruskin should have been a novelist. When he chooses to describe a man or a woman, there stands the figure before us; when he tells a story, we live it." But she is equally right in adding, "His is rather the descriptive than the constructive faculty; his mastery is over detail and quantity rather than over form." The weakness of *Marcolini* is in the arrangement and disposition of the plot : he has no playwright's eye for situations. But the conversation is animated, and the characters finely drawn, with more discrimination than one would expect from so young an author.

This work was interrupted at the end of Act III. by pressing calls to other studies, of which in the next chapter ; and then by the attempt to win the distinction he sought in the Newdigate prize at Oxford. But it was not that he had forgotten Adèle. From time to time he wrote verses to her, or about her ; and as in 1838 she was sent to school with her sisters near Chelmsford, to "finish" her in English, in that August he saw her again. She had lost some of her first girlish prettiness, but that made no difference. And when the Domecqs came to Herne Hill at Christmas to spend their holidays, he was as deeply in love as ever. He could show her the new *Friendship's Offering*, just come out, with a poem "To * * * ," which was a direct appeal enough. He followed it up with printing others of his poems to her in *The London Monthly Miscellany* for the next three months. He won his Newdigate ; he had written brilliantly, for a youth, in the *Architectural Magazine*, and was plainly a rising young man. But she still laughed at him.

It seems that the pertinacity of his passion disturbed his parents not a little; enough for them to employ the somewhat desperate expedient of throwing other girls in his way. And one gathers from tradition, putting hints together, that more than one fair damsel would have been willing enough to receive his suit. But his affections remained fixed, most unreasonably, if lovers knew such a thing as reason.

Soon after her return to France, emancipated from schoolgirlhood—greatly, no doubt, to the elder Ruskins' relief—her father died; and proposals were made for her hand by a young French Baron Duquesne; of which the unsuccessful suitor heard in September 1839. He wrote the long poem of "Farewell," dated the eve of their last meeting and parting. One sees that he has been reading his Shelley; one sees that he knows he is writing "poetry"; but at the same time one cannot but believe that his disappointment was deep, after nearly four years of hope and effort, and real fidelity at a period of life when, if ever, a lover's unfaithfulness might be easily pardoned, placed as he was among new scenes and new people, among success and flattery and awakening ambition. But in this disappointment there is no anger, no bitterness, no reproach. She is still to be his goddess of stone; calm and cold, but never to be forgotten.

At twenty, young men do not die of love: but I find that a fortnight after writing this he was taken seriously ill. During the winter the negotiations for the marriage in Paris went on. It took place in March. In May he was pronounced consumptive, and had to give up Oxford,

and all hope of distinction in the schools for which he had
laboured, and with that, any plans that might have been
entertained for his distinction in the Church. And remem-
bering how his physical illnesses have always followed upon
mental strain or grief, it is hard to believe that this first
great calamity of his life—how far-reaching cannot well be
told—was not the direct consequence of this unhappy love-
story.

For nearly two years he was dragged about from place
to place, and from doctor to doctor, in search of health ;
and thanks to wise treatment, more to new faces, and most
to a plucky determination to employ himself usefully with
his pen and his pencil, he gradually freed himself from the
spell ; and fifty years afterwards could look back upon the
story as a pretty comedy of his youthful days. How pretty
at any rate the actress must have been, if we do not believe
his own words, and taste, we can judge from a little side-
glimpse of the sequel afforded us by a writer whose
connoisseurship in pretty girls we can trust—Mrs. A.
Thackeray Ritchie (*Harper's Magazine*, March 1890) :—

"The writer can picture to herself something of the
charm of these most charming sisters ; for once, by chance
travelling on Lake Leman, she found herself watching a
lady who sat at the steamer's end, a beautiful young
woman, all dressed in pale grey, with a long veil floating
on the wind, who sat motionless and absorbed, looking
toward the distant hills, not unlike the vision of some
guiding, wistful Ariel at the prow, while the steamer sped
its way between the banks. The story of the French
sisters has gained an added interest from the remembrance
of those dark, lovely eyes, that charming countenance ; for
afterwards, when I knew her better, the lady told me that

her mother had been a Domecq, and had once lived with her sisters in Mr. Ruskin's home. Circumstances had divided them in after days, but all the children of the family had been brought up to know Mr. Ruskin by name, and to love and appreciate his books. The lady sent him many messages by me, which I delivered in after days, when, alas! it was from Mr. Ruskin himself I learned that the beautiful traveller—Isabelle, he called her—had passed away before her time to those distant hills where all our journeys end."

CHAPTER VI.

"*KATA PHUSIN.*"

(1836—1838.)

"And you, painter, who are desirous of great practice, understand, that if you do not rest it on the good foundation of Nature, you will labour with little honour and less profit : and if you do it on a good ground, your works will be many and good, to your great honour and advantage."—*Leonardo da Vinci.*

LOVE in idleness was no part of the Herne Hill programme. Beside the playwriting and song-composing, which was not exactly *work*, although it used up much time and energy, and over and above the lectures at King's College already mentioned, John Ruskin entered in 1836 upon a new and more serious phase of his study of Art.

In Switzerland and Italy, during the autumn of 1835, he had made a great many drawings, carefully outlined in pencil or pen, on grey paper, and sparsely touched with body colour, in direct imitation of the Prout lithographs. Prout's original coloured sketches he had seen, no doubt, in the exhibition ; but he does not seem to have thought of imitating them, for his work in this kind was all intended to be for illustration. The "Italy" vignettes likewise, with all their inspiration, suggested to him only pen-etching ; he was hardly conscious that somewhere there existed the tiny, delicious coloured pictures that Turner had made for the engraver. Still, now that he could draw really well, his father, who painted in water-colours himself, wished him to be promoted to a colour box ; and as he always got the best of everything, went straight to the President of the Old Water Colour Society, and engaged him for the usual course of half a dozen lessons at a guinea. Copley Fielding, besides being Presi-dent, could draw mountains as nobody else but Turner could, in water colour ; he had enough mystery and poetry to interest the younger Ruskin, and enough resemblance to ordinary views of nature to please the elder.

So they both went to Newman Street to his painting-room, and John worked through the course, and a few extra lessons ; but, after all, found that he could no more pick up this trick from a teacher than he could formerly pick up the orthodox method of reading and writing. The stronger a man's individuality is, the less he is likely, and even *able*, to comply with common means and aims. Such a man sometimes thinks it very stupid in himself that he cannot do what other people find so easy : Wagner, for instance, always hoping to succeed, next time, in hitting the popular taste ; and Beethoven, labouring in vain to throw some lightness into his great overture, to please the manager of the opera. So Ruskin must be him-self, or nothing ; and his way of work remained for him to devise for himself, by following at first the highest masters he knew, and by superadding to the lessons he could get from them an expression of his own sincere feeling.

One such lesson was given in the Royal Academy Ex-hibition of 1836, when Turner showed the first striking examples of his later style in the "Juliet and her Nurse," the "Mercury and Argus," and the "Rome from Mount Aventine." The strange idealism, the unusualness, the mystery of these pictures, united with evidence of intense significance and subtle observation, appealed to young Ruskin as it appealed to few other spectators. Here was Venice as he saw her in his own dreams; here were mountains and skies such as he had watched and studied, and attempted to describe in his own poems. It was not for nothing that he had been devoted to Nature, that he had tried to set down her phenomena in writing, and to represent her forms with severe draughtsmanship; that he had studied the geology of mountains as well as the poetry of them. In Turner's work he saw both sides of his own character reflected, both aspects of Nature recorded. It was not the mere matter-of-fact map of the place, which would have appealed to merely matter-of-fact people, interested in science. Nor was it simply a vague Miltonian imagination, which would have appealed to the mere sentimentalist. But Turner had been able to show, and young Ruskin to appreciate, the combination of two attitudes with regard to Nature : the scientific, inquisitive about her facts, her detail ; and the poetical, expatiating in effect, in breadth and mystery.

There may have been other people who appreciated these pictures : if so, they said nothing. On the contrary, public opinion regretted this change for the worse in its old favourite, the draughtsman of Oxford colleges, the painter of shipwrecks and castles. And *Blackwood's Magazine*, which the Ruskins, as Edinburgh people and admirers of Christopher North, read with respect, spoke about Turner, in a review of the picture-season, with that

freedom of speech which Scotch reviewers claim as a
heritage from the days of Jeffrey. Young Ruskin at once
dashed off an answer, indignant not so much that Turner
was attacked, but that he should have been attacked by a
writer whose article showed that he was not a qualified
critic of art, and that this should have been printed in
" Maga."

The critic had found that Turner was " out of nature " :
Ruskin tried to show that the pictures were full of facts,
studied on the spot and thoroughly understood, but treated
with poetical licence ; Turner being, like Shakespeare, an
idealist, in the sense of allowing himself a free treatment
of his material. The critic pronounced Turner's colour bad,
his execution neglected, and his chiaroscuro childish ; in
answer to which Ruskin explained that Turner's reasoned
system was to represent light and shade by the contrast of
warm and cold colour, rather than by the opposition of
white and black which other painters used ; he denied that
his execution was other than his aims necessitated, and
maintained that the critic had no right to force his cut-and-
dried Academic rules of composition on a great genius ; at
the same time admitting that " the faults of Turner are
numerous, and perhaps more egregious than those of any
other great existing artist ; but if he has greater faults, he
has also greater beauties.

" His imagination is Shakespearian in its mightiness.
Had the scene of ' Juliet and her Nurse ' risen up before
the mind of a poet, and been described in ' words that
burn,' it had been the admiration of the world. . . . Many-
coloured mists are floating above the distant city, but such
mists as you might imagine to be ethereal spirits, souls of
the mighty dead breathed out of the tombs of Italy into

the blue of her bright heaven, and wandering in vague and
infinite glory around the earth that they have loved. Instinct with the beauty of uncertain light, they move and
mingle among the pale stars, and rise up into the bright-
ness of the illimitable heaven, whose soft, sad blue eye
gazes down into the deep waters of the sea for ever,—that
sea whose motionless and silent transparency is beaming
with phosphor light, that emanates out of its sapphire
serenity like bright dreams breathed into the spirit of a
deep sleep. And the spires of the glorious city rise indis-
tinctly bright into those living mists, like pyramids of pale
fire from some vast altar ; and amidst the glory of the
dream, there is as it were the voice of a multitude entering
by the eye—arising from the stillness of the city like the
summer wind passing over the leaves of the forest, when
a murmur is heard amidst their multitudes.

"This, oh Maga, is the picture which your critic has
pronounced to be like ' models of different parts of Venice,
streaked blue and white, and thrown into a flour-tub ' ! "

Before sending this reply to the editor of *Blackwood*,
as had been intended, it was thought only right that Turner
should be consulted, as he was the person most interested.
The MS. was enclosed to his address in London, with a
courteous note from Mr. John James Ruskin, asking his
permission to publish. Turner replied, expressing the scorn
which such a man would be sure to feel for anonymous
attacks ; and jestingly hinting that the art-critics of the old
Scotch school found their " meal-tub " in danger from his
" flour-tub " : but " he never moved in such matters," so he
sent on the MS. to Mr. Munro of Novar, who had bought
the picture.

Thus the essay was lost, until another copy turned up

among old papers, enabling us to add an important link to the history of a great enterprise ; for this was the " first chapter," the germ of *Modern Painters*, and indeed of all Mr. Ruskin's work as an exponent of painting.

Turner was quite right in silencing his young champion. The essay, though extremely clever for a boy of seventeen, was naturally immature, and it would have done little except prolong the discussion, for which John Ruskin was hardly ripe. And then, instead of *Modern Painters*, we should have had only a few unsatisfactory passages of repartee in the pages of forgotten reviews. Turner did not even ask to see his young champion ; for he was shy of the world ; always either overworking himself or seeking violent relaxation ; and he did not like the sort of people who talked about art, even when they complimented him. It is always futile discussing what might have been : if Turner had taken the young writer kindly and frankly by the hand, he might have saved him from many errors both about himself and about art : but perhaps—most likely— the greater and weightier individuality would have crushed or bent the younger and more pliable ; and instead of a Turner and a Ruskin we should have had only a Turner, and his biographer.

Ten days or so after this episode John Ruskin was matriculated at Oxford. He tells the story of his first appearance as a gownsman in one of those gossiping letters in verse which show his improvisational humorous talent to the best advantage :

"A night, a day past o'er—the time drew near,—
The morning came—I felt a little queer ;
Came to the push ; paid some tremendous fees ;
Past ; and was capped and gowned with marvellous ease.

Then went to the Vice-Chancellor to swear
Not to wear boots, nor cut or comb my hair
Fantastically,—to shun all such sins
As playing marbles or frequenting inns ;
Always to walk with breeches black or brown on ;
When I go out, to put my cap and gown on ;
With other regulations of the sort, meant
For the just ordering of my comportment.
Which done, in less time than I can rehearse it, I
Found myself member of the University ! "

In pursuance of his plan of getting the best of everything, his father had chosen the best college, as far as he knew, and the best position in it—that of gentleman-commoner. Nowadays, no doubt, he would have wished his son to be a scholar of Balliol, or whatever college has the highest record in the last examination. But at that time Oxford was rather the fashionable finishing-school for young gentlemen than the scene of intellectual struggle-for-life which it has since become. Mr. Ruskin hints that one reason for entering him as gentleman-commoner was a fear that he might not pass the ordinary matriculation examination. But, although his teaching had been desultory, it would have been strange if any college had refused a candidate with such evidence of brains and the will to use them.

After matriculation he did not go into residence until January 1837. Part of the winter was spent on his Newdigate, part on his " Smalls." The long vacation was passed in a tour through the north of England, during which his advanced knowledge of art was shown in a series of admirable drawings, so Proutesque in manner as almost to pass for the master's work, except for traces of a strong individuality which could not be concealed. Their subjects are chiefly architectural, though a few mountain drawings are found in his sketch-book for that summer.

The interest in ancient and picturesque buildings was no new thing, and it seems to have been the branch of art-study which was chiefly encouraged by his father. During this tour among Cumberland cottages and Yorkshire abbeys, a plan was formed of a series of papers on archi-tecture; perhaps in answer to an invitation from Mr. Loudon, who had started an architectural magazine, and knew John Ruskin from previous contributions to the *Magazine* of *Natural History*. And so in the summer he began to write "The Poetry of Architecture; or, the Architecture of the Nations of Europe considered in its association with Natural Scenery and National Character"; and the papers were worked off, month by month, from Oxford or wherever he might be, with a steadiness that showed his power of detaching himself from immediate surroundings, like any experienced littérateur. This piece of work, buried in a rarely seen periodical, is a valuable link in the development of his *Seven Lamps*; anticipating many of his conclusions of later days, and exhibiting his literary style as very near maturity. It deals chiefly with the countries he had visited—the English Lakeland, France, Switzerland and North Italy; but some little notice of Spain suggests occasional collaboration with his father.

He begins by deploring the want of taste in modern buildings—the " Swiss châlets " in suburban brickfields, and the Regent's Park boxes on Derwentwater : and he shows that it is the public who are to blame, for though utility is the first requirement, it does not preclude taste. Then he contrasts, with something of the power of analysis which he afterwards displayed, the snug neatness of south-

country English cottages, with the historical and sentimental interest of dilapidated French farms, and the
pensive poetry of half-ruined Italian country-houses. He
shows how each style arises naturally from the requirements and circumstances of the inhabitants, and therefore
is in harmony with the surroundings. Still more perfect
examples are the cottages of the Alps and the Cumbrian
hills. He is not so kind to the Swiss and their châlets
as one might expect; but he describes the rugged home-
steads of the Lake district with affection: " The un-
cultivated mountaineer of Cumberland has no ' taste,' and
no idea what architecture means; he never thinks of what
is right, or what is beautiful; but he builds what is most
adapted to his purpose, and most easily erected. By
suiting the building to the uses of his own life, he gives
it humility; and by raising it with the nearest material,
adapts it to its situation. That is all that is required."

He proceeds to formulate a few principles by which a
builder of cottages, conscious of what he is doing, should
be guided. In " A Chapter on Chimneys " he explains why
they should not be ornamented, holding tight to the notion
of the development of beauty from use, and illustrating
with a sketch of " an old building called Coniston Hall."

The second half of the series discusses the Villa—that is,
the gentleman's country-house as distinct from the cottage
and from the castle or palace. He describes the shores
of Windermere with sarcastic humour; and contrasts the
villas of Como, slyly quoting—or misquoting—a couple of
lines from one of his own unpublished poems. In developing the subject, he anticipates many of his later views, and
balances the commonsense utilitarianism of his first part
by saying, as he did .in the *Seven Lamps*—" The mere

preparation of convenience is not architecture in which
man can take pride, or ought to take delight ; but the
high and ennobling part of architecture is that of giving
to buildings whose parts are determined by necessity such
forms and colours as shall delight the mind." And he
concludes by expounding at length the principles that
should guide the builder of country-houses, insisting on
their thoughtful adaptation to the scenery and position,
as opposed to the mere following of arbitrary style and
blind fashion.

The papers terminate with the termination of the magazine, which ran for those two years only. They are bright
and amusing, full of pretty description and shrewd thoughts.
They parade a good deal of classical learning and travelled
experience ; so much so that no doubt the readers of the
magazine took their author for some dilettante don at
Oxford ; and the editor did not wish the illusion to be
dispelled. So John Ruskin had to choose a *nom de plume.*
He called himself *Kata Phusin* (" according to nature "), for
he had begun to read some Aristotle after his " Smalls." No
phrase would have better expressed his point of view, that
of common sense extended by experience, and confirmed
by the appeal to matters of fact, rather than to any authority,
or tradition, or committee of taste, or abstract principles.

While these papers were in process of publication *Kata
Phusin* plunged into his first controversy. Mr. Arthur
Parsey had published a treatise on *Perspective Rectified,*
with a new discovery that was to upset all previous practice.
He said, in effect, that when you look at a tower, the top
is farther from the eye than the bottom ; therefore it must
look narrower ; therefore it should be drawn so. This was
" Parsey's Convergence of Perpendiculars " ; according to

which vertical lines should have a vanishing point, even
though they are assumed to be parallel to the plane of
the picture.

He had been discussed by one, and ridiculed by another
of the contributors to the magazine, when *Kata Phusin*
joined in, with the remark that the convergence is per-
ceptible only when we stand too close to the tower to draw
it (when, of course, the verticals are *not* parallel to the
plane of the picture); and that we never can draw it at
all until we are so far away that the eye is practically
equidistant from all parts, top and bottom. You see that
in reflections too, he said : the vertical lines do converge,
when your eye ranges round the horizon, and from zenith
to nadir ; but as a matter of fact, in a picture we include
so small a piece of the whole field of vision that the
convergence is practically reduced to *nil.*

A writer signing himself " Q." gravely reviews the situation, and gives the palm to *Kata Phusin* ; yet, he says, the
convergence is there. To which *Kata Phusin* answers that
of course it is, and all artists know it, but they know also
that the limited angle of their picture's scope makes away
with the difficulty.

Parsey was not satisfied. *Kata Phusin* appeals to observation. He says he is looking out of his window at one
of the most noble buildings in Oxford, and the vertical lines
of it do fall exactly on the sashes of his window-frame.
He suggests a new line of defence : that to see a picture
properly, the eye must be opposite the point of sight, and
the angle of vision is the same for the picture, placed at
the right distance, as for the actual scene ; so whatever
convergence there is in the scene, there is also in the
picture, when rightly viewed. And so the discussion

dragged on; *Kata Phusin* appealing to common sense and common practice as against the mathematicians and the theorists; and the editor gave him the last word to conclude the magazine.

None of the disputants were bold enough to remark that the great science of perspective was after all only an abstraction; that the "plane of the picture" is a mere assumption, made for the convenience of geometrical draughtsmen; and that if you draw what you really see, you would draw the top of a tower *broader* than its base! —for such is the position of the question in its latest phase, as discussed with curious experiment and improved knowledge of optics, by Dr. P. H. Emerson and Mr. Goodall in a recent tract.

During this controversy, and just before the summer tour of 1838 to Scotland, John Ruskin was introduced to Miss Charlotte Withers, a young lady who was as fond of music as he was of drawing. They discussed their favourite studies with eagerness; and to settle the matter, he wrote a long essay on "The Comparative Advantages of the Studies of Music and Painting," in which he sets painting as a means of recreation and of education far above music. He allows to music a greater power of stirring emotion, but finds that power strongest in proportion as the art is diminished; so that the Æolian harp is the most touching of all melody, and next to it, owing partly to associations, the Alp-horn. "The shepherds on the high Alps live for months in perfect solitude, not perhaps seeing the face of a human being for weeks together. Among these men there is a very beautiful custom—the manner in which they celebrate their evening devotions. When the sun is just setting, and the peaks

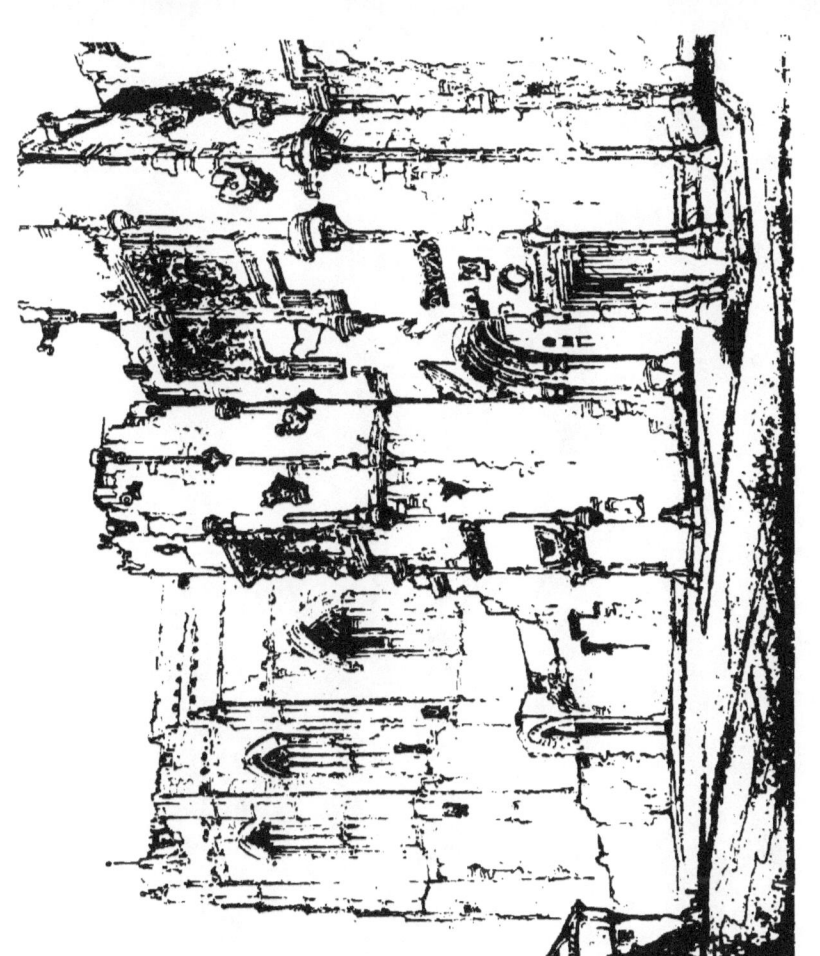

STIRLING PALACE AND CHURCH.

of eternal snow become tinted of a pale but bright rose-colour by his dying beams, the shepherd who is highest upon the mountains takes his horn, and sounds through it a few simple but melodious notes signifying 'Glory be to God.' Far and wide on the pure air floats the sound. The nearest shepherd hears, and replies; and from man to man, over the illimitable deserts of a hundred hills, passes on the voice of worship. Then there is a silence— a deep, dead silence. Every head is uncovered; every knee bowed. And from the stillness of the solitude rises the voice of supplication, heard by God only. Again the highest shepherd sounds through his horn, 'Thanks be to God.' Again is the sound taken up, and passed on from man to man along the mountains. It dies away; the twilight comes dimly down, and every one betakes himself to repose."

To the higher forms of music he awards no such power of compelling emotion, and finds no intellectual interest in them to make up for the loss; whereas in painting, the higher the art, the stronger the appeal both to the senses and the intellect. He describes an ideal "Crucifixion by Vandyke or Guido," insisting on the complexity of emotions and trains of thought roused by such a picture. He goes into ecstasies over a typical "Madonna of Raphael"; discusses David's "Horatii," and concludes that even in Landscape this double office of painting, at once artistic and literary, gives it a supremacy to which music has no claim. As a practical means of education, he finds little difficulty in showing that "with regard to drawing, the labour and time required is the same [as for music], but the advantages gained will," he thinks, "be found considerably superior. These are four: namely (1) the power

of appreciating fine pictures ; (2) the agreeable and interesting occupation of many hours ; (3) the habit of quick
observation, and exquisite perception of the beauties of
Nature ; and lastly, the power of amusing and gratifying
others."

In the examples chosen, we see the boy who admired
as yet without full discrimination ; in the line of thought
taken, we see the man. He never was a musician : he
learnt to play and sing a little, and he has composed a
few pretty little melodies as an amusement of his later
years. He takes great delight in ballad singing and in
the simpler forms of old operatic music. But he has no
ear for the higher efforts of the art ; is not what we call
musical. But what do we ask ? Surely not that one
man should combine in himself every possible power,—for
that would make but a neutral mixture.

As a forecast of his art-criticism this essay is important.
We see him giving scrupulous attention to the demands
of the artistic side, but more honestly interested, then, in
the literary subject. It was his double sympathy that
enabled him in later years to introduce the public, on the
one hand, to the aims of the artist ; and, on the other hand,
to press upon artists the admission that the public, after
all, are right in demanding that, as a picture sets out with
some suggestion of representing nature, the representation
ought to be as complete as it can be. There will always be
people who can see one side of the question only ; and
such people will always think Ruskin inconsistent.

Already at nineteen, then, we see him as a writer on
art, not full-fledged, but sturdily taking his own line and
making up his mind upon the first great questions. As
Kata Phusin he was attracting some notice. Towards

the end of 1838, a question arose as to the best site for
the proposed Scott memorial at Edinburgh ; and a writer
in the *Architectural Magazine* quotes *Kata Phusin* as the
authority in such matters ; saying that it was obvious,
after those papers of his, that design and site should be
simultaneously considered. On which the editor "begs
the favour of *Kata Phusin* to let our readers have his
opinion on the subject, which we certainly think of considerable importance."

And so he discusses the question of monuments in
general, and of this one in particular, in a long paper ;
unsatisfactorily coming to no very decided opinion ; preferring, on the whole, a statue group with a colossal Scott
on a rough pedestal, to be placed on Salisbury Crags,
"where the range gets low and broken towards the North,
at about the height of St. Anthony's Chapel." But he
finds that, after all, the climate—and, more effectually,
the sentiment of the north,—militate against this kind of
monument.

We often think we have nicely disposed of our idealists
when we have asked them to practise what they preach,
to better what they criticise. And against Mr. Ruskin it
has been urged, time and again, that his plans are fine, but
impracticable. We see him here already stopped on the
threshold by his inability to put his own principles into
action. When he is asked, "Well, now, and what are
we to do?" he replies vaguely, and in general terms, or
proposes something that won't work! The reason is
simple enough. An ideal, to be an ideal, is something
out of reach ; something to aim at, not as yet to attain.
The rest of us are content to be opportunists, to do the
best we can with the materials we have. He has all his

life been an idealist ; his counsels are counsels of perfection.
In art, in ethics, all the various departments of life that he
has touched, his work has been to set the standard higher,
not to drag it down within easy reach.   Without such men
among us, should we not be like wanderers on a waste and
dangerous moorland, making sure, indeed, of each next
step ; but to what goal tending?

CHAPTER VII.

SIR ROGER NEWDIGATE'S PRIZE.

(1837—1839.)

'Ὡς οἱ παῖδες ἄεισδον· ὁ δ' αἰπόλος ὧδ' ἀγόρευεν·
'Αδύ τι τὸ στόμα τοι, καὶ ἐφίμερος ὧ Δάφνι φωνά·
Λάσδεο τὰς σύριγγας· ἐνίκησας γὰρ ἀείδων.

Theocritus.

OXFORD in the 'Thirties has been often described.
It was beginning to awake from the torpor of its
traditional "classic groves" and cloistered erudition, and
to take upon itself the burden of educating England. It
was stirring especially in two directions: in religion, and
in physical science. The movement which created the
modern High Church and Broad Church parties was
already afoot; and it would be natural to suppose that
any active mind, thrown into the thick of the fight,
would be sure to take a side, and share the experiences
of Newman or Pusey, Pattison or Clough.

But in all these matters John Ruskin the undergraduate
was a Gallio. It seems strange that a man who had been
brought up on constant Bible-reading and sermon-hearing,
who was destined for the Church, whose eventual mission
has been to refer everything to the language and principles
of religion,—it seems strange that he, of all people, should

79

have looked on unmoved while great questions were being
agitated, consciences wrung, and souls torn asunder between
faith and doubt.

But there were reasons why he was not drawn into
the struggle. He was pious; and yet his piety was not
an affair of speculation, but of habit, a branch of ethical
practice. He had no "call" to doubt; he observed his
religious duties, and went on his way. During his career
at Oxford, also, his mother lived near him, in the High
Street, and he saw her constantly. Nothing keeps up a
habit so much as intercourse with persons who have been
accustomed to enforce it. And it was only when he got
away from his parents' company, as we shall hereafter
find, that he wandered from his parents' religion.

In the question, as between Church and Church, he
accepted what he had been taught, and all the more
easily because he had not been fostered in any of the
narrower sects, though always in the strictest Protestantism. He had not been fettered even to the Church of
England; for the Scottish traditions of his family, partly
descended from the hereditary keepers of the "Solemn
League and Covenant," the Tweddales, and partly from
old-time Jacobites, saved him from any exclusive devotion
to one party, or even nationality, in religion. He had
seen the good sides of more than one school of Protestant
Christianity, and their weak points as well. So that an
ecclesiastical contest had no interest for him; he could
take neither side.

But the other movement, then less heard of, was destined to make a greater impression on the world. The
beginning of modern Physical Science was not confined
to Oxford, but it was well represented there. And it

happened that at Christ Church there were two leading
workers in the cause : among the elder men, Dr. Buckland,
the veteran geologist ; and among the younger men, Henry
W. Acland, who was already beginning his life's work in
Physiology.

The latter—so the story runs—while crossing the Quad.
one day, spied a noble lord riding a freshman round the
place, to the great amusement and gratification of other
noble lords, the senior gentlemen-commoners. The freshman took his initiatory bullying with good nature ; and
though he had never been to school, to speak of, and
though he was too given to reading and writing, and though
his father was only a wine-merchant, he soon won a place
in the miniature republic, where, while ordinary advantages
of course have their weight, still the best man is more
frankly recognised than in the bigger world.   And if our
freshman had found no other company at Christ Church
but this, it would still have been good for him to be there.
As a self-educated dilettante in art and a bourgeois
reformer of society he could never have attained that
breadth of outlook, that freedom of expression, which he
got by mixing with all classes, from the highest to the
·lowest ; gauging all tastes, testing all pretensions, comparing all ideals.

But to meet a man like Mr. Acland, to be placed at
the outset in necessary comradeship with so fine a nature,
was a true stroke of luck ; without which young Ruskin
would have been left to fight his way alone in an uncon-
genial world.   He was too able a man to be neglected
but too thoughtful to be content with merely aristocratic
and fashionable companions.   If he had not found real
comrades in his own college and at his own table in

Hall, he might have been obliged to seek them elsewhere, to have become perhaps the hero of an inferior set of men, which is the worst thing that can happen to a clever undergraduate.

To Mr. (now Sir) Henry Acland, and Dr. Buckland, who took notice of a young geologist and made him useful in drawing diagrams for lectures, he owed his first encouragement in science. To Sir Charles Newton, now famous as our leading authority on classical archæology, and at that time an undergraduate antiquary of Christ Church, young Ruskin owed sympathy in his artistic tastes. So that, by the best of fortune, no side of his nature was left undeveloped, and he began his career as the junior comrade of the best men in each walk of life.

The dons of his college were not interesting to him, nor interested in him. His college-tutor, indeed, the Rev. Walter Brown, remained his friend ; and his private tutor, the Rev. Osborne Gordon, famous for his scholarship but still more for his tact, was always regarded with affectionate respect. Habits of study and an extremely good memory made his reading easy to him. He was always at a disadvantage in the nicer points of classical scholarship ; but he made up for that by a much more vivid interest in the subjects he read—Herodotus and Thucydides, the tragedians and Aristophanes, with some Plato and Aristotle. To him they were not merely school-books : they were authors and inspirers of original thought, which in the end is more valuable than grammatical minutiæ. But, even so, he was a safe candidate for examinations, and could have won any ordinary success by mere force of intelligence and application, if his health had permitted. So little was he overworked by the usual course of reading, that he had to look for other subjects to employ his mind upon : such as the *Kata Phusin* papers, and Science. But the chief by-play of his Oxford years was poetry.

He had made up his mind to win the Newdigate ; and he had not been in residence a term before he sent in his first trial-poem—" The Gipsies " : an essay in rhyme in the style of the eighteenth century, very well devised and full of neat lines and passages of shrewd reflection. He describes the encampment in the woods ; the vagrant's feats and the fortune-teller's power, too often abused but sometimes used for kindly ends. Then he turns suddenly to contrast this beggarly function of modern astrology and palmistry with the widespread belief in such things of old ; and to compare the despairing superstition of the gipsies with enlightened faith in

> " That Great One whose spirit interweaves
> The pathless forests with their life of leaves ;
> And lifts the lowly blossoms, bright in birth,
> Out of the cold, black, rotting charnel earth :
> Walks on the moon-bewildered waves at night,
> Breathes in the morning breeze, burns in the evening light ;
> Feeds the young ravens when they cry ; uplifts
> The pale-lipped clouds among the mountain clifts ;
> Moves the pale glacier on its restless path ;
> Lives in the desert's universal death ;
> And fills, with that one glance which none elude,
> The grave, the city, and the solitude."

And he concludes by showing how far removed from true liberty is the unrestrained and lawless life, which some have sentimentally praised and unreflectingly envied ; in which he anticipates his own doctrine of the *Seven Lamps*, and his consistent belief that only in service is perfect freedom to be found and used.

This poem is much above the average of such exercises, and would have won the prize had it not been for the still stronger work of a senior member of his own college, Arthur Penrhyn Stanley, afterwards Dean of Westminster. Ruskin was not to be beaten, but with " a perseverance worthy of a better cause " tried again and again until he was successful. We may be allowed to regret this success, not so much for the sake of the time spent upon writing, re-writing and polishing those useless essays in verse, as because it fixed the young poet in a habit of treating his art merely as an art ; writing to order without waiting for inspiration. We have already seen him supplying verses for a picture—the " Salzburg " of *Friendship's Offering* : and, strange as it may seem in a man like Ruskin, we find him repeatedly doing the same kind of thing, as in " The Two Paths "—the poem of that name, and " The Departed Light." This was owing partly to his " fatal facility," partly to his humility in accepting advice and meeting the requirements of any one who assumed to be his critic and censor. He was sincerely anxious to learn the art of literature, to improve himself ; and generously ready to please. So he laid aside his own standards for those of his father, of Mr. Pringle, of Mr. Harrison, of the Newdigate examiners : a dangerous thing to do, even with his powers. And he succeeded in adapting his verse to the fashion of the day so well that his own individuality in it was lost, all the spontaneity of his earlier work vanished ; while in the meantime Tennyson and Browning were steering their own courses in sturdy independence toward ultimate success.

The second Newdigate, " The Exile of St. Helena," though it treated of a subject familiar to him, was more stilted, more strained and unreal than the first. This time the prize was won by his old schoolfellow at Mr. Dale's, Henry Dart of Exeter College. He was at any rate beaten by a friend, and by a poem which his honourable sympathy and assistance had helped to perfect.

The third try won it, with " Salsette and Elephanta " : in which, though it deals with scenes of which he had no experience, there is an artificial gorgeousness of description, carefully extracted from books of travel, and an exaltation of phrase copied from the " best models," enough to justify the award. No doubt the examiners were further influenced by the orthodoxy of the closing passage, which prophesies the prompt extermination of Brahminism by the missionaries.

In this poem there is a strong tinge of the horrible, which, to judge from Mr. Ruskin's expressed opinions on art, we should hardly suspect ever to have been his taste. But during all his boyhood and youth there were moments of weakness when he allowed himself to be carried away by a sort of nightmare, the reaction from healthy delight in natural beauty. In later life the same tendency led him at times to brood over the sufferings of the poor and the crimes of society until a too sensitive brain could no longer bear the tension and the torture.

But by that time he had learnt to put limits to art, and to refuse the merely horrible as its material. As an undergraduate, however, writing for effect, he gave free rein to the morbid imaginations to which his unhappy *affaire de cœur* and the mental excitement of the period predisposed him. In his first year he was reading Herodotus, and was struck—as who is not?—by the romantic picturesqueness of the incomparable old chronicler. Several passages of Greek history—the story of the Athenian fugitive from the

massacre at Ægina, and the death of Aristodemus at Platæa
—offered telling subjects for lyrical verse : the death of
Arion and the dethronement of Psammenitus were treated,
later, at length ; but above all, the account of the Scythians,
with their wild primitive life and manners, fascinated him.
Instead of gathering from their history such an idyl as
Mr. William Morris would have made, he fixed upon only
the most gruesome points—their fierce struggle with the
Persians, cruelty and slavery, burial-rites and skull-
goblets—which he set himself to picture with ghastly
realism.

Mr. Harrison, his literary mentor, approved these poems,
and inserted them in *Friendship's Offering*, along with love-
songs to Adèle. One had a great success and was freely
copied—plagiarism being then, as always, the most favourable criticism : and the preface to the annual for 1840 publicly
thanked the " gifted writer " for his " valuable aid." What
with that, and the Newdigate just gained, it surely seemed
that John Ruskin had found his vocation at last, and that
he was on the high road to reputation as a poet. But
" the great difficulty about making verses," as Dr. Johnson
sagely observed, "is to know when you have made good
ones." Was there nobody among those friends, whose
criticism he anxiously courted and whose advice he so
humbly followed, to tell him that if he would keep clear of
Græcisms in syntax and Latinisms in etymology,* and if
he would condescend to be as explicit in verse as he could

---

* To wit, "the scatheless keel," for "the keel without scathe," and
" prore " for " prow." The subject of the song is obscure until, on re-
reading, one sees some great Indiaman, homeward bound with troops
aboard, striking an unknown rock and sinking with all hands, in sight
of shore.

be in prose, then he would charm the world with such music
as we hear in *The Wreck* ?—

> " Its masts of might, its sails so free
>   Had borne the scatheless keel
> Through many a day of darkened sea,
>   And many a storm of steel.
> When all the winds were calm, it met
> (With home-returning prore)
>   With the lull
>   Of the waves
> On a low lee shore.
>
> " The crest of the conqueror
>   On many a brow was bright ;
> The dew of many an exile's eye
>   Had dimmed the dancing sight.
> But for love, and for victory,
> One welcome was in store,
>   . . . In the lull
>   Of the waves
> On a low lee shore."

CHAPTER VIII.

THE BROKEN CHAIN.

(1840—1841.)

"But never more the same two sister pearls
Ran down the silken thread to kiss each other
On her white neck ;—so is it with this rhyme."
Tennyson.

"WHEN all the seas were calm ; "—so it seemed to
the friends who celebrated John Ruskin's coming-
of-age, on Feb. 8th, 1840. He was not far, now, from his
desired haven. A very few months, and he would be passing his final examinations, taking his degree, and preparing
for honourable settlement in a dignified profession in which
life would be congenial, advancement easy, and success
anticipated. He had wealth, which he owed to his father ;
health, to all appearance, which he owed to his mother's
constant care ; friends of the best, and fame already much
wider and more appreciable than the strictly academic
reputation of the ordinary successful undergraduate. For
was he not the authority of one magazine, the "gifted
contributor" of another, winner of the most popular University prize, and, in circles where such tastes are current,
welcomed as a clever young artist and an eager student
of science ? If, as he was bidden, he "counted up his

mercies," there was much to be thankful for ; it was indeed an auspicious coming-of-age.

His father, who had sympathised with his admiration for Turner enough to buy two pictures—the " Richmond Bridge " and the " Gosport "—for their Herne Hill drawing-room, now gave him a picture all to himself for his rooms in St. Aldate's—the " Winchelsea "; and settled on him an allowance of pocket-money of £200 a year. The first use he made of his wealth was to buy another Turner. In the Easter vacation he met Mr. Griffith, the dealer, at the private view of the Old Water-colour Society ; and hearing that the " Harlech Castle " was for sale, he bought it there and then, with the characteristic disregard for money which has always made the vendors of pictures and books and minerals find him extremely pleasant to deal with. But as his love-affair had shown his mother how little he had taken to heart her chiefest care for him, so this first business transaction was a painful awakening to his father, the canny Scotch merchant, who had heaped up riches hoping that his son would gather them.

This " Harlech Castle " transaction, however, was not altogether unlucky. It brought him an introduction to the painter, whom he met when he was next in town, at Mr. Griffith's house. He knew well enough the popular idea of Turner, as a morose and niggardly, inexplicable man. As he had seen faults in Turner's painting, so he was ready to acknowledge the faults in his character. But while the rest of the world, with a very few exceptions, dwelt upon the faults, Ruskin had penetration to discern the virtues which they hid. Few passages in his auto-biography are more striking than the transcript from his journal of the same evening recording his first impression :—

" ' I found in him a somewhat eccentric, keen-mannered, matter-of-fact, English-minded—gentleman ; good-natured evidently, bad-tempered evidently, hating humbug of all sorts, shrewd, perhaps a little selfish, highly intellectual, the powers of the mind not brought out with any delight in their manifestation, or intention of display, but flashing out occasionally in a word or a look.'   Pretty close, that," he adds, later, " and full, to be set down at the first glimpse, and set down the same evening."

Turner was not a man to make an intimate of, all at once : the acquaintanceship continued, and it ripened into as close a confidence as the eccentric painter's habits of life permitted.   He seems to have been more at home with the father than with the son ; but even when the young man took to writing books about him, he did not, as Carlyle is reported to have done in a parallel case, show his exponent to the door.

The occasion of John Ruskin's coming to town this time was not a pleasant one : nothing less than the complete break-down of his health,—we have heard the reasons why, in the last chapter but one.   It is true that he was working very hard during this spring ; but hard reading does not —of itself—kill people : only when it is combined with real and prolonged mental distress, acting upon a sensitive temperament.   The case was thought serious ; reading was stopped, and the patient was ordered abroad for the winter.

From February to May, and such a change !   Then he had seemed so near the top of the hill, and the prospect was opening out before him ; now, cloud and storm had come suddenly down ; the path was lost, the future blotted out.   Disappointed in love after four years of hope and effort ; disappointed in ambition after so nearly gathering the fruits of his labour ; to be laid aside, to be sent away out of the battlefield as a wounded man,—perhaps, to die.

We have seen how this young man bore himself when he met Love face to face ; watch him now, encountering Death.

For that summer there was no hurry to be gone : rest was more needful than change, at first. Late in September the same family-party crossed the sea to Calais : how different a voyage for them all from the merry departures of bygone Mays ! Which way should they turn ? Not to Paris, for *there* was the cause of all these ills ; so they went straight southwards through Normandy to the Loire, and saw the chateaux and churches from Orleans to Tours ; famous for their Renaissance architecture, and for the romance of their chivalric history. Amboise especially made a strong impression upon even the languid and unwilling invalid. It stirred him up to write, in easy verse, the tale of love and death that his own situation too readily suggested. In "The Broken Chain," he indulged his gloomy fancy, turning, as it was sure to do, into a morbid nightmare of mysterious horror, not without reminiscence of Coleridge's *Christabel*. But through it all he preserved, so to speak, his dramatic *incognito* : his own disappointment and his own antici- pated death were the motives of the tale ; but treated in such a manner as not to betray his secret, nor even to wound the feelings of the lady who now was beyond appeal from an honourable lover—taking his punishment like a man.

This poem lasted him, for private writing, all through that journey : a fit emblem of the broken life which it

records.   A healthier source of distraction was his drawing,
in which he had received a fresh impetus from the exhibition of David Roberts' sketches in the East.   More delicate
than Prout's work, entering into the detail of architectural
form more thoroughly, and yet suggesting chiaroscuro with
broad washes of quiet tone and touches of light, cleverly
introduced—"that marvellous *pop* of light across the
foreground" Harding said of the picture of the Great
Pyramid—these drawings were a mean between the limited
manner of Prout and the inimitable fulness of Turner.
Ruskin took up the fine pencil and the broad brush, and
with that blessed habit of industry which has helped so
many a one through times of trial, made sketch after
sketch on the half-imperial board, finished just so far as
his strength and time allowed, as they passed from the
Loire to the mountains of Auvergne, and to the valley
of the Rhone, and thence slowly round the Riviera to
Pisa and Florence and Rome.

He was not in a mood to sympathise readily with the
enthusiasms of other people.   They expected him to be
delighted with the scenery, the buildings, the picture-
galleries of Italy, and to forget himself in admiration.
He did admire Michelangelo, and he was interested in
the back streets and slums of the cities.   Something
piquant was needed to arouse him; the mild ecstasies of
common connoisseurship hardly appeal to a young man
between life and death.   He met the friends to whom
he had brought introductions: Mr. Joseph Severn, who
had been Keats' companion, and was afterwards to be
the genial consul at Rome; and the two Messrs. Richmond,
then studying art in the regular professional way—one
of them to become a celebrated portrait painter, and the

other a canon of Carlisle. But his views on art were not theirs; he was already too independent and outspoken in praise of his own heroes, and too sick in mind and body to be patient and to learn.

They had not been a month in Rome before he took the fever. As soon as he was recovered, they went still farther south, and loitered for a couple of months in the neighbourhood of Naples, visiting the various scenes of interest—Sorrento, Amalfi, Salerno. They did not drag the patient up Vesuvius, of course; and perhaps even if he had been strong he would not have cared for the excursion,—for just as he loved the Alps and found nothing but beauty and beneficence in their crags and glaciers, so he saw in the crumbling soil and lurid smoke of the volcanic region—in spite of its scientific interest—" the image of visible hell." It was not only sentimentalism, but a sensitiveness to form, especially to the details of curvature, which gave him this impression : a quality of his taste which had been early shown in his awe of the twining roots of Friar's Crag, and which has determined most of his judgments on art. Where, in nature, the subject admits, or, in art, the painter perceives, what he calls " infinite curves," springing lines of life, he has always recognised beauty ; but where the normal exquisiteness of vital form is replaced by lines suggesting inertness or decay, he has scented " a form of death."

On the way to Naples he had noted the winter scene at La Riccia which he afterwards used for a glowing passage in *Modern Painters*; and he had ventured into a village of brigands to draw such a castle as he had once imagined in his *Leoni*. From Naples he wrote an account of a landslip near Giagnano, which was sent

home to the Ashmolean Society.   He seemed better;
they turned homewards, when suddenly he was seized with
all the old symptoms, worse than ever.   After another
month at Rome, they travelled slowly northwards from
town to town ; spent ten days of May at Venice, and
passed through Milan and Turin, and over the Mont
Cenis to Geneva.

At last he was among the mountains again—the Alps
that he loved. It was not only that the air of the Alps
braced him, but the spirit of mountain-worship stirred
him as nothing else could. At last he seemed himself,
after more than a year of intense depression ; and he
records that one day, in church at Geneva, he resolved
to *do* something, to *be* something useful. That he could
make such a resolve was a sign of returning health ; but
if, as I have heard, he had just been reading Carlyle's
lately published lectures " on Heroes," though he did not
accept Carlyle's conclusions nor admire his style, might
he not, in spite of his judgment, have been spurred the
more into energy by that enthusiastic gospel of action ?

They travelled home by Basle and Laon ; but London
in August, and the premature attempt to be energetic,
brought on a recurrence of the symptoms of consumption.
He wished to try the mountain-cure again, and set out
with his friend Richard Fall for a tour in Wales.   But his
father recalled him to Leamington, to try iron and dieting
under Dr. Jephson, who, if he was called a quack, was a
sensible one, and successful in subduing, for several years
to come, the more serious phases of the disease.   The
patient was not cured : he suffered from time to time from
his chest, and still more from a weakness of the spine,
which during all the period of his early manhood gave

him trouble, and finished by bending his tall and lithe figure into something that, were it not for his face, would be deformity. In 1847 he was again at Leamington under Jephson, in consequence of a relapse into the consumptive symptoms ; after which we hear no more of it. He outgrew the tendency, as so many do. But nevertheless the alarm had been justifiable, and the malady had left traces which, in one way and another, haunted him ever after. For one of the worst effects of consumption is to be thought consumptive, and marked down as an invalid.

At Leamington, then, in September 1841, he was finding a new life under the Doctor's dieting, and new aims in life, which were eventually to resolder, for a while, the broken chain. Among the Scotch friends of the Ruskins there was a family at Perth whose daughter came to visit at 'Herne Hill—more lovely, and more lively, than his Spanish princess had been. The story goes that she challenged the melancholy John, engrossed in his drawing and geology, to write a fairy-tale—as the least likely task for him to fulfil. Upon which he produced at a couple of sittings *The King of the Golden River,* a pretty medley of Grimm's grotesque and Dickens' kindliness and the true Ruskinian ecstasy of the Alps.

He had come through the valley of the shadow, that terrible experience which so few survive ; fewer still emerge from it without loss of all that makes their life worth the living. But though for a while he was "hard bested," he fought a good fight, and kept his faith in God, and in Nature, and—but too fond a faith, in the human heart.

CHAPTER IX.

THE GRADUATE OF OXFORD.

(1841—1842.)

"Enough of Science and of Art ;
    Close up those barren leaves ;
  Come forth, and bring with you a heart
      That watches and receives." *Wordsworth.*

R EADY for work again, and in reasonable health of
mind and body, John Ruskin sat down in his little
study at Herne Hill in November 1841, with his wise tutor,
Osborne Gordon.   There was eighteen months' leeway to
make up ; and the dates of ancient history, the details of
schematised Aristotelianism, soon slip out of mind when
one is sketching in Italy.   But he was more serious now
about his work ; and aware of his deficiencies.   To be
useful in the world, is it not necessary, first, to understand
all possible Greek constructions?   So said the voice of
Oxford ; but our undergraduate was saved, both now and
afterwards, from this vain ambition.   " I think it would
hardly be worth your while," said Gordon, with Delphic
double-entendre.

Ruskin could not now go in for honours, for his lost year
had superannuated him.   So in May he went up for a pass.
In those times, when a pass-man showed unusual powers,
they could give him an honorary class : not a high class,

because the range of the examination was less than in the honour-school. This candidate wrote a poor Latin prose, it seems ; but his divinity, philosophy, and mathematics were so good that they gave him the best they could, an honorary double fourth. Upon which he took his B.A. degree, and could describe himself as " A Graduate of Oxford."

It is noteworthy that Ruskin wrote a bad Latin prose. He knew Latin well ; it was Greek that he was deficient in. He knew French, and read it constantly ; which is a help to Latin writing. He was a clever imitator of style, and surely never workman handled his tools with readier skill. But he was inaccurate. His early writing was full of thought, of sonority, of effect ; but risking strange irregularities of grammar, not to say blunders, from which he has never quite cleared his paragraphs. That freedom of touch is a trick of his literary art.

The divinity, by which is meant Bible-knowledge, was thoroughly learnt from his mother's early lessons. Not long after he was contemptuously amused at a Scotch reviewer who did not know what a " chrysoprase " was : as the word occurs in the Revelation, he assumed that every one ought to know it, whether mineralogist or not. And his works teem with Biblical quotations—see their indexes for the catalogue. The mathematics were not elaborate in the old Oxford pass-school ; geometry and the elements of trigonometry and conics, thoroughly got by heart, and frequently alluded to in early works, sum up his studies. The philosophy meant the usual Logic from Aldrich, with Bacon and Locke, Aristotle and Plato, analysed into rather thin abstract. But Ruskin, with his thoroughness in all matters of general interest, took in the teaching of his books and inwardly digested it. *Modern Painters*, even in its literary style, is imbued with Locke ; Aristotle is his leader and antagonist, alternately, throughout the earlier period of art criticism ; and Plato his guide and philosopher ever after. Some Scotch philosophy he had read : Thomas Brown, his parents' old friend ; Dugald Stewart, and the rest of the school ; and their teaching comes out in the scheme of thought that underlies his artistic theories.

It is worth while dwelling upon his acquirements at this moment, taking stock, as it were, because he was on the brink of his first great work. *Modern Painters* has been usually looked upon as the sudden outburst of a genius ; young, but mature; complex, but inexplicable ; to be accepted as a gospel, or to be decried as the raving of a heretic. But we cannot trace the author's life without seeing that the book is only one episode in an interesting development. We have been gradually led up to it ; and as gradually we shall be led away from it. And the better we understand the circumstances of its production, the better we shall be able to appreciate it, to weigh it, and to keep what is permanent in it. That will be true criticism, the only possible criticism for an intelligent reader, who sees no authority in the impudent assumption of an extemporised black cap.

All this religious and useful learning was very lightly carried by our Oxford graduate. He could now take no high academic position, and the continued weakness of his health kept him from entering either commerce or the Church. And his real interest in art was not crowded out even by the last studies for his examination. While he was working with Gordon, in the autumn of 1841, he was also taking lessons from J. D. Harding; and the famous study of ivy, his first naturalistic sketching, to which we must revert,—this must have been done a week or two before going up for his " finals."

The lessons from Harding were a useful counter-stroke to the excessive and exaggerated Turnerism in which he had been indulging during his illness.   The drawings of Amboise, the coast of Genoa, and the Glacier des Bois, though published later, were made before he had exchanged fancy for fact; and they bear, on the face of them, the obvious marks of an unhealthy state of mind.   Harding, whose robust common sense and breezy mannerism endeared him to the British amateur of his generation, was just the man to .correct any morbid tendency.   He had religious views in sympathy with his pupil; and he soon inoculated Ruskin with his contempt for the minor Dutch school; those bituminous landscapes—so unlike the sparkling fresh-ness that Harding's own water colour illustrated; and those vulgar tavern-scenes, painted, he declared, by sots who disgraced art alike in their works and in their lives.

Until this epoch, John Ruskin had found much that interested him in the Dutch and Flemish painters of the seventeenth century.   He had classed them all together as the school of which Rubens, Vandyck and Rembrandt were the chief masters,—and those as names to rank with Raphael and Michelangelo and Velasquez.   He was a humorist, not without boyish delight in a good Sam-Wellerism; and so could be amused with the "drolls," until Harding appealed to his religion and morality against them.   He was a chiaroscurist, and not naturally offended by their violent light and shade, until George Richmond showed him the more excellent way in colour, the glow of

Venice ; first hinting it at Rome in 1840, and then proving
it in London in the spring of 1842, from Samuel Rogers'
treasures, of which the chief (now in the National Gallery)
was the " Christ appearing to the Magdalen."

Much as the author of *Modern Painters* owed to these
friends and teachers, and to the advantages of his varied
training, he would never have written his great work without a farther inspiration.   Harding's especial *forte* was his
method of drawing trees.   He looked at nature with an
eye which, for his period, was singularly fresh and un-
prejudiced ; he had a strong feeling for truth of structure
as well as for picturesque effect ; and he taught his pupils
to observe as well as to draw.   But in his own practice he
rested too much on *having observed* ; formed a style ; and
copied himself if he did not copy the old masters.   Hence
he held to rules of composition, and conscious graces of
arrangement ; and while he taught naturalism in study, he
followed it up with teaching artifice in practice.

Turner, who was not a drawing-master, lay under no
necessity to formulate his principles and stick to them.
On the contrary, his style developed like a kaleidoscope,
ever changing into something more rich and strange.   He
had been in Switzerland and on the Rhine in 1841,
" painting his impressions," making watercolour notes from
memory of effects that had struck him.   From one of these,
" Splügen," he had made a finished picture, and now wished
to get commissions for more of the same class.   Ruskin
was greatly interested in this series, because they were
not landscapes of the ordinary type, scenes from nature
squeezed into the mould of recognised artistic composition ;
nor on the other hand mere photographic transcripts ; but
dreams, as it were, of the mountains and sunsets, in which

Turner's wealth of detail was suggested, and his intuitive knowledge of form expressed, together with the unity which comes of the faithful record of a single impression. Nothing had been done like them before, in landscape. They showed that an artistic result might be obtained without the use of the ordinary tricks and professional rules ; that there was a sort of composition possible, of which the usual hackneyed arrangements were merely frigid and vapid imitations ; and that this higher kind of art was only to be learnt by long watching of Nature and sincere rendering of her motives, of her supreme moments, of the spirit of her scenes.

The lesson was soon enforced upon his mind by example. One day, while taking his student's constitutional, he noticed a tree-stem with ivy upon it, which seemed not ungraceful, and invited a sketch. As he drew, he fell into the spirit of its natural arrangement, and soon perceived how much finer it was as a piece of design than any conventional rearrangement would be. Harding had tried to show him how to generalise foliage ; but in this example he saw that not generalisation was needed to get at its beauty, but truth. If he could express his sense of the charm of the natural arrangement, what use in substituting an artificial composition ?

In that discovery lay the germ of his whole theory of art, the gist of his mission. Understanding the importance of it, we shall understand his subsequent writing, the grounds of his criticism and the text of his art-teaching. If it can be summed in a word, the word is " Sincerity." Be sincere with Nature, and take her as she is ; neither casually glancing at her " effects," nor dully labouring at her parts, with the intention of improving and blending

them into something better : but taking her all in all.   On
the other hand, be sincere with yourself ; knowing what
you truly admire, and painting that : refusing the hypocrisy
of any "grand style" or "high art" just as much as you
refuse to pander to vulgar tastes.   And then vital art is
produced ; and if the workman be a man of great powers,
great art.

All this follows from the ivy-sketch on Tulse Hill in
May 1842.   It did not follow all at once : repeated experiment was needed to give the grounds from which the induc-
tion was drawn.   At Fontainebleau soon after, under much
the same circumstances, a study of an aspen-tree, idly
begun, but carried out with interest and patience, confirmed
the principle.   At Geneva, once more in the church where
he had formed such resolutions the year before, the desire
came over him with renewed force : now not only to be
usefully employed, but to be employed in the service of
a definite mission ; which, be it observed, was, in art,
exactly what Carlyle had preached in every other sphere
of life in that book of *Heroes* : the gospel of sincerity ; the
reference of greatness in any form to honesty of purpose
as the underlying motive of a perspicuous intellect and
a resolute will,—these last being necessary conditions of
success ; but the sincerity being the chief thing needful.

The design took shape.   At Chamouni he studied plants
and rocks and clouds, not as an artist, to make pictures out
of them, nor as a scientist, to class them and analyse them ;
but to learn their aspects and enter into the spirit of their
growth and structure.   And though on his way home
through Switzerland and down the Rhine he made a few
drawings in his old style for admiring friends, they were
the last of the kind that he attempted.   Thenceforward his

path was marked out ; he had found his vocation.   He
was not to be a poet—that was too definitely bound up
with the past which he wanted to forget, and with conven-
tionalities of art which he wished to shake off ; not to be
an artist, struggling with the rest to please a public which
he felt himself called upon to teach ; not a man of science,
for his botany and geology were to be the means and not
the ends of his teaching ; but the mission was laid upon
him to tell the world that Art, no less than the other
spheres of life, had its Heroes ; that the mainspring of their
energy was Sincerity, and the burden of their utterance,
Truth.

BOOK II.

THE ART CRITIC.

(1842—1860.)

"The almost unparalleled example of a man winning for himself the unanimous plaudits of his generation and time, and then casting them away like dust, that he may build his monument—*ære perennius.*"

Ruskin on Turner, 1844.

RUSKIN'S HOME AT HERNE HILL.

By Arthur Severn, R.I.

[Vol. L, p 107.]

CHAPTER I.

"TURNER AND THE ANCIENTS."

(1842—1844.)

Ἀρχὴ γὰρ τὸ ὅτι.
Aristotle, Eth. i. 4.

THE neighbour, or the Oxonian friend, who climbed the steps of the Herne Hill house and called upon Mrs. Ruskin, in the autumn and winter of 1842, would learn that Mr. John was hard at work in his own study overhead. Those were its windows, on the second floor, looking out upon the front garden : the big dormer-window above was his bedroom, from which he had his grand view of lowland, and far horizon, and unconfined sky, comparatively clear of London smoke. In the study itself, screened from the road by russet foliage and thick evergreens, great things were going on. But Mr. John could be interrupted ; would come running lightly downstairs, with both hands out to greet the visitor ; would show the pictures, eagerly demonstrating the beauties of the last new Turners, Ehrenbreitstein and Lucerne, just acquired ; and anticipating the sunset glories and mountain gloom of the Goldau and Dazio Grande, which the great artist was "realising" for him from sketches he had chosen at Queen Anne Street. He was very busy, but never too busy to see his friends; writing a book; and yet not to be "pumped" about it, for he had already adopted a motto which he has often repeated, "Don't talk about your work, but do it."

And, the visitor gone, he would run up to his room and his writing, sure of the thread of his ideas and the flow of his language, with none of that misery and despair of soul which an interruption brings to many another author. In the afternoon his careful mother would turn him out for a tramp round the Norwood lanes; he might look in at the Poussins and Claudes of the Dulwich Gallery; or, for a longer excursion, go over to Mr. Thomas Windus, F.S.A., and his roomful of Turner drawings; or sit to Mr. George Richmond for the second of the two portraits, the full length with desk and portfolio, and Mont Blanc in the background. After dinner, another hour or two's writing; and early to bed after finishing his chapter with a flourish of eloquence, to be read next morning at breakfast to father and mother and Mary—for from them it was no secret. The vivid descriptions of scenes yet fresh in their memory, or of pictures they treasured, the "thoughts" as they used to be called, allusions to sincere beliefs and cherished hopes, never failed to win the praise that pleased the young writer most, in happy tears of unrestrained emotion. These old-fashioned folk had not learnt the trick of *nil admirari*. Quite honestly they would say, with the German musician, "When I hear good music, then must I always weep."

We can look into the little study, and see what this writing was, that went on so busily and steadily. It was the long meditated defence of Turner, provoked by *Blackwoods Magazine* six years before, encouraged by

THE AUTHOR OF "MODERN PAINTERS."

By George Richmond, R.A. -1842.

[Vol. I., p. 108.]

Carlyle's *Heroes,* and necessitated by the silence, on this topic, of the more enlightened leaders of thought in an age of cut and dry connoisseurship and critical cant. There were teachers like Prout and Harding, right, but narrow in range ; and the moment any author ventured upon the subject of "high art," his principles of beauty and theories of sublimity stood in the way of candour and common sense.

But *Kata Phusin* had been to college, and read his "Ethics" : and he had marked such a passage as this :— "We must not forget the difference between reasoning *from* principles and reasoning *to* principles. Plato was quite right in pointing this out, and in saying that it is as important in philosophy as in running races, to know where your starting-point is to be. Now you and I," quoth Aristotle, "can reason only upon what we know,—not on what we *ought* to know, or might be *supposed* to know ; but upon what each of us has ascertained to be matter of fact. Fact, then—the particular fact—is our starting-point. Take care of the facts," he says, to put him into plain English, "and the principles will take care of themselves."

Which Aristotle did, and in the sphere of Ethics found that the observed facts of conscience and conduct were not truly explained by the old moral philosophy of the Sophists and the Academy. Just in the same way, our young Aristotelian, by beginning with the observed facts of nature,—truths, he called them, and the practice, not the precept, of great artists, superseded the eighteenth-century Academic art-theories, and created a perfectly new school of criticism ; which, however erring or incomplete in details, or misapplied in corollaries, did for English art what Aristotle did for Greek Ethics. He brought the whole subject to the bar of common sense and common understanding. He took it out of the hands of adepts and initiated jargoners, and made it public property, the right and the responsibility of all.

Though Ruskin had the honour of doing this work in the world of art, others were doing similar work in other spheres. Most of our soundest thinkers of the middle of the nineteenth century were brought up on the " Ethics," and learnt to take fact for their starting-point. The physical-science school, whether classically trained or not, was working in the same cause,—the substitution of observation and experiment for generalisation and *à priori* theories. And it is curious, as showing how accurately the young John Ruskin was representative of the spirit of his age, that at the very moment when he was propounding his revolutionary art-philosophy, John Stuart Mill was writing that *Logic* which was to convert the old hocus-pocus of Scholasticism into the method of modern scientific inquiry.

Nowadays we think of Mr. Ruskin as somewhat of a reactionary, *laudator temporis acti*, opponent of modernism. But, like many men of note, he began as a Progressist, the preacher of hope, the darter of new lights, the destroyer of pythons—chaos-bred tyrannic superstitions *quibus lumen ademptum*. His youth was an epoch of intellectual reform ; one of many such epochs, when the house of life was being set in order for another cycle's work and wage-earning.; no new thing, but necessary.

There had been such a clearance begun a hundred and seventy years before by John Locke, when *he* took fact for his starting-point in a revolt from the tyranny of philosophical dogma. And it was not at all strange that our young author should model his manifesto upon so renowned a precedent; that his style, in the opening chapters of his work, his arrangement in divisions and subdivisions, even his marginal summaries, should recall the *Essay on the Human Understanding*, from which the scheme and system of his thought were derived.

He began, like Locke, by showing that public opinion and the dicta of tradition were no valid authorities. If painting be an expression of the human mind—as, in another way, language is;—and if the contents of the mind are Ideas; then, he said, the best painting is that which contains the greatest number of the greatest Ideas. Locke had shown that all Ideas are derived from Sensation, from Reflection, and from the combination of both: the Ideas which painting can express must be similarly derived. And since the mind which we share with the Deity is nobler than the senses which we share with beasts, it was logical to conclude that, in proportion as the Ideas expressed in painting are intellectual and moral, the art that expresses them is fuller and higher. Ideas of Imitation, involving only the illusion of the senses, are the lowest of all; those of Power, artistic execution, are a step higher, but still so much in the realm of sensation as to be hardly matter of argument; and therefore the Ideas of Truth, of Beauty, and of Relation (or the imaginative presentment of poetical thought in the language of painting) are the three chief topics of his inquiry.

For the present he will discuss Truth; the more readily as it was the general complaint that Turner was untrue to Nature. What is Truth?

Aristotle had stated plainly enough—"particular fact

is our starting-point." But unfortunately Sir Joshua Reynolds, our old friend Northcote's master, the greatest English artist and art-theorist, had taught a modified Academic doctrine of Ideas, not Lockeian, but Platonic : and our young philosopher lost his way, for the time, in trying to reconcile one favourite authority with another. But he was able to show that old-fashioned generalisation was not Truth : and quitting the formal doctrinaire tone of his opening chapters, plunged eagerly into the illustration of his theme—namely, that Truth in landscape-art was the expression of natural law, by exhibiting such facts as tell the story of the scene. For example ; Canaletto, with all his wonderful mechanism, when he painted Venice lost the fulness of detail and glory of light and colour ; Prout secured only the picturesqueness with his five strokes of a reed pen ; Stanfield only the detail ; while Turner gave the full character of the place in its detail, colour, light, mystery and poetical effect.

In the analysis of natural fact as shown in painting, there was full scope for the power of descriptive writing which, as we have seen, was Ruskin's peculiar gift and study. When he came to compare Gaspar Poussin's picture of La Riccia with the real scene as he had witnessed it, he had the description ready to hand in his journal of two years before ; and a careful drawing on the spot—not indeed realising the colour, which he could not then attempt—but recording "the noonday sun slanting down the rocky slopes of La Riccia, and its masses of entangled and tall foliage," with their autumnal tints suggested so far as his water-colour wash on grey paper allowed.

A still happier adaptation of accumulated material was his word-picture of a night on the Rigi, with all its wonderful successive effects of gathering thunder, sunset in tempest, serene starlight, and the magic glories of Alpine sunrise : taken from the true story of his visit there, eight years before, as described in a rhyming letter to Richard Fall ; and ingeniously embroidered with a running commentary on a series of drawings by Turner.

Then passing to the forms of mountains, he warmed with his old enthusiasm. Years of study and travel had taught him to combine scientific geology with the mystery and poetry of the Alps. Byron and Shelley had touched the poetry of them ; a crowd of earnest investigators were working at geology. But none beside this youth of twenty-three had made them the topic of literature so lofty in aim and so masterly in execution.

And as the year ran out, he was ending his work, happy in the applause of his little domestic circle, and conscious that he was preaching the crusade of Sincerity, the cause of justice for the greatest landscape artist of any age, and justice, at the hands of a heedless public, for the glorious works of the supreme Artist of the universe. Let our young painters, he concluded, go humbly to Nature, "rejecting nothing, selecting nothing, and scorning nothing," in spite of Academic theorists ; and in time we should have a school of landscape worthy of the inspiration they would find.

There was his book : the title of it, *Turner and the Ancients*. Before publishing, to get more experienced criticism than that of the breakfast-table, he submitted it to his friend, Mr. W. H. Harrison. The title, it seemed, was not explicit enough ; and after debate they substituted one which was too explicit to be neat : "Modern Painters, their superiority in the Art of Landscape Painting to all the

VOL. I.   8

Ancient Masters proved by Examples of the True, the Beautiful, and the Intellectual, from the works of Modern Artists, especially from those of J. M. W. Turner, Esq., R.A." And as the severe tone of many remarks was felt to be hardly supported by the age and standing of so young an author, he was content to sign himself " A Graduate of Oxford."

Mr. Harrison did much for Mr. Ruskin's early work. For thirty years he revised proofs, and acted as censor in all matters of grammar and punctuation. There are few authors who can say of any good piece of work, " Alone I did it" : but whatever young Ruskin owed to Locke and to Coleridge, to Reynolds and Johnson, to Harding and Harrison, the work was such as none but he could have planned and carried through. . And for the Egoist they call him, is it not surprising that he should have submitted to the pruning of his pet periods by the editor of *Friendship's Offering*?

It is odd how easily men of note become the heroes of myths. The too common discouragement of young geniuses, the old story of the rejected manuscript, disdainful publishers, and hope deferred, experienced by so many as to be typical of the tadpole stage of a literary reputation, all this has been tacked on to Mr. Ruskin's supposed first start. Anecdotes are told of his father hawking the MS. from office to office until it found acceptance with Messrs. Smith & Elder,—absurd, since young Ruskin had been doing business for seven years past with that firm ; he was perfectly well known to them as one of the most " rising " youths of the time, and their own literary editor, Mr. Harrison, was his private mentor. And yet there is the half truth in it, that his business dealings with the publishers were generally conducted through his father, who made very fair terms for him, as things went then.

In April 1843 *Modern Painters*, vol. i., was published ; and it was soon the talk of the art-world. It was meant to be audacious, and naturally created a storm. The free criticisms of public favourites made an impression, not because they were put into strong language, for the tone of the press was stronger then than it is now, as a whole ; but because they were backed up by illustration and argument. It was evident that the author knew something of his subject, even if he were all wrong in his conclusions. He could not be neglected, though he might be protested against, decried, controverted. Artists especially, who do not usually see themselves as others see them, and are not accustomed to think of themselves and their school as mere dots and spangles in the perspective of history, could not be entirely content to be classed as Turner's satellites. Even the gentle Prout was indignant, not so much at the "five strokes of a reed pen," but at the want of reverence with which his masters and friends were treated. Harding thought that his teaching ought to have been more fully acknowledged. Turner was embarrassed at the greatness thrust upon him. And while the book contained something that promised to suit every kind of reader, every one found something to shock him. Critics were scandalised at the depreciation of Claude ; the religious were outraged at the comparison of Turner, in a passage omitted from later editions, to the Angel of the Sun, in the Apocalypse.

But readers survive a few shocks ; very literally, they first endured, then pitied, then embraced : for the descriptive passages were such as had never appeared before in prose ; and the obvious usefulness of the analyses of natural form and effect made many an artist read on, while he shook his head. Of professed connoisseurs, such as reviewed the book adversely in *Blackwood* and the *Athenæum*, not one undertook to refute it seriously with a full restatement of the Academic theory. They merely attacked a detail here and there, which the author discussed in two or three replies, with a patience that showed how confident he was in his position.* Next year a second edition appeared.

He had the good word of some of the best judges of literature. *Modern Painters* lay on Rogers' table; and Tennyson, who a few years before had beaten young Ruskin out of the field of poetry, was so taken with it that he wrote to his publisher to borrow it for him, "as he longed very much to see it," but could not afford to buy it. When the secret of the "Oxford Graduate" leaked out, as it did very soon, through the proud father, Mr. John was lionised. During the winter of 1843, he met all the celebrities of the day at fashionable dinner-tables; and now that his parents were established in their grander house on Denmark Hill, they could duly return the hospitalities of the great world.

It was one very satisfactory result of the success that the father was more or less converted to Turnerism; and

---

* Of these minor battles, one of the hardest fought was about Reflections in Water. Mr. J. H. Maw, then of Hastings, an enlightened patron of art, and an accomplished amateur (to say nothing, here, of his earnestness and ability in many other spheres), maintained that Mr. Ruskin was wrong in believing that the reflecting surface of clear water receives no shadow: and even after the reply which can now be read in *Arrows of the Chace*, stuck to his opinion. It was a good instance of simple misunderstanding: the experiment can be tried with any shiny object, such as a watch. What seems to be shadow disappears when you look *across* it, and catch a bright reflection in it.

RUSKIN'S HOUSE AT DENMARK HILL.

By Arthur Severn, R.I.

lined his walls with Turner drawings, which became the great attraction of the house, far outshining its seven acres of garden and orchard and shrubbery, and the ampler air of cultured ease. For a new year's gift to his son, he bought *The Slave Ship*, one of Turner's latest and most disputed works, since then taken to America; and he was all eagerness to see the next volume in preparation.

The intention was to carry on the discussion of "Truth," with further illustrations of mountain-form, trees and skies. And so in May 1844 they all went away again, that the artist-author might prepare drawings for his plates. He was going to begin with the geology and botany of Chamouni, and work through the Alps, eastward.

At Chamouni they had the good fortune to meet with Joseph Couttet, a superannuated guide, whom they engaged to accompany the eager but inexperienced mountaineer. Couttet was one of those men of natural ability and kindliness, whose friendship is worth more than much intercourse with worldly celebrities: and for many years afterwards Mr. Ruskin had the advantage of his care, and something more than mere attendance. At any rate, under such guidance he could climb where he pleased, free from the feeling that somebody at home was anxious about him.

He was not unadventurous in his scramblings; but with no ambition to get to the top of everything. He wanted to observe the aspects of mountain-form; and his careful outlines, slightly coloured, as his manner then was, and never aiming at picturesque treatment, record the structure of the rocks and the state of the snow with more than photographic accuracy. A photograph often confuses the eye with unnecessary detail; these drawings seized the leading lines, the important features, the interesting points. For example, in his Matterhorn (a drawing of 1849), as Mr. Whymper remarks in *Scrambles among the Alps*, there are particulars noted which the mere sketcher neglects, but the climber finds out, on closer intercourse, to be the essential facts of the mountain's anatomy.   All this is not picture-making ; but it is a very valuable contribution and preliminary to criticism.

From Chamouni this year they went to Simplon, and met J. D. Forbes the geologist, whose " viscous theory " of glaciers Mr. Ruskin adopted and defended with warmth ever after : and then to the Bell' Alp, long before it had been made a place of popular resort by Professor Tyndall's notice.   The Panorama of the Simplon from the Bell' Alp is still to be found in the Sheffield Museum as a record of Mr. Ruskin's draughtsmanship in this period.   Thence to Zermatt with Osborne Gordon ; Zermatt, too, unknown to the fashionable tourist, and innocent of hotel luxuries. It is curious that, at first sight, Mr. Ruskin did not like the Matterhorn.   It was too altogether unlike his ideal of mountains.   It was not at all like Cumberland !   But he was not long in learning to appreciate the Alps for their own sake : so that he could write to Miss Mitford from Keswick (in 1848, I believe): " As for our mountains and lakes, it is in vain that they are defended for their finish or their prettiness.   The people who admire them after Switzerland do not understand Switzerland,—even Wordsworth does not."

After another visit to Chamouni he went home by way of Paris, where something awaited him that upset all his plans, and turned his energies into an unexpected channel.

CHAPTER II.

CHRISTIAN ART.

(1845—1847.)

> " They might chirp and chatter, come and go
>   For pleasure or profit, her men alive—
>   My business was hardly with them, I trow,
>   But with empty cells of the human hive ;
>   With the chapter-room, the cloister-porch,
>   The church's apsis, aisle or nave,
>   Its crypt, one fingers along with a torch,
>   Its face, set full for the sun to shave."
>
> *Old Pictures in Florence.*

AT Paris, on the way home in 1844, Mr. Ruskin had spent some days in studying Titian and Bellini and Perugino. They were not new to him ; but now that he was an Art-critic, it behoved him to improve his acquaintance with the Old Masters. "To admire the works of Pietro Perugino " was one thing ; but to understand them was another,—a thing which was hardly attempted by "the Landscape Artists of England " to whom the author of *Modern Painters* had so far dedicated his services. He had been extolling modernism, and depreciating " the Ancients " because they could not draw rocks and clouds and trees : and he was fresh from his scientific sketching in the happy hunting ground of the modern world. A few days in the Louvre made him the devotee of ancient art, and taught him to lay aside his geology, for history.

119

In one way the development was easy. The patient attempt to copy mountain-form had made him sensitive to harmony of line ; and in the great composers of Florence and Venice he found a quality of abstract design which tallied with his experience of what was beautiful in nature. Aiguilles and glaciers, drawn as he drew them, and the figure-subjects of severe Italian draughtsmen, are beautiful by the same laws of composition, however different the associations they suggest. With the general public, and with many artists, associations easily outweigh abstractions : but this was an analytic mind, bent, then, upon the problems of form, and ready to acknowledge them no less in Madonnas than in mountains.

But *he* had been learning these laws of beauty from Turner and from the Alps ; how did the ancients come by them ? That could be found only in a thorough study of their lives and times, to begin with ; to which he devoted his winter, with Rio and Lord Lindsay and Mrs. Jameson for his authorities. He found that his foes, Gaspar Poussin and Canaletto and the Dutch landscapists, were not the real Old Masters ; that there had been a great age of art before the era of Vandyck and Rubens,—even before Michelangelo and Raphael ; and that towards setting up as a critic of the present, he must understand the past, out of which it had grown. So he determined to go to Florence and Venice, and study the religious painters at first hand.

Mountain-study and Turner were not to be dropped. For example, to explain the obvious and notorious licences which Turner took with topography, it was necessary to see in what these licences consisted. Of the later Swiss drawings, one of the wildest and most impressive was the

OLIVE AT CARRARA.

John Ruskin,—1845.

St. Gothard; Ruskin wanted to find Turner's point of view, and to see what alterations he had made. He told Turner so; and the artist, who knew that his picture had been realised from a very slight sketch, was naturally rather opposed to this test, as being, from his point of view, merely a waste of time and trouble. He tried to persuade the Ruskins that, as the Swiss Sonderbund war was beginning, travelling would not be safe, and so forth. But in vain. Mr. John was allowed to go, for the first time, alone, without his parents, taking only a servant, and meeting the trustworthy Couttet at Geneva.

With seven months at his own disposal, he did a vast amount of work, especially in drawing. The studies of mountain-form and Italian design, in the year before, had given him a greater interest in the *Liber Studiorum*, Turner's early book of Essays in Composition. He found there that use of the pure line, about which he has since said so much; together with a thoughtfully devised scheme of light and shade in mezzotint, devoted to the treatment of landscape in the same spirit as that in which the Italian masters treated figure-subjects in their pen-and-bistre studies. And just as he had imitated the Rogers vignettes in his boyhood, now in his youth he tried to emulate the fine abstract flow and searching expressiveness of the etched line, and the studied breadth of shade, by using the quill pen with washes of monochrome, or sometimes with subdued colour. This dwelling upon outline as not only representative, but decorative in itself, has sometimes led Mr. Ruskin into over-emphasis and a mannered grace; but the value of his pen-and-wash style has never been fairly tested in landscape. His best drawings are known to very few; some of his finest work was thrown away on subjects which were never completed, or were ruined by rough experiments when he had tired of them, and no other man with half his feeling and knowledge has attempted to work in the same method.

At first he kept pretty closely to monochrome. His object was form, and his special talent for draughtsmanship rather than for colour, which developed quite late in his life. But it is this winter's study of the *Liber Studiorum* that started him on his own characteristic course ; and while we have no pen-and-wash work of his before 1845 (except a few experiments after Prout), we find him now using the pen continually during all the *Modern Painters* period.

On reaching the Lake of Geneva he wrote, or sketched, one of his best-known pieces of verse, *Mont Blanc Revisited* ; and a few others followed, the last of the long series of poems, which had once been his chief interest and aim in life. With this lonely journey there seemed to come new and deeper feelings ; with his increased literary power, fresh resources of diction ; and he was never so near being a poet as when he gave up writing verse. Too condensed to be easily understood, too solemn in their movement to be trippingly read, the lines on *The Arve at Cluse*, on *Mont Blanc*, and *The Glacier*, should not be passed over as nothing more than rhetorical. And the reflections on the loungers at Conflans are full of significance of the spirit in which he was gradually approaching the great problems of his life, to pass through art into the earnest study of human conduct and its final cause.

"Why stand ye here all the day idle ?"

Have you in heaven no hope—on earth no care—
No foe in hell, ye things of stye and stall,

That congregate like flies, and make the air
  Rank with your fevered sloth ; that hourly call
The sun, which should your servant be, to bear
  Dread witness on you, with uncounted wane
And unregarded rays, from peak to peak
  Of fiery-gnomoned mountain moved in vain ?
Behold, the very shadows that ye seek
  For slumber, write along the wasted wall
Your condemnation. They forget not, they,
  Their ordered functions ; and determined fall,
Nor useless perish. But *you* count your day
By sins, and write your difference from clay
In bonds you break, and laws you disobey.

God! who hast given the rocks their fortitude,
Their sap unto the forests, and their food
  And vigour to the busy tenantry
  Of happy soulless things that wait on Thee,
Hast Thou no blessing where Thou gav'st Thy blood ?
  Wilt Thou not make Thy fair creation whole ?
Behold and visit this Thy vine for good, —
  Breathe in this human dust its living soul.

He was still deeply religious—more deeply so than
before ; and found the echo of his own thoughts in George
Herbert, with whom he "communed in spirit" while he
travelled through the Alps. But the forms of outward
religion were losing their hold over him, in proportion as
his inward religion became more real and intense. It was
only a few days after writing these lines that he "broke
the Sabbath" for the first time in his life, by climbing a
hill after church. That was the first shot fired in a war, in
one of the strangest and saddest wars between conscience
and reason that biography records ; strange, because the
opposing forces were so nearly matched, and sad because
the struggle lasted until their field of battle was desolated,
before either won a victory. Thirty years later, the

cleverest of his Oxford hearers* drew his portrait under
the name of the man whose sacred verse was his guide
and mainstay in this youthful pilgrim's progress: and the
words put into his mouth summed up with merciless
insight the issue of those conflicts. "'For I! who am I
that speak to you? Am I a believer? No. I am a
doubter too. Once I could pray every morning, and go
forth to my day's labour stayed and comforted. But now
I can pray no longer. You have taken my God away
from me, and I know not where you have laid Him. My
only consolation in my misery is that I am inconsolable
for His loss. Yes,' cried Mr. Herbert, his voice rising into
a kind of threatening wail, 'though you have made me
miserable, I am not yet content with my misery. And
though I too have said in my heart that there is no God,
and that there is no more profit in wisdom than in folly,
yet there is one folly that I will not give tongue to. I will
not say Peace, peace, when there is no peace.'"

Later on we have to tell how he dwelt in Doubting
Castle, and how he escaped. But the pilgrim had not yet
met Giant Despair; and his progress was very pleasant in
that spring of 1845, the year of fine weather, as he drove
round the Riviera, and the cities of Tuscany opened out
their treasures to him. There was Lucca, with San
Frediano and the glories of twelfth-century architecture;
with Fra Bartolommeo's picture of the Madonna with the
Magdalen and St. Catherine of Siena, his initiation into
the significance of early religious painting; and, taking
hold of his imagination, in her marble sleep, more power-
fully than any flesh and blood, the dead lady of St.
Martin's church, Ilaria di Caretto. There was Pisa, with

* W. H. Mallock, *The New Republic.*

the jewel shrine of Sta. Maria della Spina, then undestroyed; the excitement of street sketching among a sympathetic crowd of fraternising Italians; the Abbé Rosini, Professor of Fine Arts, whom he made friends with, endured as lecturer, and persuaded into scaffold-building in the Campo Santo, for study of the frescoes. And there was Florence, with Giotto's campanile, where the young Protestant frequented the monasteries, and made hay with monks, and sketched with his new-found friends Rudolf Durheim of Berne and Dieudonné the French purist; and spent long days copying Angelico and annotating Ghirlandajo, fevered with the sun of Italy at its strongest, and with the rapture of discovery "which turns the unaccustomed head like Chianti wine."

Couttet got him away, at last, to the Alps; worn out and in despondent reaction after all this excitement. He spent a month at Macugnaga, reading Shakespeare and trying to draw boulders; drifting gradually back into strength enough to attack the next piece of work, the study of Turner sites on the St. Gothard. There he made the drawings afterwards engraved in *Modern Painters*; and hearing that J. D. Harding, who, it seems, had quite forgiven him his criticisms, was going to Venice, he arranged for a meeting at Baveno on the Lago Maggiore. They sketched together; Ruskin perhaps emulating his friend's slap-dash style in the "Sunset" reproduced in his "Poems," and illustrating his own in the "Water-mill." And so they drove together to Verona and thence to Venice.

At Venice they stayed in Danieli's hotel on the Riva degli Schiavoni, and began by sketching picturesque canal-life. Mr. Boxall, R.A., and Mrs. Jameson, the historian of Sacred and Legendary Art, were their companions. Another old friend, Joseph Severn, had in 1843 gained one of the prizes at the Westminster Hall Cartoons Competition ; and a letter from Mr. Ruskin, referring to the work there, shows how he still pondered on the subject that had been haunting him in the Alps. "With your hopes for the elevation of English art by means of fresco I cannot sympathise. . . . It is not the material nor the space that can give us thoughts, passions, or power. I see on our Academy walls nothing but what is ignoble in small pictures, and would be disgusting in large ones. . . . It is not the love of fresco that we want ; it is the love of God and His creatures ; it is humility, and charity, and self-denial, and fasting, and prayer ; it is a total change of character. We want more faith and less reasoning, less strength and more trust. You want neither walls, nor plaster, nor colours—*ça ne fait rien à l'affaire* ; it is Giotto, and Ghirlandajo, and Angelico that you want, and that you will and must want until this disgusting nineteenth century has—I can't say breathed, but steamed its last." So early he had taken up, and wrapped around him, the mantle of Cassandra.

But he was suddenly to find the sincerity of Ghirlandajo and the religious significance of Angelico united with the matured power of art. Without knowing what they were to meet, Harding and he found themselves one day in the Scuola di S. Rocco, and face to face with Tintoret.

It was the fashion before Mr. Ruskin's time, and it has been the fashion since, to undervalue Tintoret. He is not pious enough for the purists, nor decorative enough for the Pre-Raphaelites. The ruin or the restoration of almost

all his pictures makes it impossible for the ordinary amateur
to judge them ; they need reconstruction in the mind's eye,
and that is a dangerous process.   Mr. Ruskin himself, as
he grew older, found more interest in the playful industry
of Carpaccio than in the laborious games, the stupendous
Titan-feats, of Tintoret.   But at this moment, solemnised
before the problems of life, he found these problems hinted
in the mystic symbolism of the School of S. Rocco ; a
recent convert to pre-Reformation Christianity, he found
its completed outcome in Tintoret's interpretation of the
life of Christ and the types of the Old Testament ; fresh
from the stormy grandeur of the St. Gothard, he found
the lurid skies and looming giants of the Visitation, or
the Baptism, or the Crucifixion, re-echoing the subjects of
Turner as "deep answering to deep " ; and, with Harding of
the Broad Brush, he recognised the mastery of landscape-
execution in the Flight into Egypt, and the St. Mary in
the Desert.

He devoted the rest of his time chiefly to cataloguing
and copying Tintoret.   The catalogue appeared in *Stones
of Venice*, which was suggested by this visit, and begun by
some sketches of architectural detail, and the acquisition
of daguerreotypes—a new invention, which delighted Mr.
Ruskin immensely, as it had delighted Turner, with trustworthy records of detail which sometimes eluded even his
industry and accuracy.

At last his friends were gone ; and, left alone, he overworked himself, as usual, before leaving Venice with
crammed portfolios and closely-written notebooks.   At
Padua, he was stopped by a fever ; all through France he
was pursued by what, from his account, appears to have
been some form of diphtheria, averted only, as he believed,

in direct answer to earnest prayer. At last his eventful pilgrimage was ended, and he was restored to his home and his parents.

It was not long before he was at work again in his new study ; looking out upon the quiet meadow and grazing cows of Denmark Hill, and rapidly throwing into form the fresh impressions of the summer. Still thoroughly Aristotelian and Lockeian in method, he found no difficulty in making his philosophy the vehicle of religious thought. He was strongly influenced by the sermons of Canon Melvill—the same preacher whom Browning in his youth admired ; a good orator and sound analytic expositor, though not a great or independent thinker. Osborne Gordon had recommended him to read Hooker ; and he caught the tone and style of the *Ecclesiastical Polity* only too readily, so that much of his work of that winter, the more philosophical part of Vol. II., was damaged by inversions, and Elizabethan quaintness as of ruff and train, long epexegetical sentences, and far-sought pomposity of diction. It was only when he had waded through the philosophic chaos, which he set himself to survey, that he could lay aside his borrowed stilts, and stand on his own feet, in the Tintoret descriptions,—rather stiff, yet, from foregone efforts. But, after all, who writes philosophy in graceful English ?

For one must remember that this was really a philosophical work, and not simply a volume of Essays, or Sermons, which any preacher or journalist could turn out by the piece. It may be wrongly founded ; but it is founded on Locke and Aristotle, like the first volume. The division of Pleasures into higher and lower may be illusory ; but it is the logical outcome of the division of

Ideas into those of Sensation and those of Reflection. It may be foolish to mix the whole question up with Morals : but so do Kant and Schopenhauer. It may be absurd to express a theory of Art in terms of Theology : but so do Plato and Hegel, without reproof. In short, the significance of the work, as a reflex of the great movement of German philosophy, and as the completion of the English school of æsthetics begun by Coleridge,—as a last attempt at a metaphysic of the subject, before a new era of materialistic thinking set in, all this can only be grasped by a reader who has taken some interest in the history of thought. He will see, what we can hardly loiter to explain, whence Ruskin gets his *Theoria*, and why he opposes it to *Æsthesis*; how the sense of rightness, law-abiding, dominates him, so that he finds that all our pleasure is to be traced to acquiescence in it; how he identifies this natural law with the Divine method of creation, in all its various moods, such as Infinity, Unity, Repose, and so forth; and traces its effects in animated beings as well as in stocks and stones; producing what we call Beauty as the outward and visible sign of a certain all-round rightness, the object of admiration, hope and love, not of the lust of the flesh and the merely sensual desire of the eye. And in the same way the student of philosophy will recognise a train of systematic thought in Ruskin's treatment of the imagination as something beyond the mere effect of sensation,—as simple conception would be, which, in excess, is insanity. And he will find this defence of genius more and more interesting, when he has disentangled it from the cumbrous ornaments in which it is enveloped ; more and more valuable, as being quite unique in English thought ; while, on re-reading, the appositeness of the illustrative

passages becomes more evident ; and, the thread of the
idea once held, you can look about you at the varied hedges
and vistas and nooks in the labyrinth of thought through
which John Ruskin first wandered—that winter of 1845,
with beating heart and earnest outlook, in pursuit of the
Minotaur of materialism, the hidden, pampered brute-
instinct to which his contemporaries immolated the virgin-
tribute of poetry and art.

When his book came out he was away again in Italy,
trying to show his father all that he had seen in the Campo
Santo and Giotto's Tower, and to explain "why it more
than startled him." The good man hardly felt the force
of it all at once. How should he ? And there were little
passages of arms and some heart-quaking and head-
shaking ; until Mr. Dale, the old schoolmaster, wrote that
he had heard no less a man than Sydney Smith mention
the new book in public, in the presence of "distinguished
literary characters," as a work of "transcendent talent,
presenting the most original views, in the most elegant
and powerful language, which would work a complete
revolution in the world of taste."

When the chief of the critics nodded approval, what
could the rest of the mandarin-college do, but nod ? The
first volume had paved the way to success ; and during
this journey, the young author was correcting the proofs
of a third edition. Turner was already a household word ;
Angelico and the Primitives were coming into notice :
Ruskin never claimed to have discovered them ; only to
have expounded them. And Tintoret was a great unknown. There were plain folk who wondered at this
strange association of subjects so apparently diverse in
all nameable qualities ; but the best men saw that the

young writer had taken a firm and defensible position akin to Carlyle's; that like Carlyle he was talking and thinking over the heads of the crowd; and they forgave what there was to forgive—some affectation and hasty dogmatism—for the sake of the " fundamental brain-work " which they saw in this book.

When he returned home, it was to find a respectful welcome. His word on matters of Art was now really worth something; and before long it was called for. The National Gallery was comparatively in its infancy. It had been established less than twenty-five years, and its manager, Mr. Eastlake (afterwards Sir Charles) had his hands full, what with rascally dealers in forged old masters, and incompetent picture-cleaners, and an economical government, and a public that did not know its own mind and would not trust his judgment. A great outcry was set up against him for buying bad works, and spoiling the best by restoration. Mr. Ruskin wrote very temperately to the *Times*, pointing out that the damage had been slight compared with what was being done everywhere else; and suggesting that, prevention being better than cure, the pictures should be put under glass, for then they would not need the recurring attentions of the restorer. But he blamed the management for spending large sums on added examples of Guido and Rubens, while , they had no Angelico, no Ghirlandajo, no good Perugino, only one Bellini; and, in a word, left his new friends, the early Christian artists, unrepresented. He suggested that pictures might be picked up for next to nothing in Italy; and he begged that the collection might be made historical and educational by being fully representative, and chronologically arranged.

Such ideals cannot be realised at a stroke ; but as we walk round our Gallery now, we can be thankful that his voice was raised, and not in vain ; and rejoice that in many a case justice has been done to "the wronged great soul of an ancient master."

CHAPTER III.

THE SEVEN LAMPS.

(1847—1849.)

"They dreamt not of a perishable home
Who thus could build."
Wordsworth.

OF the leading men who acknowledged the rising star,
it was natural that the foremost in their recognition
should be Scotsmen. Hogg and Pringle had been the
boy-poet's first encouragers; and now the art-critic was
hailed by Sydney Smith, a former Edinburgh professor;
patronised by John Murray, who got him to write notes on
pictures for his "Guide"; and employed by Lockhart on
the staff of the *Quarterly.* "The happiest lot on earth is
to be born a Scotchman," says R. L. Stevenson; and it is
certainly convenient for the aspirant to artistic or literary
fame.

Lockhart was a person of great interest to young Ruskin,
who so worshipped Scott: and Lockhart's daughter, even
without her personal charm, would have attracted him, as
the actual grandchild of the great Sir Walter. It was for
her sake, rather than for the honour of writing in the
famous *Quarterly,* that he went, after a fatiguing winter in
London society, to Ambleside, to get peace and quiet for
his review of Lord Lindsay's "Christian Art." It was not

133

only society that had fatigued him.   He had never quite
recovered from the tendency to consumption which had
sent him down from Oxford ; and a weakness of the spine
was now keeping him always more or less of an invalid.
The writing of his second volume, during several months
of mental tension and emotional excitement, had wearied
him out, and the tour that followed had not sufficed for
relaxation—chiefly because he was beginning to find himself drifting away from that earlier happy confidence in his
parents' beliefs, and reliance on their sympathy.   His father
and he pulled different ways—not openly, not admitting
such a thing even to themselves ; for, some years after, the
father wrote that his son had "never cost him a single
pang that could be avoided."   But that was because the
son never hesitated to sacrifice himself and his wishes to
please his father.   And now, it was not the least trying
sacrifice, that his father should be opposed to the idea he
had entertained, of recommending himself to Lockhart and
his daughter ; and that he should find his parents, with the
best intentions in the world, arranging his affairs with an
eye to what they believed to be his interests, and not with
regard to his inclinations.

With all his intellectual independence Mr. Ruskin was,
and is, the least selfish of men.   The fact has been obvious
to many a one who has taken advantage of it, and scorned
it as a weakness.   But there have been people at all times
to whom his character was more estimable than his genius :
people like Miss Mitford, who wrote (early in this year
1847) that he was "certainly the most charming person
she had ever known."   With unselfishness there generally
goes an unsuspicious habit, too little on its guard against
vulgar knavery and folly ; and a passion for abstract justice,

that does not stop to weigh consequences or circumstances, and is liable to end in disappointment and bitterness, like Shakespeare's Timon, " When man's worst sin is, he does too much good."

After a summer visit to Oxford, working in the Geological section at a meeting of the British Association, Mr. Ruskin's health broke down again, and he was sent to Leamington to his old Doctor, Jephson, once more a consumption-patient. Dr. Jephson again dieted him into health ; and he went to Scotland with a new-found friend, Mr. William Macdonald Macdonald of St. Martin's. He had no taste for sport : one battue was enough for him ; and the rest of the visit was spent in digging thistles, and thinking over them, and the significance of the curse of Eden, so strangely now at last interwoven with his own life, —" thorns also and thistles."

On his way back he stopped at Bower's Well, Perth, where his parents had been married ; and in accordance with their wishes proposed marriage to the young lady for whom, some years earlier, he had written *The King of the Golden River*. She had grown up into a perfect Scotch beauty, another Fair Maid of Perth, with every gift of health and spirits which would compensate, as they thought, his retiring and morbid nature. And if she, by obedience to her own parents, got the wealth and position they sought for her, on the other hand the dutiful son easily persuaded himself that he was, after all, the luckiest of mortals. He was ready to do anything, to promise anything, for so charming a prize. The parents on each side had their several conditions to make ; but united in hastening on the event, alike " dreaming of a perishable home."

In the Notes on Exhibitions added to a new edition of *Modern Painters* then in the press, the author mentions a "hurried visit to Scotland in the spring" of 1848. An old newspaper-cutting betrays the reason of the journey, by recording his marriage on the 10th of April. The young couple went to Keswick, whence on Good Friday he wrote to his friend Miss Mitford,—"I begin to feel that all the work I have been doing, and all the loves I have been cherishing, are ineffective and frivolous—that these are not times for watching clouds or dreaming over quiet waters; that more serious work is to be done; and that the time for endurance has come rather than for meditation, and for hope rather than for happiness. Happy those whose hope, without this severe and tearful rending away of all the props and stability of earthly enjoyments, has been fixed 'where the wicked cease from troubling.' Mine was not; it was based on 'those pillars of the earth' which are 'astonished at His reproof.' I have, however, passed this week very happily here. We have a good clergyman, Mr. Myers; and I am recovering trust and tranquillity. I had been wiser to have come to your fair English pastures and flowering meadows, rather than to these moorlands, for they make me feel too painfully the splendour, not to be in any wise resembled or replaced, of those mighty scenes which I can reach no more—at least for a time. I am thinking, however, of a tour among our English abbeys."

The pilgrimage began with Salisbury, where a few days' sketching in the damp and draughts of the cathedral laid the bridegroom low, and brought the wedding tour to an untimely end. When he was thought to be recovered, the whole family started for the Continent, but a relapse in the patient's condition brought them back. At last, in August, the young people were seen safely off to Normandy, where they went by easy stages from town to town, studying the remains of Gothic building. In October they returned, and settled in a house of their own, at 31, Park Street, where during the winter Mr. Ruskin wrote *The Seven Lamps of Architecture*, and as a bit of bye-work, a notice of Samuel Prout for the *Art Journal*.

"The Seven Lamps"—or Laws " of Architecture,"—"Thy word is a lamp unto my feet," the Psalmist said ;—and so, not practical rules of art, but Divine conditions affecting man as a building creature, and the work of his hands as the expression of his mind ; complicated too with those seven lamps which are the churches of latter-day Christianity, and their light of warning, of reproof or of encouragement ;—" The Seven Lamps " was not meant to be either an instructive manual or an historical essay. Something of the sort had been promised as part of *Modern Painters*, an inquiry upon the aspects of Architecture as seen by the artist, just as the author was writing on the aspects of Mountains or Waves ; and this book is practically one volume of the greater work, illustrating the theory of beauty and imagination stated in Vol. II. But the feelings with which he had written three years before had gathered strength, both through the personal experiences he had been undergoing, and through the increasing seriousness of public turmoil and discontent in that memorable year of Chartism at home and Revolutions abroad, 1848.

" The aspect of the years that approach us," he writes, " is as solemn as it is full of mystery ; and the weight of evil against which we have to contend is increasing like the letting out of water. It is no time for the idleness of

metaphysics, or the entertainment of the arts. The blas-
phemies of the earth are waxing louder, and its miseries
heaped heavier, every day." This was his plea for con-
sidering Architecture in a new light, as a language of the
human mind ; in the past, bearing witness to faith and
sincerity, and in the present, as a means of testing the
moral symptoms of the nation " that thus could build."

He showed, as he had done in the " Poetry of Architecture," that the word meant more than " building " ; it
meant the expression of thought and feeling in, and upon,
buildings ; and that this was seen especially in sacred
buildings, for it was upon such that the greatest care and
the most significant symbolism had been lavished. For
example, the first intent of building a house for God was a
form of *Sacrifice*, and involved the giving of the best work
and the costliest materials, that the sacrifice might be
acceptable. He could show how this had been done by
the Gothic builders of ancient Italy and France ; and he
could contrast the luxury of modern private houses with
the shoddy of their sham Gothic churches. Next, the
sincerity of the worship which sacred architecture meant
to illustrate was reflected in its *Truth*, refusing all architectural deceits, in structure, in material, or in the substitution of cheap machine-made ornament for the honest
result of truly artistic labour. The Lamps of *Power* and
Beauty were the expressions of seriousness, in sympathy
with human pain and struggle, and of pleasure, in sympathy
with Divine law made visible in nature. *Life* was the
result of spontaneous and unaffected art, dying out at once
when the workman became a formal imitator or a soulless
mechanist. *Memory* was the documentary character of
ancient buildings, destroyed by restoration ; and finally

Obedience was shown in the refusal of impudent attempts at mere *bizarrerie*, and novelty for its own sake ; for a great style could only spring up as the unconscious expression of national character and circumstances, developing out of the received inheritance of the traditional school.

This was Mr. Ruskin's first illustrated volume. The plates were engraved by himself in soft-ground etching, such as Prout had used, from drawings he had made in 1846 and 1848. Some are scrappy combinations of various detail, but others, such as the Byzantine capital, the window in Giotto's Campanile, the arches from St. Lo in Normandy, from S. Michele at Lucca, and from the Ca' Foscari at Venice, are effective studies of the actual look of old buildings, seen as they are shown us in Nature, with her light and shade added to all the facts of form, and her own last touches in the way of weather-softening, and settling-faults, and tufted, nestling plants.

The book was announced for his father's birthday, May 10th, 1849 ; but there was still one plate to finish,— that of Giotto's tower,—when the whole family went abroad again, the new Mrs. John replacing Cousin Mary, who also had been married the year before. Mr. Ruskin worked at his plate on the way through France, and bit it hastily in his wash-hand-basin at the Hôtel de la Cloche at Dijon (perhaps on April 17th). These sketchy and unprofessionally manipulated plates were thought to be not a success ; and in the second edition more elaborate engravings were given, with an exquisite frontispiece by Armytage from a new drawing. But, apart from their merely fancy value as rarities, the autograph etchings are fine bold work, and especially interesting as a new departure in the way of architectural illustration. The

cover of the original editions, also, was happier than Mr.
Ruskin's book-covers have usually been; stamped with
an arabesque which Mr. W. Harry Rogers designed from
the author's sketches of the floor of San Miniato.

As to the reception of the work, or at any rate the
anticipation of it, Charlotte Brontë bears witness in a letter
to the publishers. "I have lately been reading *Modern
Painters*, and have derived from the work much genuine
pleasure, and, I hope, some edification; at any rate it has
made me feel how ignorant I had previously been on the
subject which it treats. Hitherto I have only had instinct
to guide me in judging of art; I feel now as if I had been
walking blindfold—this book seems to give me new eyes.
I *do* wish I had pictures within reach by which to test the
new sense. Who can read these glowing descriptions of
Turner's work without longing to see them?

"I like this author's style much; there is both energy
and beauty in it. I like himself, too, because he is such
a hearty admirer. He does not give half-measure of praise
or veneration. He eulogises, he reverences, with his whole
soul. One can sympathise with that sort of devout, serious
admiration, for he is no rhapsodist; one can respect it;
yet, possibly, many people would laugh at it.

"I congratulate you on the approaching publication of
Mr. Ruskin's new work. If the *Seven Lamps of Architecture* resemble their predecessor, *Modern Painters*, they
will be no lamps at all, but a new constellation—seven
bright stars, for whose rising the reading world ought to
be anxiously agape."

The author's own opinion, thirty years later, was that the
book had become the most useless he ever wrote; "the
buildings it describes with so much delight being now

either knocked down, or scraped and patched up into smugness and smoothness more tragic than uttermost ruin. But I find the public still like the book, and will read it, when they won't look at what would be really useful and helpful to them ; . . . the germ of what I have since written is indeed here, however overlaid with gilding, and overshot, too splashily and cascade-fashion, with gushing of words."

CHAPTER IV.

STONES OF VENICE.

(1849—1851.)

"I stood in Venice, on the Bridge of Sighs,
A palace and a prison on each hand ;
I saw from out the wave her structures rise
As from the stroke of the enchanter's wand."—*Byron*.

" And I, John, saw the holy city, New Jerusalem, coming down from God,
out of heaven."—REV. xxi. 2.

A BOOK about Venice had been planned in 1845,
during Mr. Ruskin's first long working visit. He
had made so many notes and sketches both of architecture
and painting that the material seemed ready to hand ;
another visit would fill up the gaps in his information ; and
two or three months' hard writing would work the subject
off, and set him free to continue *Modern Painters*. So
before leaving home in 1849, he had made up his mind
that the next work would be *The Stones of Venice* ; which,
on the appearance of *The Seven Lamps*, was announced
by the publishers as in preparation.

Like the *Seven Lamps*, this new book was not to be a
manual of practical architecture, but the further illustration
of doctrines peculiar to the author ; the reaction, that is
to say, of society upon art ; the close connection, in this
case, of style in architecture with the life, the religious

142

tone, the moral aims, of the people who produced it. Venice was chosen as the special ground of inquiry, not because Venetian architecture was better than Florentine or French ; but because it presented a conveniently isolated school, neatly continuous, with none of those breaks and catastrophes which destroy the full value, as specimens of development, of most other schools ; just as flaws and interruptions destroy the museum-value of a mineral, as specimen of crystallisation.   Venice was a perfectly normal development, under favourable circumstances.   And there was this added interest, that the character of Venice was the nearest analogy in the past, and among the great influential nations of history, to our own country.   It was free, but aristocratic and conservative ; Christian, but independent of the Pope ; it pursued a course of " spirited foreign policy " in contrast with—but as a consequence of —its apparently peaceful function of commerce.   So that, by its example, the lessons of national virtue which, since 1845, the author had felt called on to preach, could be illustrated and enforced in a far more interesting way than if he had merely written a volume of essays on political morality ; at least, so he felt and intended.   But in the end, the inquiry branched out into so many directions that the main purpose was all but hidden in flowers of rhetoric and foliage of technical detail, which most readers took for the sum and substance of its teaching.

In the summer of 1849 Mr. Ruskin was with his family and friends in Switzerland from the beginning of May until the end of October.   He spent a busy and eventful time,—whether well or ill, happy or distressed, he was always busy ; some of his most careful drawings of the Alps were made this year, and their accuracy was checked

by the daguerreotype-camera which he carried about with
him. I do not know if he can claim to be the actual
pioneer of Alpine photography, but he was the first to
photograph the Matterhorn,—I believe, early in August,
1849.

Part of November was spent at Verona, and by the end
of the month he was settled with his wife at Venice for
the winter. He expected to find without much trouble
all the information he wanted as to the dates and styles
and history of Venetian buildings ; but after consulting
and comparing all the native writers, it appeared that the
questions he asked of them were just the questions they
were unprepared to answer, and that he must go into the
whole matter afresh. So he laid himself out, that winter,
for a thorough examination of St. Mark's and the Ducal
Palace and the other remains—drawing, and measuring,
and comparing their details ; only to find that the work
he had undertaken was like a sea " chi sempre si fa
maggiore." The old buildings were a patchwork of all
styles and all periods. In St. Mark's alone, every pinnacle
called for separate study ; every capital and balustrade, on
minute inquiry, turned out to have its own independent
history. So that after all his labour he could give no
complete and generalised survey of his subject, chronological and systematised, without much more time and
thought. But at any rate the details he had in his
notebooks were the result of personal observation ; he was
no longer trusting to second-hand information or the
vague traditions of the tribe of ciceroni.

His father had gone back to England in September,
out of health ; and the letters from home did not report
improvement. His mother, too, was beginning to fear the

loss of her sight; and he could not stay away from them any longer, to pursue what he thought to be his own selfish aims. And so, in February 1850, he broke off his work in the middle of it, and returned to London. The rest of the year he spent in writing the first volume of *Stones of Venice* and in preparing the illustrations, and the *Examples of the Architecture of Venice,* a portfolio of large lithographs and engravings in mezzotint and line, to accompany the work.

The illustrations to the new book were a great advance upon the rough soft-ground etchings of the *Seven Lamps.* He secured the services of some of the finest engravers who ever handled the tools of their art. The English school of engravers was then in its last and most accomplished period. Photography had not yet begun to supersede it; and the demand for delicate work in book-illustration had encouraged minuteness and precision of handling to the last degree. In this excessive refinement there were the symptoms of decline; but it was most fortunate for Mr. Ruskin that his drawings could be interpreted by such men as Armytage and Cousen, Cuff and Le Keux, Boys and Lupton, and not without advantage to them that their masterpieces should be preserved in his works, and praised as they deserved in his prefaces. Sometimes, as it often happens when engravers work for an artist who sets the standard high, they found Mr. Ruskin a hard taskmaster. The mere fact of their skill in translating a sketch from a notebook into a gem-like vignette, encouraged him to ask for more; so that some of the subjects which became the most elaborate were at first comparatively rough drawings, and were gradually worked up from successive retouchings of the proofs, by the infinite patience of both parties. In other cases, working drawings were prepared by Mr. Ruskin, as refined as the plates. How steady his hand was, and how trained his eye, can be seen by any one who looks carefully at the etchings by him—not *after* him—in *Modern Painters*; which show that he was fully competent to have produced his own illustrations, had it been worth his while; and any one who has turned over a portfolio of his best drawings will bear witness that, while in one mood he does those roughly-handled chiaroscuro studies like the *Seven Lamps* illustrations, at other times he can " curb the liberal hand" and rival a cameo in refinement. His limitation as an artist was owing to no want of executive skill. His own apology is that " he has no imagination," and fails in composition, especially in the arrangement of colour. With which explanation one is puzzled, seeing how many are in the same case; but no doubt he has not been ambitious to be of their number.

He could have been a painter if he had devoted himself to painting—not a Turner or a Titian, but a sound practitioner, much above the average. The same may be said of his verse-writing. In this year, 1850, his father collected and printed his poems, with a number of pieces that still remained in MS.; the author taking no part in this revival of bygones, which for many reasons, then, he was not anxious to recall,—though his father still believed that he *might* have been a poet, and *ought* to have been one. He, however, knew that he had found his vocation.

Another resurrection was *The King of the Golden River*, which had lain hidden for the nine years of the Ars Poetica. He allowed it to be published, with woodcuts by the famous " Dicky " Doyle. I say " allowed it to be published," not that there was any reason for suppressing the work on the score of triviality or juvenility. Mr. Ruskin has repeatedly said that he has no desire to suppress anything he has written, and proved it by sanctioning the collection of his letters to newspapers, and to private friends; without, as some might think, enough regard to consequences. In this case the venture was a success; the little book ran through three editions that year, and, partly because School Boards have adopted it as one of their prizes, it still finds a steady sale. The first issue must have been torn to rags in the nurseries of the last generation, since copies are so rare as to bring ten guineas apiece instead of the six shillings at which they were advertised in 1850.

Living in London this year, and already one of the most important literary celebrities, Mr. Ruskin could not avoid entertaining society and being entertained, even on the plea of book-writing. He mixed with an artistic circle, on good terms with men both in and out of the Academy; a literary circle of the old-fashioned gentleman-author type, such as rallied round the veteran Rogers; and in the third place a religious circle, or rather circles of various opinions in religion, from the more pronounced Evangelicals like Spurgeon to the most evasive of the early Broad Church-men. Puseyites and Roman Catholics were still as heathen men and publicans to him; and he noted with interest, while writing his review of Venetian history, that the strength of Venice was distinctly Anti-Papal, and her virtues Catholic but not Roman. Reflections on this subject were to have formed part of his great work, but the first volume was taken up with the à priori develop-ment of architectural forms; and the treatment in especial of Venetian matters had to be indefinitely postponed, until another visit should complete his material. Meanwhile he noticed with growing uneasiness—as many others did—the divided aims of professing Christians. Even in the Church of England, not to speak of the innumerable phases of dissenting Protestants, there were at least three opposing classes, pulling different ways and setting up different standards of theological and ecclesiastical thought. And all the while, the energy that might have made head against Popery and Infidelity, as it seemed to him, and to many, was being spent in discussing the Thirty-Nine Articles, or the history of the Reformation, or the Early Fathers, with every prospect of disastrous and irremediable schism.

His study of Venice had shown him the political importance of an acknowledged religion ; and the possibility of such a religion maintaining its influence for good, while still wedded to the state, and in external things remaining under state-direction. He saw that the Church, as it was regarded by the Apostles, was simply the assembly of professing Christians, the flock of Christ, for whom there was but one fold, with room for all. And he believed that if these discussions about Church history and post-Apostolic opinion were dropped, and if people would go candidly to the New Testament for its simple teaching, there ought to be no difficulty in finding a common ground upon which all could meet. If that were possible, then all that his writings had been pleading for, the habitual sincerity of thought and the standard simplicity of life, which would produce, among other things, a revival of the right spirit of art,—all this would be greatly helped and forwarded. He could think so, and say so, without apology ; for in those days religion was still treated with some show of

respect, and agnostic morality had scarcely been formulated.

Accordingly he put together his thoughts in a pamphlet
on the text " There shall be one fold and one shepherd,"
calling it, in allusion to his architectural studies, " Notes
on the Construction of Sheepfolds." He proposed a
compromise ; trying to prove that the pretensions to
priesthood on the high Anglican side, and the objections
to episcopacy on the Presbyterian, were alike untenable ;
and hoped that, when once these differences—such little
things, he thought them—were arranged, a united Church
of England might become the nucleus of a world-wide
federation of Protestants, a *civitas Dei*, a New Jerusalem.

There were many who agreed with his aspirations ; he
received shoals of letters from sympathising readers, most
of them praising his aims and criticising his means. For
it was just these little differences that stood in the way of
what all at every time have professed to desire. Others
objected, rather to his manner than to his matter : the title
savoured of levity, and an art-critic was supposed to be
wandering out of his province,—it was the *ne sutor* upside
down. Tradition says that the Notes were freely bought
by Border-farmers under a rather laughable mistake ; but
surely it was no new thing for a Scotch reader to find a
religious tract under a catching title ; and their two shillings
might have been worse spent. There were a few replies ;
one by Mr. Dyce, the clerical R.A., who defended the
Anglican view with mild persiflage and the usual common-
places. And there the matter ended, for the public. For
Mr. Ruskin, it was the beginning of a train of thought
which led him far. He gradually learnt that his error was
not in asking too much, but in asking too little. He

wished for a union of Protestants, forgetting the sheep that
are not of *that* fold, and little dreaming of the answer he
got, after many days, in "Christ's Folk in the Apennine."

Meanwhile the first volume of *Stones of Venice* had
appeared.   Its reception was indirectly described in a
pamphlet entitled "Something on Ruskinism, with ·a
'Vestibule' in Rhyme, by an Architect," a Puginist, it
seems, who felt that his craft was in danger.   He complains
bitterly of the "ecstasies of rapture" into which the newspapers had been thrown by the new work :—

> "Your book—since Reviewers so swear—may be rational,
>   Still, 'tis certainly not either loyal or national ; "

for it did not join in the chorus of congratulation to Prince
Albert and the British public on the Great Exhibition of
1851, the apotheosis of trade and machinery.   The "Architect" finds also—what may surprise the modern reader
who has not noticed that many an able writer has been
thought unreadable on his first appearance—that he cannot
understand Mr. Ruskin's language and ideas :—

> "Your style is so soaring—and some it makes sore—
>   That plain folks can't make out your strange mystical lore."

He will allow the author to be quite right, when he finds
something to agree with ; but the moment a sore point
is touched, then Ruskin is "insane."   In one respect the
"Architect" hit the nail on the head :—"Readers who are
not reviewers by profession can hardly fail to perceive that
Ruskinism is violently inimical to *sundry existing interests.*"
A more comprehensive answer to Mr. Ruskin's critics was
never given.   Before leaving the "Architect" one may
notice that his attack was printed at "Bell Yard, Temple

Bar," where forty years afterwards the *Stones of Venice* is re-issued, while the angry outcries it evoked are forgotten by all but the laborious biographer.

The best men, we said, were the first to recognise Mr. Ruskin's genius. Let us throw into the opposite scale an opinion of more weight than the Architect's, in a transcript from the original letter from Carlyle.

"CHELSEA, 9 *March*, 1851.

" DEAR RUSKIN,—

"I did not know yesterday till your servant was gone that there was any note in the parcel; nor at all what a feat you had done! A loan of the gallant young man's Memoirs was what I expected; and here, in the most chivalrous style, comes a gift of them. This, I think, must be in the style *prior* to the Renaissance! What can I do but accept your kindness with pleasure and gratitude, though it is far beyond my deserts? Perhaps the next man I meet will use me as much below them; and so bring matters straight again! Truly I am much obliged, and return you many hearty thanks.

"I was already deep in the *Stones*; and clearly purpose to hold on there. A strange, unexpected, and I believe, most true and excellent *Sermon* in Stones—as well as the best piece of School-mastering in Architectonics; from which I hope to learn in a great many ways. The spirit and purport of these Critical Studies of yours are a singular sign of the times to me, and a very gratifying one. Right good speed to you, and victorious arrival on the farther shore! It is a quite new ' renaissance,' I believe, we are getting into just now : either towards new, *wider* manhood, high again as the eternal stars; or else into final death, and the mask of Gehenna for evermore! A dreadful process, but a needful and inevitable one; nor do I doubt at all which way the issue will be, though which of the extant nations are to get included in it, and which to be trampled out and abolished in the process, may be very doubtful. God is great :—and sure enough, the changes in the *Construction of Sheepfolds* as well as in other things, will require to be very considerable.

" We are still labouring under the foul kind of Influenza here, I not far from emancipated, my poor Wife still deep in the business, though I hope past the deepest. Am I to understand that you too are seized? In a day or two I hope to ascertain that you are well again. Adieu: here is an interruption, here also is the end of the paper.

" With many thanks and regards,"

[Signature cut away.]

Another reader who was not a reviewer by profession took a different view. Charlotte Brontë wrote to one of her friends :—" The ' Stones of Venice ' seem nobly laid and chiselled. How grandly the quarry * of vast marbles is disclosed! Mr. Ruskin seems to me one of the few genuine writers, as distinguished from book-makers, of this age. His earnestness even amuses me in certain passages, for I cannot help laughing to think how utilitarians will fume and fret over his deep, serious, and (as they will think) fanatical reverence for Art."

But I do not share Charlotte Brontë's view altogether, nor her contempt for the utilitarians. A short while ago, one of her own people, a Yorkshire working-man not far from Haworth, got up in a public discussion, and said that he had once talked with Mr. Ruskin and tried to say how much he had enjoyed his works. " And he said to me, ' I don't care whether you *enjoyed* them : did they do you any good? ' "

They have at any rate done us the good, little valued by Mr. Ruskin, but greatly by many a dweller in modern towns, of reforming our street-architecture. And a greater outcome of this work the next chapter must unfold.

As soon as the first volume of *Stones of Venice* and the

---

* An allusion to the title of the first chapter of this first volume.

Notes on the Construction of Sheepfolds were published, Mr. Ruskin took a short Easter holiday at Matlock, and set to work at a new edition of *Modern Painters.* This was the fifth reprint of the first volume, and the third of Vol. II. They were carefully and conscientiously revised ; some passages of rough youthful criticism were cancelled, and wisely ; for more lasting good is done by expounding what is noble, than by satirising what is base. The work was left in its final form, except for notes added in later years ; and the Postscript indulges, most justifiably, in a little triumph at the changed tone of public criticism upon Turner.

But it was too late to have been any service to the great artist himself. In 1845—after saying good-bye and " Why *will* you go to Switzerland? There will be such a *fidge* about you when you're gone"—Turner was attacked, no one knows how, with some paralysis or mental decay, and was never himself again. The last drawings he did for Mr. Ruskin (Jan. 1848), the " Brünig " and the " Descent from the St. Gothard to Airolo," showed his condition unmistakably ; and the lonely restlessness of the last, disappointing years were, for all his friends, a melancholy ending to a brilliant career.

"This year (1851) he has no picture on the walls of the Academy ; and the *Times* of May 3rd says, 'We miss those works of INSPIRATION !'

" *We* miss ! Who misses? The populace of England rolls by to weary itself in the great bazaar of Kensington, little thinking that a day will come when those veiled vestals and prancing amazons, and goodly merchandise of precious stones and gold, will all be forgotten as though they had not been ; but that the light which has faded from the walls of the Academy is one which a million Koh-i-noors could not re-kindle ; and that the year 1851 will, in the far future, be remembered less for what it has displayed, than for what it has withdrawn."

Too truly prophesied ; for Turner was in his last illness, hiding like a wild animal, wounded to death.   On December the 19th, in the evening, the sunset shone upon his dishonoured corpse through the chamber window in Chelsea. Just so it shone upon another deathbed, for the sainted maid of Florence prefiguring, they said, the aureole.

"The Sun is God, my dear," Turner had told his housekeeper.   Was there no " healing in his wings " for the fallen hero ? or was *that* reserved only for the spotless soul of Ida ?   Were there still *other* sheep ? stones which the builders of sheepfolds rejected,—all manner of precious stones ?

CHAPTER V.

PRE-RAPHAELITISM.

(1851—1853.)

"Don't go yet! Are you aware that there will be a torch-race this evening on horseback, to the glory of Artemis?

"That is entirely new to me, said Socrates. And do you mean that they will really have torches, and pass them from rider to rider in the race?"—*Plato, Rep.* 328.

THE Academy-critic of the *Times*, in May 1851, who missed "those works of inspiration," as Ruskin had at last taught him to call Turner's pictures,—the acknowledged mouthpiece of public opinion found consolation in castigating a school of young artists who had "unfortunately become notorious by addicting themselves to an antiquated style and an affected simplicity in painting. . . . We can extend no toleration to a mere servile imitation of the cramped style, false perspective, and crude colour of remote antiquity. We want not to see what Fuseli termed drapery 'snapped instead of folded'; faces bloated into apoplexy, or extenuated into skeletons; colour borrowed from the jars in a druggist's shop, and expression forced into caricature. . . . That morbid infatuation which sacrifices truth, beauty, and genuine feeling to mere eccentricity, deserves no quarter at the hand of the public."

"Certainly, without doubt," said Henny-penny, Cocky-

locky, and the whole farm-yard.   And observe how cleverly
the *vox populi* had learnt to quack in the cadences of
Modern Painters, Vol. II., and the *Seven Lamps* :—" We
want not to see," and so forth, quoth he ; and re-reading
his proof, beheld, if I mistake not, by the eye of con-
templative imagination,—or was it associative ? these
distinctions being somewhat difficult,—beheld Mr. Ruskin's
graceful wave of the hand—" *Thank* you, my Dear Sir,
for your noble. . . ."

Mr. Ruskin read his *Times* that May morning at Park
Street ; smiled at " his own thunder" in the Thunderer's
hands ; remembered that last year he had not quite approved
of the obviously Popish tendency, as he took it, of a picture
called " Ecce Ancilla Domini " by an Italian of the name
of Rossetti ; nor of the Holy Family in the Carpenter's
Shop by a—Frenchman ?—called Millais ; nor of the thin
end of the Puseyite wedge in the " Early Christian
Missionary" signed W. H. Hunt,—no relative of his old
friend of the Water-colour Society.   The year before he
had been abroad ; all these months he had been closely
kept to his *Sheepfolds* and *Stones of Venice* ; and now he
was correcting the proofs of *Modern Painters*, Vol. I., as
thus :—

" Chapter the last : section 21.   *The duty and after
privileges of all students* . . . Go to Nature in all singleness
of heart, and walk with her laboriously and trustingly,
having no other thoughts but how best to penetrate her
meaning, and remember her instruction ; rejecting nothing,
selecting nothing, and scorning nothing ; believing all
things to be right and good, and rejoicing always in the
truth."

He went round to the Academy to look at the false

perspective, and snapped draperies, and infatuated untruth, and eccentric ugliness. Yes ; the faces were ugly : Millais' *Mariana* was a piece of idolatrous Papistry, and there was a mistake in the perspective. Collins' *Convent Thoughts*— more Popery ; but very careful,—the tadpole "too small for its age "; but what studies of plants ! And there was his own *Alisma Plantago*, which he had been drawing for *Stones of Venice* (vol. i., plate 7) and describing : " the lines through its body, which are of peculiar beauty, mark the different expansions of its fibres, and are, I think, exactly the same as those which would be traced by the currents of a river entering a lake of the shape of the leaf, at the end where the stalk is, and passing out at its point." Curvature was one of the special subjects of Mr. Ruskin, the one he found most neglected by ordinary artists. The *Alisma* was a test of observation and draughtsmanship. He had never seen it so thoroughly or so well drawn, and heartily wished the study were his.

Looking again at the other works of the school, he found that the one mistake in the *Mariana* was the only error in perspective in the whole series of pictures ; which could not be said of any twelve works, containing archi- tecture, by popular artists in the exhibition ; and that, as studies both of drapery and of every other minor detail, there had been nothing in art so earnest or so complete as these pictures since the days of Albert Dürer.

He went home, and wrote his verdict in a letter to the *Times*, and after farther examination of Hunt's "Two Gentlemen of Verona " and Millais' " Return of the Dove " wrote again, pointing out beauties, and indications of power in conception, and observation of nature, and handling, where at first he, like the rest of the public, had been

repelled by the wilful ugliness of the faces.   Meanwhile the
Pre-Raphaelites wrote to tell him that they were neither
Papists nor Puseyites.   The day after his second letter was
published he received an ill-spelt missive, anonymously
abusing them.   This was the sort of thing to interest his
love of poetical justice.   He made the acquaintance of
several of the Brethren.   "Charley" Collins, as his friends
affectionately called him, was the son of a respected R.A.,
and the brother of Wilkie Collins ; himself afterwards the
author of a delightful book of travel in France, *A Cruise
upon Wheels.*   Mr. Millais turned out to be the most
gifted, charming and handsome of young artists.   Mr.
Holman Hunt was already a Ruskin-reader, serious and
earnest in his religious nature as in his painting.

The Pre-Raphaelites were not, originally, Mr. Ruskin's
pupils, nor was their movement, directly, of his creation.
But it was the outcome of a general tendency which he,
more than any man, had helped to start ; and it was the
fulfilment, though in a way he had not intended, of his
wishes.   His advice to go to nature, selecting nothing,
rejecting nothing and scorning nothing, had been offered
to landscape students, and it had involved the acceptance
of Turner as their great exemplar and ultimate standard.
It was beginning to be accepted by many, but with timidity
and modifications ; and, to indulge for a moment in the
" might have been," if the Pre-Raphaelite revolution had
not happened, a school of modern landscape, naturalistic
on the one hand, idealistic and poetical on the other, would
probably have developed *constitutionally*, so to speak ; with
Mr. Ruskin as its prophet and Turner as its forerunner,—a
school which would have been as truly national as the
great school of portraiture had been, and as representative

in one direction of the spirit of the age, as the sixteenth-century Venetians.

But history does not behave so reasonably. There are more wheels in the machine than we can count, " cycle on epicycle," not to hint at cometary orbits unknown to the almanac. The naturalistic movement, which had engaged Mr. Ruskin's whole attention at his start, was only one side of the nation's life. The other side was reactionary, leading to Tractarianism in some, in others to historical research, to Gothic revivals in architecture and painting and poetry ; in all cases betraying itself in the harking back to bygones, rather than in progressist modernism. The lower class of minds took one side or the other, and became merely radical or materialist, and Puseyite or roman-tic, as their sympathies led them. But the problem, to a thinker, was to mediate between these opposing tendencies ; to find the higher term that embraced them both ; to unite the two aims without compromise. And in proportion as a man was great, he found the problem, with widening issues, there for him to attempt.

So Mr. Ruskin, who began as a naturalist, was met first by ancient Christian art, and spent his early manhood in dissolving the antithesis between modern English landscape-study and the standpoint of Angelico. No sooner had he succeeded than a new element appeared—an element of life, as he perceived, and therefore necessary to accept—but at first sight irreconcilable with his arrangement of the world. So he brought it into his scheme, bit by bit : first the naturalism of the Pre-Raphaelites, which he tried to consider the essence of the movement.

But they, too, were attempting the great problem, from their own side, like rival Matterhorn-pioneers : and they

shouted to him, as it were, to leave the *arête* he was
following, and its ups and downs and dizzy descent on
either hand, and to join them in their *couloir*. There the
little band toiled together, until some gave up the enterprise ; some were struck down by the stones that always
make a *couloir* unsafe ; some never struggled out of the
narrow chimney.   He regained his *arête*, stronger when
free from the rope, and safer on the dangerous edge.

His conversion to Pre-Raphaelitism was none the less
sincere because it was sudden, and brought about partly
by the personal influence of his new allies.   And in re-
arranging his art-theory to take them in, he had before his
mind rather what he hoped they would become, than what
they were.   For a time, his influence over them was great ;
their first three years were their own ; their next three
years were practically his ; and some of them, the weaker
brethren, leant upon him until they lost command of their
own powers.   No artist can afford to use another man's
eyes ; still less, another man's brain and heart.   Mr. Ruskin,
great as an exponent, was in no sense a master of artists.
His business was to set up the target, and register the
shot : not to sight and aim the guns.   And if he cheered
on the men who, he believed, were the best of the time, it
did not follow that he should be saddled with the responsibility of directing them.   In so far as he meddled with it,
he brought about their defeat.   I do not think he would
have been defeated as leader of a party which was truly
his own.   The Pre-Raphaelites were not his men ; he was
not their natural leader.   He was like some good knight
generously heading an insurrection, for the sake of fair
play.   The worse for him, whichever side won ; and his
allies would have been wiser to trust to bills and bows.

The famous pamphlet on *Pre-Raphaelitism* of August 1851 was the apology for his conversion, and a first attempt to reconcile his old principles with his new professions. He showed that the same motives of Sincerity impelled both the Pre-Raphaelite Brethren and Turner, and in a degree, men so different as Prout, old Hunt and Lewis. All these were opposed to the Academical School who worked by rule of thumb; and they differed among one another only in differences of physical power and moral aim. Which was all perfectly true, and much deeper and truer insight than the cheap criticism which could not see beyond superficial differences, or the fossil theories of the old school, defended in the pamphlet war by men like Rippingille, his old Editor, a useful populariser of art, but not a philosophic thinker. But Pre-Raphaelitism was an unstable compound; liable to explode upon the experimenter; and its component parts to return to their old antithesis of crude naturalism on the one hand and affectation, whether of piety or poetry or simple reactionary antiquarianism, on the other. And *that* Mr. Ruskin did not then foresee. All he knew was that, just when he was sadly leaving the scene, Turner gone and night coming on, new lights arose. It was really far more noteworthy that Millais and Rossetti and Hunt were *men of genius*, than that the "principles" they tried to illustrate were sound. And Mr. Ruskin, always safe in his intuitions, divined their power, and generously applauded the dexterous troop in their unexpected Lampadephoria.

Indirectly he found his reward. For, like Socrates in the dialogue, by joining in the festival he found youths to discourse with, and with them gradually evolved his own Republic, the ideal of life which is his real contribution to

humanity: . . . " What *good* have his writings done us? "
Hitherto they had been for our enjoyment; or, like the
Seven Lamps, vague outcries; or, like the *Sheepfolds*, tenta-
tive ideals.   In the later volumes of *Stones of Venice* we
find distinct aims prefigured.

Immediately after finishing the pamphlet on *Pre-Raphaelitism*, he left for the Continent with his wife and a friend,
the Rev. Daniel Moore; spent a fortnight in his beloved
Savoy; and then crossed the Alps with Mr. Newton.   On
the first of September he was at Venice again, for a final
spell of labour on the palaces and churches.   He tells the
story of his ten months' stay in a letter to his venerable
friend Rogers the poet, dated 23rd June (1852).

" I was out of health and out of heart when I first got
here.   There came much painful news from home,* and
then such a determined course of bad weather, and every
other kind of annoyance, that I never was in a temper fit to
write to any one; the worst of it was that I lost all *feeling*
of Venice, and this was the reason both of my not writing
to you and of my thinking of you so often.   For whenever
I found myself getting utterly hard -and indifferent, I
used to read over a little bit of the ' Venice ' in the ' Italy,'
and it put me always into the right tone of thought
again, and for this I cannot be enough grateful to you.
For though I believe that in the summer, when Venice is
indeed lovely, when pomegranate blossoms hang over every
garden-wall, and green sunlight shoots through every wave,
custom will not destroy, or even weaken, the impression
conveyed at first; it is far otherwise in the length and bitterness of the Venetian winters.   Fighting with frosty winds

* Among other things, the deaths of Turner in December, and of
Prout in February.

at every turn of the canals takes away all the old feeling of peace and stillness ; the protracted cold makes the dash of the water on the walls a sound of simple discomfort, and some wild and dark day in February one starts to find oneself actually balancing in one's mind the relative advantages of land and water carriage, comparing the Canal with Piccadilly, and even hesitating whether for the rest of one's life one would rather have a gondola within call or a hansom. When I used to get into this humour I *always* had recourse to those lines of yours :—

> 'The sea is in the broad, the narrow streets,
>   Ebbing and flowing,' etc. ;

and they did me good service for many a day ; but at last a time came when the sea was *not* in the narrow streets, and was always ebbing and not flowing ; and one day, when I found just a foot and a half of muddy water left under the Bridge of Sighs, and ran aground in the Grand Canal as I was going home, I was obliged to give the canals up. I have never recovered the feeling of them."

He then goes on to lament the decay of Venice, the idleness and the dissipation of the populace, the lottery-gambling ; and to forebode the "destruction of old buildings and erection of new" changing the place "into a modern town—a bad imitation of Paris." Better than that he thinks would be utter neglect; St. Mark's Place would again be, what it was in the early ages, a green field, and the front of the Ducal Palace and the marble shafts of St. Mark's would be rooted in wild violets and wreathed with vines. "She will be beautiful again then, and I could almost wish that the time might come quickly, were it not that so many noble pictures must be destroyed

first. . . . I love Venetian pictures more and more, and
wonder at them every day with greater wonder ; compared
with all other paintings they are so easy, so instructive, so
natural ; everything that the men of other schools did by
rule and called composition, done here by instinct and only
called truth.

" I don't know when I have envied anybody more than
I did the other day the directors and clerks of the Zecca.
There they sit at inky deal desks, counting out rolls of
money, and curiously weighing the irregular and battered
coinage of which Venice boasts ; and just over their heads,
occupying the place which in a London counting-house
would be occupied by a commercial almanack, a glorious
Bonifazio—' Solomon and the Queen of Sheba '; and in a
less honourable corner three *old* directors of the Zecca,
very mercantile-looking men indeed, counting money also,
like the living ones, only a little *more* living, painted by
Tintoret ; not to speak of the scattered Palma Vecchios,
and a lovely Benedetto Diana which no one ever looks
at. I wonder when the European mind will again awake
to the great fact that a noble picture was not painted
to be *hung*, but to be *seen* ? I only saw these by accident,
having been detained in Venice by some obliging person
who abstracted some [of his wife's jewels] and brought
me thereby into various relations with the respectable
body of people who live at the wrong end of the Bridge of
Sighs—the police, whom, in spite of traditions of terror, I
would very willingly have changed for some of those their
predecessors whom you have honoured by a note in the
Italy. The present police appear to act on exactly
contrary principles : yours found the purse and banished
the loser ; these *don't* find the jewels, and won't let me go

away. I am afraid no punishment is appointed in Venetian law for people who steal *time*."

Mr. Ruskin returned to England in July 1852, and settled next door to his old home on Herne Hill. He said he could not live any more in Park Street, with a dead brick wall opposite his windows. And so, in the old place where he wrote the first volume of *Modern Painters*, he finished *Stones of Venice*, with a thorough account of St. Mark's and the Ducal Palace and other ancient buildings ; a complete catalogue of Tintoret's pictures,—the list he had begun in 1845 ; and a history of the successive styles of architecture, Byzantine, Gothic and Renaissance, interweaving illustrations of the human life and character that made the art what it was.

The kernel of the work was the chapter on the Nature of Gothic ; in which he showed, more distinctly than in the *Seven Lamps*, and connected with a wider range of thought, suggested by Pre-Raphaelitism, the great doctrine that art cannot be produced except by artists ; that architecture, in so far as it is an art, does not mean the mechanical execution, by unintelligent workmen, of vapid working-drawings from an architect's office ; that, just as Socrates postponed the day of justice until philosophers should be kings and kings philosophers, so Ruskin postponed the reign of art until workmen should be artists, and artists workmen.

A phrase ? A formula ? As much a phrase as Napoleon's *carrière ouverte aux talens*. As much a formula as Luther's justification by faith. It was at length the frontier of his battle-field reached ; a real object in life, a motive of action attained ; a text to teach from, a creed to hold by. And out of that idea the whole of his doctrine could be evolved, with all its safeguardings and widening vistas. For if the workman must be made an artist he must have the experience, the feelings of an artist, as well as the skill : and that involves every circumstance of education and opportunity which may make for his truest well-being. And when Mr. Ruskin came to examine into this subject practically, he found that mere drawing-schools and charitable efforts could not make an artist out of a town mechanic or a country bumpkin ; far wider questions were complicated with this of art—nothing short of the fundamental principles of human intercourse and social economy. Now for the first time, after much sinking of trial-shafts, he had reached the true ore of thought, in the deep-lying strata ; and the working of his mine was begun. As we explore the scene of his labours, we can pick out samples from the heaps that mark his progress, and roughly assay them and partly reckon up the results. But all the while we must remember that the results are not here before us : they have gone out into the world ; they are in circulation, current coin of the realm of modern life ; won, or spent, gambled for, or bribed with ; hoarded, or wasted ; until the mint mark, often, has been worn away, or the image and superscription wilfully defaced.

But that matters little to the man who found the gold ; and it would matter less, could he see that his wealth and his work are being worthily inherited. It was that chapter on the Nature of Gothic that served for the first message of peace, as we shall hear, to the labouring classes in the beginning of the campaign of conciliation ; and it is not without curious significance that our greatest artist-workman, whom, with all his circle and their achievements and aspirations, these labours of Mr. Ruskin and his

Pre-Raphaelite friends created—William Morris should
now have chosen this chapter to reproduce, for love of it,
and of the art in which he has enshrined it.

"And do you mean, said Socrates, that they will be
Light-bearers; and hand the light on from man to man
in the race? Yes, said War-duke; do stay with us, and
don't sulk. And Bright-eyes,—It seems, he said, you must
wait."

CHAPTER VI.

THE EDINBURGH LECTURES.

(1853—1854.)

" The general history of art and literature shows that the highest achievements of the human mind are, as a rule, not favourably received at first."—*Schopenhauer* (*Lebensweisheit*).

BY the end of July 1853 *Stones of Venice* was finished, as well as a description of Giotto's works at Padua, written|for the Arundel Society. The social duties of the season were over ; and Mr. Ruskin took a cottage in Glenfinlas, where to spend a well-earned holiday. He invited Mr. Millais, by this time an intimate and heartily admired friend, to go down into Scotland with him for the summer's rest,—such rest as two men of energy and talent take, in the change of scene without giving up the habit of work. Mr. Ruskin devoted himself first to foreground studies, and made careful drawings of rock-detail ; and then, being invited to give a course of lectures before the Philosophical Society of Edinburgh, he was soon busy writing once more, and preparing the cartoon-sketches, "diagrams" as he calls them, to illustrate his subjects. Dr. Acland had joined the party ; and one day, in the ravine, it is said that he asked Millais to sketch their host as he stood contemplatively on the rocks, with the torrent thundering beside him. The sketch was produced at a

168

sitting ; and, with additional work in the following winter, became the well-known portrait now at Oxford in the possession of Sir Henry Acland, much the best likeness of this early period.

Another portrait of Mr. Ruskin, not so highly finished, but cleverly sketched, was painted—in words—by one of his audience at Edinburgh on November 1st, when he gave the opening lecture of his course, his first appearance on the platform. The account is extracted from the *Edinburgh Guardian* of November 19th, 1853 :—

" Before you can see the lecturer, however, you must get into the hall, and that is not an easy matter, for, long before the doors are opened, the fortunate holders of season tickets begin to assemble, so that the crowd not only fills the passage, but occupies the pavement in front of the entrance and overflows into the road. At length the doors open, and you are carried through the passage into the hall, where you take up, of course, the best available position for seeing and hearing. . . . After waiting a weary time . . . the door by the side of the platform opens, and a thin gentleman with light hair, a stiff white cravat, dark overcoat with velvet collar, walking, too, with a slight stoop, goes up to the desk, and looking round with a self-possessed and somewhat formal air, proceeds to take off his greatcoat, revealing thereby, in addition to the orthodox white cravat, the most orthodox of white waistcoats. . . . ' Dark hair, pale face, and massive marble brow—that is my ideal of Mr. Ruskin,' said a young lady near us. This proved to be quite a fancy portrait, as unlike the reality as could well be imagined. Mr. Ruskin has light sand-coloured hair ; his face is more red than pale ; the mouth well cut, with a good deal of decision in its curve, though somewhat wanting in sustained dignity and strength ; an aquiline nose ; his forehead by no means broad or massive, but the brows full and well bound together ; the eye we could not see, in consequence of the shadows that fell upon his countenance from the lights overhead, but we are sure that the poetry and passion we looked for almost in vain in other features must be concentrated there. After sitting for a moment or two, and glancing round at the sheets on the wall as he takes off his gloves, he rises, and leaning slightly over the desk, with his hands folded across, begins at once,—'You are proud of your good city of Edinburgh,' etc.

"And now for the style of the lecture. Properly speaking, there were two styles essentially distinct, and not well blended,—a speaking and a writing style ; the former colloquial and spoken off-hand ; the latter rhetorical and carefully read in quite a different voice,—we had almost said intoned. . . . His elocution is peculiar ; he has a difficulty in sounding the letter 'r'; and there is a peculiar tone in the rising and falling of his voice at measured intervals, in a way scarcely ever heard, except in the public lection of the service appointed to be read in churches. These are the two things with which, perhaps, you are most surprised,—his dress and manner of speaking —both of which (the white waistcoat notwithstanding) are eminently clerical. You naturally expect, in one so in-dependent, a manner free from conventional restraint, and an utterance, whatever may be the power of voice, at least expressive of a strong individuality ; and you find instead a Christ Church man of ten years' standing, who has not· yet taken orders ; his dress and manner derived from his college tutor, and his elocution from the chapel-reader."

The lectures were a summing-up, in popular form, of the chief topics of Mr. Ruskin's thought during the last two years. The first stated, with more decision and warmth than part of his audience approved, or than would have been expected from the impression he made upon the writer in the *Guardian*, his plea for the Gothic Revival, for the use of Gothic as a domestic style. He tried to show by the analogy of natural forms that the Gothic arch and gable were in themselves more beautiful, and more logical in construction, than the horizontal lintel and low pediment of the ordinary Renaissance-Classic then in vogue. The next lecture, given three days later, went on to contrast the wealth of ornament in mediæval buildings with the poor survivals of conventionalised patterns which did duty for decoration in nineteenth-century "Greek" architecture; and he raised a laugh by comparing a typical stonemason's lion with a real tiger's head, drawn in the Edinburgh zoological gardens by Mr. Millais. He showed how a gradual Gothicising of the common dwelling-house was possible, by introducing a porch here and an oriel window there, piece by piece, as indeed had been done in Venice. And he pointed out that this kind of work would give opportunities for freer and more artistic workmanship; it would be an education in itself, and raise the builder's man from a mere mechanical drudge into an intelligent and interested craftsman.

The last two lectures, on November 15th and 18th, were on Painting; briefly reviewing the history of landscape and the life and aims of Turner; and, finally, Christian art and Sincerity in imagination, which was now put forth as the guiding principle of Pre-Raphaelitism. The proud possessor of a cut and dry creed,—and such, in spite of much talk about progress, we have always with us,—will be stumbled by this new milestone in Mr. Ruskin's intellectual pilgrimage. But no educated reader, or writer, would accompany the rubbing of his shins with quite so unrestrained an outcry as was possible in the younger days of the century. It is most difficult to understand the violence of language—the fanaticism of partisanship, which were common, then, in controversies about poor innocent Art: it would be impossible to understand them, unless one knew that the public was very eager after pictures and architecture, but very ill-informed about them : and that, consequently, certain " existing interests " existed beautifully on the very darkness and decay of the world they adorned, like orchids in the Amazonian woods. To let in the light was to cut at the roots of these pretty parasites ; and fear for their pets, if not for their own arbours, caused men of position and education, writers in the best newspapers and magazines, to use terms of childlike passion,—to lose their critical coolheadedness,—in a way which the respectable editor of to-day would rule out of order.

For instance, while these lectures were being prepared, the Rev. Edward Young, M.A., gave a lecture at Bristol on the Pre-Raphaelites, in which he arraigned their *arrogance*, *bigotry*, and *destructiveness* ; labelled them *unwholesome* and *ungenerous* ; declared that they were *pandering to the downward tendencies of the age*, and cried, " Woe, woe, woe, to ' exceedingly young men of stubborn instincts ' "—a quotation, without the context, from Mr. Ruskin,—the *Woe, woe, woe*, being his own, of course ; rather profane, for a clergyman.

This lecture, when printed, the *Athenæum* reviewed at length, as a serious contribution to literature. It began by calling Mr. Young *sensible and eloquent* ; after a paragraph or two it doubted his fairness and impartiality, and "thought he went rather far." For its own part, it objected to the antiquarian spirit of the age : "What do we know of Tubal Cain or Nimrod, of Assur or Menes ? We cannot unravel the Pyramid mystery, and we know not who built them. So must it ever be." That was the *Athenæum's* notion of archæology and of impartiality : and so frank a confession of onesidedness—of adhesion to the utilitarian *éclaircisse-ment*—conveniently relieves us of the trouble of analysing its authority, forty years ago.

When the *Lectures on Architecture and Painting* were published, the *Athenæum* showed its impartiality thus :— " Mr. Ruskin has outdone himself in these lectures. Cleverness and absurdity—deep insight in one direction, stone blindness in every other—vigour and weakness—power of explanation and unfairness of statement—are found on every page, from frontispiece to *finis*. The absence of logic has seldom been so conspicuously paraded. . . . Why are these heads placed in this conspicuous contrast ? To prove that the Greeks did not copy from nature. See the absurdity here involved. A Greek lion is not like a Scotch tiger ; hence, Greek art is not natural !"

And so on, for eleven columns ; for though Ruskin is of course absurd, he is an uncommonly interesting and plausible fellow, and we can't afford to miss the chance of sprinkling his name about our pages. Indeed, however, there were weak points in these lectures, considered as an argumentative essay. They were not the unfolding of the train of thought by which Mr. Ruskin reached his conclusions : he is not a good exponent of such trains of thought, and continually does himself injustice by stating the

conclusion without the premisses ; though now and then he
works out a lesson in analysis as nobody else can.   They
were written under peculiar circumstances of domestic
anxiety which would have completely paralysed another
man : the marvel is that he was able to deliver these
lectures at all, " looking round with a self-possessed air."
And while they sum up his standpoint at the time, they
must have been wholly unintelligible to any who had not
read his previous works.   Perhaps, too, it was hasty of
the writer to suppose that the modern Scotch have John
Knox's respect for the authority of the Bible : or that the
slight suggestive touches, with which he sketched contrast-
ing ages of thought and schools of art, would be easily
recognised and read by people who, in the surprise of his
sudden raid, so far forgot their schooling as to declare, with
the *Athenæum*, that the Middle Ages were characterised by
cannibalism and obscenity, and that Dante seldom drew
an image from nature ; who, in the act of defending Greek
art against Ruskin the Goth, had never heard of the important Stele of Aristion, known as " The Soldier of
Marathon " ; who, as judges of modern art, found that
" water-colour painting can scarcely satisfy the mind craving
for human action and human passion " ; and " objected to
the painting of contemporary history because we have
had enough of portraits, and as for modern battles, they
are mere affairs of smoke and feathers."

Why do I rake up these old quarrels?   Because the
modern Ruskin-reader, innocent of history, is often surprised
and pained at indications of bitterness he cannot explain,
and suspects some cankering grudge on the author's part,
some moral defect which invalidates his judgment and
impairs his argument.   Whereas the truth is that during

these ten years (1844-54) Mr. Ruskin had to fight his way against strenuous opposition in certain quarters ; to hear language used against himself and his friends which was to the last degree personal and scurrilous ; to which the humorous petulancies of his own old age, as calling Mr. Goldwin Smith a " goose," and such *obiter dicta*, were harmless trifling, at the worst. In these earlier times, though he gave many a " smashing blow " to fallacies, he did not render railing for railing : it was measures, not men, that he attacked. Sometimes, of course, the cap fitted one or other head : that could hardly be helped.

The *argumentum ad hominem* is always illogical : and this was never shown more distinctly than in the discussion which he raised, especially in these lectures, about the relations of art and morality. He did seem to think, up to this time, that a good painter must be what is commonly called a good man. He had not clearly formulated the doctrine of his Oxford Lectures, that art simply reflects the general morality of the race and age, and that it is only indirectly connected with the individual character of the painter ; and *that*, again, only in ideal, and not in social morality. It was in this opinion that he tried to make Turner's virtues shine ; and rightly, in so far as he was doing justice to a great man whom the world had grossly misunderstood ; rightly, also, as a counterstroke to the vulgar error that proclaims genius to be another name for lunacy, and greatness merely a form of successful cunning. But I venture to think that, if Mr. Ruskin had found time to write Turner's life at full length, thoroughly balancing the different elements in that strange character, and tracing the growth of the man as he had traced the growth of Venetian art, instead of contenting himself with incomplete

notices in scattered contexts,—he would then have defined
his views more clearly, to his own great advantage ; and
written a noble work, to ours.   No doubt he did not wish
to interfere with Walter Thornbury's book, then in preparation : he certainly collected a mass of most interesting
material, which fully bears out the view he took of Turner's
character.

While staying at Edinburgh Mr. Ruskin met the various
celebrities of modern Athens, some of them at the table of
his former fellow-traveller in Venice, Mrs. Jameson.   One
lifelong friendship was begun during this time, with Dr.
John Brown, the author of *Rab and his Friends* and *Pet
Marjorie*, who corresponded with Mr. Ruskin till his death
in 1882, on terms of the greatest affection.

The next May (1854) the Pre-Raphaelites again needed
his defence.   Mr. Holman Hunt exhibited the "Light of
the World" and the "Awakening Conscience," two pictures
whose intention was misunderstood by the public, though
as serious, as sincere, as the religious paintings of the Campo
Santo of Pisa.   Mr. Ruskin made them the theme of two
more letters to the *Times* ; mentioning, by the way, the
"spurious imitations of Pre-Raphaelite work" which were
already becoming common.   And on starting for his
summer tour on the Continent, he left a new pamphlet for
publication on the opening of the Crystal Palace.   There
had been much rejoicing over the "new style of architecture" in glass and iron, and its purpose as a Palace of
Art.   Mr. Ruskin who had declined, in the last chapter of
the *Seven Lamps*, to join in the cry for a new style, was
not at all ready to accept this as any real artistic advance ;
and took the opportunity to plead again for the great
buildings of the past, which were being destroyed or

neglected, while the British public was glorifying its gigantic greenhouse. The pamphlet practically suggested the establishment of the Society for the preservation of ancient buildings which has since come into operation. Some of the critics made merry over the proposal, not foreseeing how the tide would turn. Others, like the *Builder*, to the credit of their own sagacity, approved a movement which is now doing good work in England ; and after many years has spread to Italy, as a direct result of Mr. Ruskin's work. His pupil, Signor Giacomo Boni, after recommending himself in Venice as the practical exponent of these principles at the Ducal Palace, has lately been appointed by the Government to the post of Director of the monuments of Italy, already with the happiest results. And so, in spite of opposition year by year diminishing, and withdrawing itself into the lower class of journalism, Mr. Ruskin's work went on, until he was practically acknowledged to be the leading authority upon matters of art—almost the dictator of taste. Pre-Raphaelitism won a complete victory ; Gothic forms were soon introduced into domestic architecture ; Turner became recognised as the greatest of all landscapists ; art-education was extended to the masses. And yet Mr. Ruskin was not satisfied. What more could he want?

CHAPTER VII.

THE WORKING MEN'S COLLEGE.

(1854—1855.)

> "Sighing, I turned at last to win
> Once more the London dirt and din."
> *Rossetti.*

ONE is sometimes called upon to sympathise with friends at a loss for a subject. Form, we have learnt, makes the artist ; the gifts of prophecy, we hear, have been withdrawn ; and there comes from the abodes of talent a bitter cry of " no work to do "—no interests, no excitements, no burning question to illustrate, no neglected truth to teach, no message to deliver. " The earth falls asunder, being old." With Mr. Ruskin it was not so. Time was, at the age of twelve, in a languid mood, he versified the situation in a poem on Nothing ; but he does not seem to have needed to do so again. Sometimes he has repeated himself, but in a general way every lecture he gave was a new lecture, every sketch he made was a fresh conception ; and no sooner had he finished one book than he was busy on another, like a wine-treader toiling to keep the grapes under.

This summer of 1854 he projected a study of Swiss history : to tell the tale of six chief towns—Geneva,

Fribourg, Basle, Thun, Baden and Schaffhausen, to which in 1858 he added Rheinfelden and Bellinzona. He intended to illustrate the work with pictures of the places described. He began with his drawing of Thun, a large bird's-eye view of the town with its river and bridges, roofs and towers, all exquisitely defined with the pen, and broadly coloured in fluctuating tints that seem to melt always into the same aerial blue ; the blue, high up the picture, beyond the plain, deepening into distant mountains. Suppose a Whistler etching and a Whistler colour-sketch combined upon one paper, and you form an idea of the style of this series : except that Mr. Ruskin's work, being calculated for book-illustration, and not for decoration, can only be seen in the hand, and totally loses its effect by hanging—especially by exhibition hanging. But the delicate detail and studied use of the line are there, together with a calculated unity of effect and balance of colour which by 1858 had begun to degenerate into a mannered purple.

But his father wanted to see *Modern Painters* completed ; and so he began his third volume at Vevey, with the discussion of the grand style, in which he at last broke loose from Reynolds, as he was bound to do, after his study of Pre-Raphaelitism, and all the varied experiences of the last ten years. The lesson of the Tulse Hill ivy had been brought home to him in many ways : he had found it to be more and more true that Nature is, after all, the criterion of art, and that the greatest painters were always those whose aim, so far as they were conscious of an aim, was to take fact for their starting-point. Idealism, beauty, imagination, and the rest, though necessary to art, could not, he felt, be made the object of study ; they were the gift of heredity, of circumstances, of national aspirations and virtues ; not to be produced by the best of rules, or achieved by the best of intentions.

What his own view of his own work was can be gathered from a letter to an Edinburgh student, written on August 6th, 1854 : " I am sure I never said anything to dissuade you from trying to excel or to do great things.   I only wanted you to be sure that your efforts were made with a substantial basis, so that just in the moment of push your footing might not give way beneath you ; and also I wanted you to feel that long and steady effort made in a contented way does more than violent effort made from some strong motive or under some enthusiastic impulse. And I repeat—for of this I am perfectly sure—that the best things are only to be done in this way.   It is very difficult thoroughly to understand the difference between indolence and reserve of strength, between apathy and severity, between palsy and patience ; but there is all the difference in the world ; and nearly as many men are ruined by inconsiderate exertions as by idleness itself.   To do as much as you can heartily and happily do each day in a well-determined direction, with a view to far-off results, with present enjoyment of one's work, is the only proper, the only essentially profitable way."

This habit of great industry not only enabled Mr. Ruskin to get through a vast amount of work, but it helped him over times of trouble, of which his readers and acquaintances, for the most part, had little idea.   To them he appeared as one of those deities of Epicurus, sipping his nectar and hurling his thunderbolts, or, when it pleased him, showering the sunshine of his eloquence upon delighted crowds.   He had wealth and fame, the converse of wit and genius ; the delight of travel and intense appreciation of all the pleasures that travelling afforded. The fancy of the outside public pictured him in the possession of rare works of art, of admiring friends, of a beautiful wife. They did not know, as we do, the strange ill-omened circumstances of his marriage; they had not followed him about, as we have, from place to place, and seen him in continual suffering and struggle of mind and body; they could not guess, as the thoughtful reader can, the effort needed on his part to do what he believed to be his duty toward a wife whose affection he earnestly sought, but whose tastes were discordant with his; nor, on the other hand, the disappointment and disillusioning of a young girl who found herself married, by parental arrangement, to a man with whom she had nothing in common; in habits of thought and life, though not so much in years, her senior; taking "small notice, or austerely," of the gayer world she preferred, "his mind half-buried in some weightier argument, or fancy-borne perhaps upon the rise and long roll" of his periods. And his readers and the public were intensely puzzled when she left him.

To his acquaintances, however, it was no great surprise, though, with one exception, they took his part, and fully exonerated him from blame. He, with his consciousness of having fulfilled all the obligations he had undertaken, and with an old-fashioned delicacy and chivalry which revolted alike from explanation and from recrimination, set up no defence, brought no counter-charges, and preferred to let gossip do its worst. It was only the other day that a public lecturer, who had quoted a passage of Mr. Ruskin's, was asked whether it were not true that Ruskin had run away with somebody's wife. That is a very mild version of the lies that, one time or other, have been current about him, scandals which have had all the more weight because he never cared to speak out for himself, even to people who believe that they are his intimates. There are many tales whispered behind his back that are perfectly true—*of somebody else*, of different people who have been his friends, at one time or another—people whose reputation he values, it seems, more than his own. So much so, that while he gossips about early days and youthful follies, laments the mistakes of his life and disappointments of his age, he has never let one single word escape to clear his own character at the expense of others. And this is the man they call Egoist.

In that affair of 1854, how little blame really attached to him can be gathered from the continuance of valued friendships and expressions of esteem on the part of several who would have been the most likely to judge him severely if they had found him in the wrong ;—such as Miss Mitford, who not only stood firmly by him, but introduced him to her friends the Brownings. Mrs. Browning wrote, early in 1855, " We went to Denmark Hill yesterday, to have luncheon with them (Mr. Ruskin and his parents) and see the Turners, which, by the way, are divine. I like Mr. Ruskin very much, and so does Robert : very gentle, yet earnest—refined and truthful. I like him very much. We count him one among the valuable acquaintances made this year in England."

He tells in *Præterita* how, about this time, he used to go a good deal into society, and "sometimes, indeed, an incident happened that was amusing or useful to me ;—I heard Macaulay spout the first chapter of Isaiah, without understanding a syllable of it ;—saw the Bishop of Oxford

taught by Sir Robert Inglis to drink sherry-cobbler
through a straw ;—and formed one of the worshipful
concourse invited by the Bunsen family, to hear them 'talk
Bunsenese' (Lady Trevelyan), and *see* them making
presents to—each other—from their family Christmas tree,
and private manger of German Magi. But, as a rule, the
hours given to the polite circles were an angering penance
to me." In the performance of these duties he met, however, Lady Mount Temple, who has always been one
of his best and most valued friends. It was through Mr.
Cowper Temple that he was introduced to Lord Palmerston
—not with the least result on either side, in any public
expressions of opinion ; for Mr. Ruskin was never made
for "practical" or party politics.

Another friend who stood by him, and perhaps helped
him out of himself most effectually by giving him some new
work to do, was Frederick Denison Maurice. The whole
story of the Working Men's College, and other efforts to
get into touch with the labouring classes, must be read
in the biography of Maurice by his son, and in such of
the literature of the time, like Kingsley's *Alton Locke*, as
reflects the spirit of the enterprise. It was a brave attempt,
in an age when such attempts were regarded as mere
Quixotism, to redress some of the crying evils of social
inequality ; and if it failed of great direct result, it certainly
led the way to other attempts to solve the problem of
fraternity. It was, at all events, a step towards the carrying
out of doctrines which Mr. Ruskin had been preaching—
the improvement of the intellectual life of the workman.
Indeed, his influence was very definitely acknowledged by
the fact that Mr. Furnivall (afterwards well known in the
New Shakspere and the Browning Societies) printed, and

distributed to all comers at the opening lecture,* October 30th, 1854, as a manifesto of the movement, that chapter on the Nature of Gothic from *The Stones of Venice.*

Mr. Ruskin took charge of the drawing classes at the college from the commencement, at first single-handed. He attended from November 2nd, on every Thursday evening from 8.30 to 10, until the Thursday before Christmas, when they had their two weeks' vacation. By the beginning of next term he had two allies in his work, one a friend of Maurice's, Mr. Lowes Dickinson, whose portrait of Maurice was mentioned with honour in the *Notes on the Academy*; his portrait of Kingsley hangs in the hall of the novelist-professor's college at Cambridge. The other was a friend of Mr. Ruskin's.

Only the reader who has engaged in this form of phil-anthropic labour—old-fashioned night-schools, or modern lad's clubs or carving-classes—quite understands what it involves, and how difficult it is for an artist or a literary man, after his sedentary day's work, to drag his tired brain and over-excited nerves to a crowded room in some unsavoury neighbourhood, and to endure the noise, the glare, the closeness, and, worst of all, perhaps, the indocility of a class of learners for whom the discipline of the ordinary school or college does not exist; who have no fear of deans or examiners; who must be coaxed to work, and humoured into perseverance; and for whom the lowest rung in the ladder of culture is a giddy elevation. Such work has indeed its reward, but never exceeding great; and it has

---

* At St. Martin's Hall, Long Acre. The classes were begun at 31, Red Lion Square. Mr. Ruskin also superintended classes taught by Messrs. Jeffery and E. Cooke at the Working Women's (afterwards Working Men and Women's) College, Queen Square.

more discouragements and difficulties than one cares to reckon up.

To people who know their Ruskin only as the elegant theorist of art, sentimental and egotistic, as they will have it, there must be something strange, almost irreconcilable, in his devotion, week after week and year after year, to such a labour. Still more must it astonish them to find the mystic author of the *Blessed Damozel*, the passionate painter of the *Venus Verticordia*, working by Ruskin's side in this rough navvy-labour of philanthropy.

It was early in 1854 that a drawing by D. G. Rossetti was sent to Mr. Ruskin by a friend of the painter's. The critic already knew Millais and Hunt personally, but not Rossetti. He had scarcely noticed his works, as they were not exhibited at the Academy. Mr. Ruskin was just bringing out the Edinburgh Lectures in book-form, and busy with the defence of the Pre-Raphaelites. He wrote kindly, signing himself "yours respectfully," which amused the young painter. He made acquaintance, and in the appendix to his book placed Rossetti's name with those of Millais and Hunt, especially praising the imaginative power, which he could not fail to observe at once.

He did more than that. He agreed to buy, up to a certain sum every year, any drawings that Rossetti brought him, at their market price; and his standard of money-value for works of art has never been niggardly. This sort of help, the encouragement to work, is exactly what makes progress possible to a young and independent artist; it is better for him than fortuitous exhibition-triumphs—much better than the hack-work which many have to undertake, to eke out their livelihood. And the mere fact of being bought by the eminent art-critic was enough to encourage others.   Rossetti was not a skilful economist, and it was long before his earnings were sufficient to enable him to marry and, as they call it, settle in life ; for which reason the judicious help he thus received was all the more valuable.

The artist and the critic became close friends.   In 1861 Rossetti drew a chalk portrait of Mr. Ruskin, afterwards in the possession of Dr. Pocock of Brighton.   Rossetti was often at Denmark Hill, and Ruskin used to visit the studio in Chatham Place, near Blackfriars Bridge, where he met Miss Siddall, Rossetti's pupil and model, and afterwards wife, and praised her so that it did her lover's heart good.

It was there, too, that he first met Mr. Burne-Jones, in 1856, and Mr. William Morris and other famous men of the school.   There were still other ways in which he helped.   In 1856 "The Burden of Nineveh" was published anonymously in the *Oxford and Cambridge Magazine*.   Ruskin liked it, and wrote to Rossetti to know who was the author, perhaps not without a suspicion that he was addressing the man who could tell him.   Though his Scotch morality did not approve of some phases of Rossetti's work, for instance *Jenny*,—at which many readers may not be surprised,—he tried to get Thackeray, by this time a friend of his, to print Rossetti's poems in the *Cornhill* ; but in vain.   And as editors refused them, he made himself responsible for the cost of their publication, both in the case of the *Early Italian Poets*, I believe, and also in the case of the first edition of the *Poems* in 1868.   It was only afterwards, when Rossetti gave way to chloral and misanthropy, and became inaccessible to nearly all his old friends, that he and Mr. Ruskin drifted apart.

So in the Christmas vacation of 1854 this new recruit

was enlisted, and during Lent term 1855 the three teachers worked together every Thursday evening. With the beginning of the third term, March 29th, the increase of the class made it more convenient to divide their forces. Rossetti thenceforward taught the figure on another night of the week; while the elementary and landscape class continued to meet on Thursdays under Ruskin and Lowes Dickinson. In 1856 the elementary and landscape class was further divided, Mr. Dickinson taking Tuesday evenings, and Mr. Ruskin continuing the Thursday class, with the help of Mr. William Ward as under-master. There were four terms in the Working Men's College year, the only vacation, except for the fortnight at Christmas, being from the beginning of August to the end of October. Mr. Ruskin did not always attend throughout the summer term, though sometimes his class came down to him into the country to sketch. He kept up the work without other intermission until May 1858, after which the completion of *Modern Painters* and many lecture-engagements took him away for a time. In the spring of 1860 he was back at his old post for a term; but after that he discontinued regular attendance, and went to the Working Men's College only at intervals to give addresses, or informal lectures, to students and friends. On such occasions the "drawing-room" or first floor of the house in which the College was held would be always crowded, with an audience who heard the lecturer at his best; speaking freely among friends, out of a full treasure-house, "things new and old,"—the accounts of recent travel, lately-discovered glories of art, and the growing burden of the prophecy that in those years was beginning to take more definite shape in his mind.

As a teacher, Mr. Ruskin was most engaging. What is called " personal magnetism," the attraction of a powerful mind and intensely sympathetic manner, he exercised to the highest degree over all with whom he came into personal contact. His enthusiasm for the subject in hand, his obvious devotion to his work, his unselfish readiness to take any trouble over it, his extreme consideration for the feelings of any man, woman or child, high or low, clever or stupid, in his company, his vivacity and humour and imagination, all spent, as the pupil proudly felt, " on little me," made him simply adored. But there was this drawback,—that he imputed to his pupils, in many cases, more talent than they really had ; he thought that because they could make great progress with his help, they might now and then be trusted to walk alone ; and they, too, were sometimes lifted up with pride " in little me " that went before a fall ; and then there was disappointment. He often " talked over their heads," and thought they were following him, when they were being led into misconceptions of his aims and their powers : for words, to him, meant things and ideas which only a fully educated mind was likely to grasp.

His object in the work, as he said before the Royal Commission on National Institutions, was *not to make artists,* but to make the workmen better men, to develop their powers and feelings,—to educate them, in short. And, in cases where ingrained self-conceit did not make it impossible, he did what he intended. He always has urged young people intending to study art as a profession to enter the Academy Schools, as Turner and the Pre-Raphaelites did, or to take up whatever other serious course of practical discipline was open to them. But he held very strongly that everybody could learn drawing, that their eyes could be sharpened and their hands steadied, that they could be taught to appreciate the great works of nature and of art, without wanting to make pictures and to exhibit and sell them.

It was with this intention that he wrote the *Elements of Drawing* in 1856, supplemented by the *Elements of Perspective* in 1859; which, though out of chronological order, may be noticed here as an outcome of his teaching, and a type of it. The *Elements of Drawing* are taught in three letters addressed to the general amateur; the first devoted to practice with the point and brush, suggesting various ways of making such drudgery interesting. The methods of Rembrandt's etching and Dürer's woodcut and Turner's mezzotint are illustrated, and applied to naturalistic landscape. In the next letter hints are given for sketching from Nature, especially showing the importance of matching colours, as students are now taught to do in the better schools. For the rest, the methods of old William Hunt are followed, in the use of body-colour, and broken tints. Finally, the laws of Colour and Composition are analysed—not for the sake of teaching how to colour and how to compose, but, as he says again and again, to lead to greater appreciation of good colour and good composition in the works of the masters.

In spite of the repeated statement that the book was not intended to show a short cut to becoming an artist, it has often been misused and misunderstood; so much so, that after it had proved its popularity by a sale of 8000, the author let it go out of print, intending to supersede it with a more carefully stated code of directions. But the new work, the *Laws of Fésole*, was never finished;

and meanwhile the *Elements of Drawing* remains, if not a standard text-book of Art, a model of method, a type of Object-lessons, of the greatest value to those who wish to substitute a more natural, and more truly educational, method for the old rigid learning by rote and routine.

The illustrations for the book were characteristic sketches by the author, beautifully cut by his pupil, W. H. Hooper, who was one of a band of engravers and copyists formed by these classes at the Working Men's College. In spite of the intention not to make artists by his teaching, Mr. Ruskin could not prevent some of his pupils from taking up art as a profession ; and those who did became, in their way, first-rate men. George Allen as a mezzotint engraver, Arthur Burgess as a draughtsman and wood-cutter, John Bunney as a painter of architectural detail, E. Cooke as a teacher, William Ward as a facsimile copyist, have all done work whose value deserves acknowledgment, all the more because it has not aimed at popular effect, but at the severe standard of the greater schools. But these men were only the side issue of the Working Men's College enterprise. Its real result was in the proof that the labouring classes could be interested in Art ; that the capacity shown by the Gothic workman had not entirely died out of the nation, in spite of the interregnum, for a full century, of manufacture ; and the experience led Mr. Ruskin forward to wider views on the nature of arts and the duties of philanthropic effort and social economy.

CHAPTER VIII.

"*MODERN PAINTERS*" CONTINUED.

(1855—1856.)

" Nor feared to follow, in the offence
Of false opinion, his own sense
Of justice unsubdued."

Robert, Lord Lytton.

IT was in the year 1855 that Mr. Ruskin first published *Notes on the Royal Academy and other Exhibitions.* He had been so often called upon to write his opinion upon Pre-Raphaelite pictures, either privately or to the newspapers, or to mark his friends' catalogues, that he found at last less trouble in printing his notes once for all. The new plan was immediately popular ; three editions of the pamphlet were called for between June 1st and July 1st. Next year he repeated the Notes, and six editions were sold ; which indicated a great success in those times, when literature was not spread broadcast to the millions, as it is nowadays, and when the reading public was comparatively limited.

In spite of a dissentient voice here and there, Mr. Ruskin was really by that time recognised as the leading authority upon taste in painting, and he was trusted by a great section of the public, who had not failed to notice how completely he and his friends were winning the day. The proof of it was in the fact that they were being imitated on all sides; Ruskinism in writing and Pre-Raphaelitism in painting were becoming fashionable. Many an artist, who had abused the new-fangled style three years ago, now did his best to learn the trick of it and share the success. It seemed easy : you had only to exaggerate the colour and emphasise the detail, people thought, and you could "do a Millais"; and if Millais sold, why shouldn't *they*? And thus a great mass of imitative rubbish was produced, entirely wanting in the freshness of feeling and sincerity of conception which were the real virtues of the school.

But at the same time the movement gave rise to a new method of landscape-painting, which was very much to Mr. Ruskin's mind : not based on Turner, and therefore not secured from the failure that all experiments risk ; and yet safe in so far as it kept to honest study of Nature. So that, beside the Pre-Raphaelites proper, with their poetic figure-pieces, the *Notes on the Academy* had to keep watch over the birth of the Naturalist-landscape school, a group of painters who threw overboard the traditions of Turner and Prout, and Constable and Harding, and the rest, just as the Pre-Raphaelite Brethren threw over the Academical masters. For such men their study was their picture ; they devised tents and huts in wild glens and upon waste moors, and spent weeks in elaborating their details directly from nature, instead of painting at home from sketches on the spot.

This was the fulfilment of Mr. Ruskin's advice to young artists ; and so far as young artists worked in this way, for purposes of study, he encouraged them. But he did not fail to point out that this was not all that could be required

of them.   Even such a work as Brett's *Val d'Aosta*, marvellous as it was in observation and finish, was only the
beginning of a new era, not its consummation.   It was not
the painting of detail that could make a great artist ; but
the knowledge of it, and the masterly use of such knowledge.   A great landscapist would know the facts and
effects of nature, just as Tintoret knew the form of the
human figure ; and he would treat them with the same
freedom, as the means of expressing great ideas, of affording
noble grounds for noble emotion, which, as Mr. Ruskin
had been writing at Vevey in 1854, was poetry.   Meanwhile the public and the critic ought to become familiar
with the aspects of nature, in order to recognise the difference between the true poetry of painting, and the mere
empty sentimentalism which was only the rant and bombast
of landscape art.

With such feelings as these he wrote the third and fourth
volumes of *Modern Painters*, stopped for a time by the
unhappy events of the autumn of 1854, but next year
resumed, and afterwards interrupted only by a recurrence
of his old cough, brought on by the exceptionally cold
summer of 1855.   He went down to Tunbridge Wells,
where his cousin, William Richardson of Perth, was prac-
tising as a doctor ; and it was not long before the cough
gave way to treatment, and he was as busy as ever.   About
October of that year he wrote to Carlyle as follows, in a
letter printed by Professor C. E. Norton, conveniently
summing up his year :—

" Not that I have not been busy—and very busy, too.
I have written, since May, good six hundred pages, had
them rewritten, cut up, corrected, and got fairly ready for
press—and am going to press with the first of them on

Gunpowder Plot day, with a great hope of disturbing the Public Peace in various directions.   Also, I have prepared above thirty drawings for engravers this year, retouched the engravings (generally the worst part of the business), and etched some on steel myself.   In the course of the six hundred pages I have had to make various remarks on German Metaphysics, on Poetry, Political Economy, Cookery, Music, Geology, Dress, Agriculture, Horticulture, and Navigation,* all of which subjects I have had to ' read up' accordingly, and this takes time.   Moreover, I have had my class of workmen out sketching every week in the fields during the summer ; and have been studying Spanish proverbs with my father's partner, who came over from Spain to see the Great Exhibition.   I have also designed and drawn a window for the Museum at Oxford ; and have every now and then had to look over a parcel of five or six new designs for fronts and backs to the said Museum.

"During my above-mentioned studies of horticulture I became dissatisfied with the Linnæan, Jussieuan, and Everybody-elseian arrangement of plants, and have accordingly arranged a system of my own ; and unbound my botanical book, and rebound it in brighter green, with all the pages through-other, and backside foremost—so as to cut off all the old paging numerals ; and am now printing my new arrangement in a legible manner, on interleaved foolscap. I consider this arrangement one of my great achievements of the year.   My studies of political economy have induced me to think also that nobody knows anything

---

* Most of these subjects will be easily recognised in *Modern Painters*, Vols. III. and IV.   The " Navigation " refers to the *Harbours of England.*

about that; and I am at present engaged in an investigation, on independent principles, of the natures of Money, Rent, and Taxes, in an abstract form which sometimes keeps me awake all night. My studies of German metaphysics have also induced me to think that the Germans don't know anything about *them*; and to engage in a serious enquiry into the meaning of Bunsen's great sentence in the beginning of the second volume of the *Hippolytus*, about the Finite realization of Infinity; which has given me some trouble.

" The course of my studies of Navigation necessitated my going to Deal to look at the Deal boats; and those of Geology to rearrange all my minerals (and wash a good many, which, I am sorry to say, I found wanted it). I have also several pupils, far and near, in the art of illumination : an American young lady to direct in the study of landscape painting, and a Yorkshire young lady to direct in the purchase of Turners,—and various little bye things besides. But I am coming to see you."

The tone of humorous exaggeration of his discoveries and occupations was very characteristic of Mr. Ruskin, and it was likely to be brought out all the more when writing to another humorist like Carlyle. But he was then growing into the habit of leaving the matter in hand, as he has often done since, to follow side issues, and to take up new studies with a hasty and divided attention ; the result of which was seen in his sub-title for the third volume of *Modern Painters*—" Of Many Things " : which amused his readers not a little. But that he still had time for his friends is seen in the account of a visit to Denmark Hill, written this year by James Smetham, an artist who at one time promised to do great things, but

died before he redeemed the promise. He was at any rate
a singularly charming and interesting man, admired by
Mr. Ruskin for his personal character, and known now by
the volume of his letters recently published. He wrote:
"I walked there through the wintry weather, and got in
about dusk. One or two gossiping details will interest
you before I give you what I care for; and so I will tell
you that he has a large house with a lodge, and a valet
and footman and coachman, and grand rooms glittering
with pictures, chiefly Turner's, and that his father and
mother live with him, or he with them. His father is a
fine old gentleman, who has a lot of bushy grey hair,
and eyebrows sticking up all rough and knowing, with a
comfortable way of coming up to you with his hands in
his pockets, and making *you* comfortable, and saying, in
answer to your remark, that 'John's' prose works are
pretty good. His mother is a ruddy, dignified, richly-
dressed old gentlewoman of seventy-five, who knows
Chamonix better than Camberwell; evidently a *good* old
lady, with the *Christian Treasury* tossing about on the
table. She puts 'John' down, and holds her own opinions,
and flatly contradicts him; and he receives all her opinions
with a soft reverence and gentleness that is pleasant to
witness." I will interrupt Mr. Smetham to remark, that
this respect for his mother was one of the things that
visitors always noticed as characteristic of Mr. Ruskin;
and the intimate friends of the family know that it was
something even more than respect, at all times and under
all circumstances.

"I wish I could reproduce a good impression of 'John'
for you, to give you the notion of his 'perfect gentleness
and lowlihood.' He certainly bursts out with a remark,

and in a contradictious way, but only because he believes
it, with no air of dogmatism or conceit.   He is different at
home from that which he is in a lecture before a mixed
audience, and there is a spiritual sweetness in the half-
timid expression of his eyes ; and in bowing to you, as
in taking wine, with (if I heard aright) ' I drink to thee,'
he had a look that has followed me, a look bordering on
tearful.

"He spent some time in this way.   Unhanging a Turner
from the wall of a distant room, he brought it to the table
and put it in my hands ; then we talked ; then he went up
into his study to fetch down some illustrative print or
drawing ; in one case a literal view which he had travelled
fifty miles to make, in order to compare with the picture.
And so he kept on gliding all over the house, hanging and
unhanging, and stopping a few minutes to talk."

But it was not only from his mother that he could brook
contradiction, and not only in conversation that he showed
himself—contrary to the general opinion of him—amenable
to correction, when it came from persons whom he could
respect.   As a truth-seeker, how could he be otherwise ?
And yet there were many with whom he had to deal who
did not look at things in his light ; who took his criticism
as personal attack, and resented it with a bitterness it did
not deserve.   There is a story told (but not by himself)
about one of the *Notes on the Academy*, which he was then
publishing—how he wrote to an artist therein mentioned
that he regretted he could not speak more favourably of
his picture, but he hoped it would make no difference in
their friendship.   The artist replied (so they say) in these
terms : "DEAR RUSKIN, Next time I meet you, I shall
knock you down ; but I hope it will make no difference in

our friendship." "Damn the fellow! why doesn't he stick
up for his friends?" said another disappointed acquaintance.   Perhaps Mr. Ruskin, secure in his "house with
a lodge, and a valet and footman and coachman," hardly
realised that a cold word from his pen sometimes meant
the failure of an important Academy picture, and serious
loss of income—that there was bitter truth underlying
Punch's complaint of the R.A. :—

> " I paints and paints,
> Hears no complaints,
>   And sells before I'm dry ;
> Till savage Ruskin
> Sticks his tusk in,
> And nobody will buy."

Still, as a public man, it was his duty to "be just, and
fear not " ; and, hard as it is to be just, when one looks
over those *Notes on the Academy* at this safe distance of
time, one is surprised to see with what shrewdness he put
his finger upon the weak points of the various artists, and
no less upon their strong points ; how many of the men
he praised as beginners have since risen to eminence, how
many he blamed who have sunk from a specious popularity
into oblivion.   Contrast his career as a critic with that of
other well-known men, the Jeffries and the Giffords, not
to mention writers of a later date ; and note that his error
has been always to encourage too freely, not to discourage
hastily.   The men who lay their failure to his account have
been the weaklings whom he has urged to attempts beyond
their powers, with kindly support, misconstrued into a
prophecy of success.   No article of his has snuffed out a
rising Keats, or driven a young Chatterton to suicide.
And he has never stabbed in the dark.   " Tout honnête

homme doit avouer les livres qu'il publie," says his proto-
type Rousseau : and Mr. Ruskin, after publishing his first
juvenile essays under a transparent pseudonym, has always
had the courage of his opinions and taken the consequences
of his criticisms.   I note that most of the attacks on him
have been unsigned.

In these volumes of *Modern Painters* he had to discuss
the Mediæval and Renaissance spirit in its relation to art,
and to illustrate, from Browning's poetry, "unerring in every
sentence he writes of the Middle Ages, always vital and
right and profound ; so that in the matter of art there is
hardly a principle connected with the mediæval temper
that he has not struck upon in those seemingly careless
and too rugged lines of his."   This was written twenty-five
years before the Browning Society was heard of, and at
a time when the style of Browning was an offence to most
people.   To Mr. Ruskin, also, it had been something of a
puzzle ; and he wrote to the poet, asking him to explain
himself ; which the poet accordingly did, in a letter too
interesting to remain unprinted, showing as it does the
candid intercourse of two such different minds.

"PARIS, *Dec.* 10*th,* '55.

"MY DEAR RUSKIN,—for so you let me begin, with the honest
friendliness that befits,—You never were more in the wrong than
when you professed to say 'your unpleasant things' to me.   This
is pleasant and proper at all points, over-liberal of praise here and
there, kindly and sympathetic everywhere, and with enough of
yourself in even—what I fancy—the misjudging, to make the
whole letter precious indeed.   I wanted to thank you thus much
at once,—that is, when the letter reached me ; but the strife of
lodging-hunting was too sore, and only now that I can sit down
for a minute without self-reproach do I allow my thoughts to let
go south-aspects, warm bedrooms, and the like, and begin as you

see. For the deepnesses you think you discern,—may they be more than mere blacknesses! For the hopes you entertain of what may come of subsequent readings,—all success to them! For your bewilderment more especially noted—how shall I help *that*? We don't read poetry the same way, by the same law; it is too clear. I cannot begin writing poetry till my imaginary reader has conceded licences to me which you demur at altogether. I *know* that I don't make out my conception by my language; all poetry being a putting the infinite within the finite. You would have me paint it all plain out, which can't be; but by various artifices I try to make shift with touches and bits of outlines which *succeed* if they bear the conception from me to you. You ought, I think, to keep pace with the thought tripping from ledge to ledge of my 'glaciers,' as you call them; not stand poking your alpen-stock into the holes, and demonstrating that no foot could have stood there;—suppose it sprang over there? In *prose* you may criticise so—because that is the absolute representation of portions of truth, what chronicling is to history—but in asking for more *ultimates* you must accept less *mediates*, nor expect that a Druid stone-circle will be traced for you with as few breaks to the eye as the North Crescent and South Crescent that go together so cleverly in many a suburb. Why, you look at my little song as if it were Hobbs' or Nobbs' lease of his house, or testament of his devisings, wherein, I grant you, not a 'then and there,' 'to him and his heirs,' 'to have and to hold,' and so on, would be superfluous; and so you begin:—'Stand still,—why?' * For the reason indicated in the verse, to be sure—*to let me draw him*—and because he is at present going his way, and fancying nobody notices him,—and moreover, 'going on' (as we say) against the injustice of that,—and lastly, inasmuch as one night he'll fail us, as a star is apt to drop out of heaven, in authentic astronomic records, and I want to make the most of my time. So much may be in 'stand still.' And how much more was (for instance) in that 'stay!' of Samuel's (I. xv. 16). So could I twit you through the whole series of your objurgations, but the declaring my own

* Referring to the poem "Stand still, true poet that you are," with the line "and Hobbs, Nobbs, Stokes, and Nokes combine."

notion of the law on the subject will do.   And why,—I prithee,
friend and fellow-student,—why, having told the Poet what you
read,—may I not turn to the bystanders, and tell them a bit of
my own mind about their own stupid thanklessness and mis-
taking?   Is the jump too much there?   The whole is all but a
simultaneous feeling with me.

"The other hard measure you deal me I won't bear—about my
requiring you to pronounce words short and long, exactly as I
like.   Nay, but exactly as the language likes, in this case.   *Fold-
skirts* not a trochee?   A spondee possible in English?   Two of
the 'longest monosyllables' continuing to be each of the old
length when in junction?   Sentence : let the delinquent be
forced to supply the stone-cutter with a thousand companions
to 'Affliction sore—long time he bore,' after the fashion of 'He
lost his life—by a pen-knife'—'He turned to clay—last Good
Friday,' 'Departed hence—nor owed six-pence,' and so on—so
would pronounce a jury accustomed from the nipple to say lord
and landlord, bridge and Cambridge, Gog and Magog, man and
woman, house and workhouse, coal and charcoal, cloth and broad-
cloth, skirts and fold-skirts, more and once more,—in short !
Once *more* I prayed !—is the confession of a self-searching professor !   'I stand here for law !'

"The last charge I cannot answer, for you may be right in
preferring it, however unwitting I am of the fact.   I *may* put
Robert Browning into Pippa and other men and maids.   If so,
peccavi : but I don't see myself in them, at all events.

"Do you think poetry was ever generally understood—or can
be ?   Is the business of it to tell people what they know already,
as they know it, and so precisely that they shall be able to cry
out—'Here you should supply *this—that*, you evidently pass
over, and I'll help you from my own stock' ?   It is all teaching,
on the contrary, and the people hate to be taught.   They say
otherwise,—make foolish fables about Orpheus enchanting stocks
and stones, poets standing up and being worshipped,—all nonsense
and impossible dreaming.   A poet's affair is with God, to whom
he is accountable, and of whom is his reward : look elsewhere,
and you find misery enough.   Do you believe people understand

Hamlet? The last time I saw it acted, the heartiest applause of the night went to a little by-play of the actor's own—who, to simulate madness in a hurry, plucked forth his handkerchief and flourished it hither and thither : certainly a third of the play, with no end of noble things, had been (as from time immemorial) suppressed, with the auditory's amplest acquiescence and benediction.   Are these wasted, therefore ?   No—they act upon a very few, who react upon the rest : as Goldsmith says, ' some lords, my acquaintance, that settle the nation, are pleased to be kind.'

" Don't let me lose *my* lord by any seeming self-sufficiency or petulance : I look on my own shortcomings too sorrowfully, try to remedy them too earnestly : but I shall never change my point of sight, or feel other than disconcerted and apprehensive when the public, critics and all, begin to understand and approve me. But what right have *you* to disconcert me in the other way? Why won't you ask the next perfumer for a packet of *orris*-root ? Don't everybody know 'tis a corruption of *iris*-root—the Florentine lily, the *giaggolo*, of world-wide fame as a good savour ?   And because ' iris ' means so many objects already, and I use the old word, you blame me !   But I write in the blind-dark and bitter cold, and past post-time as I fear.   Take my truest thanks, and understand at least this rough writing, and, at all events, the real affection with which I venture to regard you.   And ' I ' means my wife as well as

"Yours ever faithfully,

"ROBERT BROWNING."

That Mr. Ruskin was open to conviction and conversion could be shown from the difference in his tone of thought about poetry before and after this period ; that he was the best of friends with the man who took him to task- for narrowness, may be seen from the following letter, written on the next Christmas' Eve.

"MY DEAR MR. RUSKIN,—Your note having just arrived, Robert deputes me to write for him while he dresses to go out on an engagement.   It is the evening.   All the hours are wasted, since the morning, through our not being found at the Rue de Grenelle, but here—and our instinct of self-preservation or self-satisfaction insists on our not losing a moment more by our own fault.

"Thank you, thank you for sending us your book, and also for writing my husband's name in it.   It will be the same thing as if you had written mine—except for the pleasure, as you say, which is greater so.   How good and kind you are !

" And not well.   That is worst.   Surely you would be better if you had the summer in winter we·have here.   But I was to write only a word—Let it say how affectionately we regard you.

" ELIZABETH BARRETT BROWNING.

"3, RUE DU COLYSÉE,
" *Thursday Evening, 24th* " [Dec. 1855].

So it was true—was it?—

> " I've a Friend, over the sea ;
> I like him, but he loves me.
> It all grew out of the books I write. . . .'

CHAPTER IX.

THE POLITICAL ECONOMY OF ART.

(1857—1858.)

" Pitch thy behaviour low, thy projects high."
George Herbert.

THE humble work of the drawing-classes at Great Ormond Street was teaching Mr. Ruskin even more than he taught his pupils. It was showing him how far his plans were practicable ; how they should be modified ; how they might be improved ; and especially what more, beside drawing-classes, was needed to realise his ideal. It brought him into contact with uneducated men, and the seamy side of civilisation, as it is usually thought to be— poverty and ignorance, and, most difficult of all to treat, the incompetence and the predestinated unsuccess of too many an ambitious nature. That was, after all, the great problem which was to occupy him ; but meanwhile he was anxiously willing to co-operate with every movement, to join hands with any kind of man, to go anywhere, do anything that might promote the cause he had at heart.

Already at the end of 1854 he had given three lectures, his second course, at the Architectural Museum, specially addressed to workmen in the decorative trades. His sub-jects were design and colour, and his illustrations were chiefly drawn from mediæval illumination, which he had long been studying. His father did not care about his lecturing, then rather looked down upon as "little better than play-acting," which was distinctly not the occupation of a gentleman. So these were informal, quasi-private affairs, which nevertheless attracted notice owing to the celebrity of the speaker. It would have been better if his addresses had been carefully prepared and authentically published ; for a chance word here and there raised replies about matters of detail, in which his critics thought they had gained a technical advantage, which added weight to his father's desire not to see him "expose himself" in this way. There were no more lectures until the beginning of 1857.

On January 23rd, 1857, he spoke before the Architectural Association upon *The Influence of Imagination in Architecture*, repeating and amplifying what he had said at. Edinburgh about the subordinate value of mere proportion, and the importance of sculptured ornament based on natural forms. This of course would involve the creation of a class of stone-carvers who could be trusted with the execution of such work. Once grant the value of it, and public demand would encourage the supply, and the workmen would raise themselves in the effort.

A louder note was sounded in an address at the St. Martin's School of Art, Castle Street, Long Acre (April 2nd, 1857), where, speaking after George Cruikshank, his old friend—practically his first master (see p. 40)—and an enthusiastic philanthropist and temperance advocate, Mr. Ruskin gave his audience a wider view of art than they had known before : "the kind of painting they most wanted in London was painting cheeks red with health."

This was anticipating the standpoint of the Oxford Lectures, and showed how the inquiry was beginning to take a much broader aspect.

Another work in a similar spirit, the North London School of Design, had been prosperously started by a circle of men under Pre-Raphaelite influence, and led by Thomas Seddon. He had given up historical and poetic painting for naturalistic landscape, and had returned from the East with the most valuable studies completed, only to break down and die prematurely. His friends, among them Mr. Holman Hunt, were collecting money to buy from the widow his picture of Jerusalem from the Mount of Olives, to present it to the National Gallery as a memorial of him ; and at a meeting for the purpose, Mr. Ruskin spoke warmly of his labours in the cause of the working classes. " The blood of the martyrs is the seed of the Church," said the early Christians, and this public recognition sealed the character of the Pre-Raphaelite philanthropic movement ; though at what cost, the memoir of Thomas Seddon by his brother too amply proves.

The next step in the propaganda was of a still more public nature. In the summer of 1857 the Art Treasures Exhibition was held at Manchester, and Mr. Ruskin was invited to lecture. The theme he chose was *The Political Economy of Art*. He had been studying political economy closely for some time back, but, as we saw from his letter to Carlyle, he had found no answer in the ordinary text-books for the questions he had to put. He wanted to know what Bentham and Ricardo and Mill, the great authorities, would advise him as to the best way of employing artists, of educating workmen, of elevating public taste, of regulating patronage ; but these subjects were not in their programme. And so he put together his own thoughts into two lectures upon Art considered as Wealth : first, how to get it ; next, how to use it.

He compared the body politic to a farm, of which the " economy," in the original sense, consisted, not in sparing, still less in standing by and criticising, but in active direction and management. He thought that the government of a state, like a good farmer or housekeeper, should not be content with *laissez faire*, but should promote everything that was for the true interests of the state, and watch over all the industries and arts which make for civilisation. It should undertake education, and be responsible for the employment of the artists and craftsmen it produced, giving them work upon public buildings, as the Venetian state used to do. Meantime he showed what an enlightened public might aim at, what their standards of patronage should be : how, for example, each and all might help the cause by preferring artistic decorative work, in furniture and plate and dress, to the mechanical products of inartistic manufacture ; how they might help in preserving the great standard buildings and pictures of the past—not without advantages to their own art-production—how they might deal directly with the artist rather than the dealer ; and serve the cause of education by placing works of art in schools. And he concluded by suggesting that the mediæval guilds of craftsmen, if they could be re-established, would be of great service, especially in substituting a spirit of coöperation for that of competition.

There were very few points in these lectures that were not vigorously contested at the moment, and conceded in the sequel,—in some form or other. The paternal function of government, the right of the state to interfere in matters beyond its traditional range, its duty with regard to education,—all this was quite contrary to the prevailing habits of thought of the time, especially at Manchester, the headquarters of the *laissez faire* school : but to Mr. Ruskin, who, curiously enough, had just then been referring sarcastically to German philosophy, knowing it only at secondhand, and unaware of Hegel's political work,—to him this Platonic conception of the state was the only possible one, as it is to most people nowadays. In the same way, his practical advice has been accepted, perhaps unwittingly, by our times. We do now understand the difference between artistic decoration and machine-made wares ; we do now try to preserve ancient monuments, and to use art as a means of education. And we are in a fair way, it seems, of lowering the prices of pictures, as he bids us, to " not more than £500 for an oil picture and £100 for a water-colour."

From Manchester he went with his parents to Scotland ; for his mother, now beginning to grow old, wanted to revisit the scenes of her youth. They went to the Highlands and as far north as the Bay of Cromarty, and then returned by way of the Abbeys of the Lowlands, to look up Turner sites, as he had done in 1845 on the St. Gothard. From the enjoyment of this holiday he was recalled to London by a letter from Mr. Wornum saying that he could arrange the Turner drawings at the National Gallery.

Mr. Ruskin's first letter on the National Gallery, in 1847, has been noticed. He had written again to the *Times* (Dec. 29th, 1852), pressing the same point—namely, that if the pictures were put under glass, no cleaning nor restoring would be needed ; and that the Gallery ought not to be considered as a grand hall, decorated with pictures, but as a convenient museum, with a chronological sequence of the best works of all schools,—every picture hung on the line and accompanied by studies for it, if procurable, and engravings from it.

Now,—in 1857,—question was raised of removing the National Gallery from Trafalgar Square. The South Kensington Museum was being formed, and the whole business of arranging the national art treasures was gone into by a Royal Commission, consisting of Lord Broughton (in the chair), Dean Milman, Prof. Faraday, Prof. Cockerell, and Mr. George Richmond. Mr. Ruskin was examined before them on April 6th, and re-stated the opinions he had written to the *Times*, adding that he would like to see two National Galleries,—one of popular interest, containing such works as would catch the public eye and enlist the sympathy of the untaught ; and another containing only the cream of the collections, in pictures, sculpture and the decorative crafts, arranged for purposes of study. This was suggested as an ideal ; of course, it would involve more outlay, and less display, than any Parliamentary vote would sanction, or party leader risk.

Another question of importance was the disposal of the pictures and sketches which Turner had left to the nation. Mr. Ruskin was one of the executors under the will ; but, on finding that, though Turner's intention was plain, there were technical informalities which would make the administration anything but easy, he declined to act. It was not until 1856 that the litigation was concluded, and Turner's pictures and sketches handed over to the trustees of the National Gallery. Mr. Ruskin, whose want of legal knowledge had made his services useless before, now felt that he could carry out the spirit of Turner's will by offering to arrange the sketches; which were in such a state of confusion that only some person with knowledge of the artist's habits of work and subjects could, so to speak, *edit* them; and the editor would need no ordinary patience and skill and judgment, into the bargain. As Mr. Ruskin was, I suppose, the only man in the world fully qualified and at leisure for such a work, his offer was accepted,—the more readily, no doubt, as he would work for nothing.

Meanwhile, for that winter (1856-7) a preliminary exhibition was held of Turner's oil-paintings, with a few water-colours, at Marlborough House, then the headquarters of the Department of Science and Art, soon afterwards removed to South Kensington. Mr. Ruskin wrote a catalogue, with analysis of Turner's periods of development and characteristics; which made the collection intelligible and interesting to curious sight-seers. They showed their appreciation by taking up five editions in rapid succession.

Just before lecturing at Manchester, he wrote again on the subject to the *Times*; and in September his friend R. N. Wornum, Director of the National Gallery in succession to Eastlake and Uwins, wrote—as we saw—that he might arrange the sketches as he pleased. He returned from Scotland, and set to work on October 7th.

It was strange employment for a man of his powers; almost as removed from the Epicurean Olympus of "cultured ease" popularly assigned to him, as night-school teaching and lecturing workmen. But, beside that it was the carrying out of Turner's wishes, Mr. Ruskin has always had a certain love for experimenting in manual toil;* and

* For instance, when he scrubbed the stairs at the hotel at Sixt, because his mother complained of their dirty condition; and when he

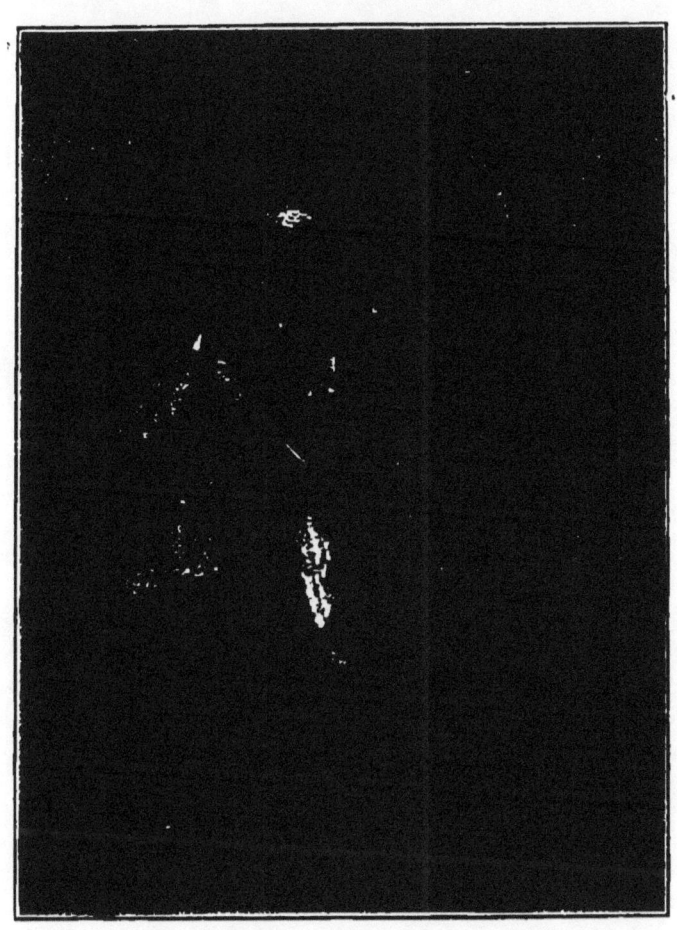

JOHN RUSKIN.

By George Richmond, R.A.—1857.

[Vol. I., p. 210.]

this was work in which his extreme neatness and deftness
of hand was needed, no less than his knowledge and
judgment.   During the winter, for full six months, he and
his two assistants worked, all day and every day, among
the masses of precious rubbish that had been removed
from Queen Anne Street to the National Gallery.

Turner used to sketch frequently on thin paper which
he folded across and across for packing, or rolled in tight
bundles to go into his pockets.   When he got his sketches
home, as they were only *pour servir* and of no value to
any one but himself, they were crammed into drawers,
anyhow, and left there, decade after decade.   His sketch-
books had rotted to pieces with the damp, their pages
pressed together into mouldering masses.   Soft chalk lay
loose among the leaves, crushed into powder when the
book was packed away.   He economised his paper by
covering both sides, and of course did not trouble to "fix"
his sketches, still less to mount and frame them, as the
proud amateur is careful to do.

Among the quantities so recklessly thrown aside for dust,
damp, soot, mice and worms to destroy—some 15,000 Mr.
Ruskin reckoned at first, 19,000 later on—there were many
fine drawings, which had been used by the engravers, and
vast numbers of interesting and valuable studies in colour
and in pencil.   Four hundred of these were extricated

took regular lessons, later on, in crossing-sweeping, stone-breaking,
carpentry and house-painting.   His neatness runs almost to excess
when, in signing a drawing or inscribing a book for presentation, he
rules triple lines and *prints*, as he used to do in his boyhood, name
and date, and all the rest, in elaborate Roman script; instead of the
scrabbled cheque-signature which is fashionable in such cases.   The
orderliness of his bookshelves and mineral drawers is quite unexcep-
tionable: his own sketches he leaves in dusty confusion.

from the chaos, and with infinite pains cleaned, flattened, mounted, dated and described, and placed in sliding frames in cabinets devised by Mr. Ruskin, or else in swivel frames, to let both sides of the paper be seen. The first results of the work were shown in an Exhibition at Marlborough House during the winter, for which Mr. Ruskin wrote another catalogue. Of the whole collection he began a more complete account, which was too elaborate to be finished in that form ; but in 1881 he published a *Catalogue of the Drawings and Sketches of J. M. W. Turner, R.A., at present exhibited in the National Gallery*, so that his plan was practically fulfilled.

The collection—a monument of one great man's genius and another's patience—is still housed in the cellars of Trafalgar Square, and it has never been so honourably viewed and so freely used as Mr. Ruskin once hoped. But in proportion to the means at the disposal of the powers that be, Turner is well treated. The sketches can at least be got at by those who know about them and care to study them, and the pictures are now far better shown than formerly. The historical arrangement of the various schools, also, has been improved with every successive rehanging ; and the primitive masters, once neglected, have now almost the lion's share of the show. Such are Time's revenges.

During 1858 Mr. Ruskin continued to lecture at various places on subjects connected with his Manchester addresses, —the relation of art to manufacture, and especially the dependence of all great architectural design upon sculpture or painting of organic form. The first of the series was given at the opening of the South Kensington Museum, January 12th, 1858, entitled " The Deteriorative Power of

Conventional Art over Nations"; in which he showed that naturalism, as opposed to meaningless pattern-making, was always a sign of life. For example, the strength of the Greek, Florentine and Venetian art arose out of the search for truth, not, as it is often supposed, art of striving after an ideal of beauty ; and as soon as nature was superseded by recipe, the greatest schools hastened to their fall. From which he concluded that modern design should always be founded on natural form, rather than upon the traditional patterns of the east or of the mediævals.

On February 16th he spoke on " The Work of Iron, in Nature, Art and Policy," at Tunbridge Wells ; a subject similar to that of his address to the St. Martin's School of the year before, but amplified into a plea for the use of wrought iron ornament, as in the new Oxford Museum, then building.

The Oxford Museum was an experiment in the true Gothic revival. There had been plenty of so-called Gothic architecture ever since Horace Walpole ; but it had aimed rather at imitating the forms of the Middle Ages than at reviving the spirit. The architects at Oxford, Sir Thomas Deane and Mr. Woodward, had allowed their workmen to design parts of the detail, such as capitals and spandrils, quite in the spirit of Mr. Ruskin's teaching, and the work was accordingly of deep interest to him. So far back as April 1856, he had given an address to the men employed at the Museum, whom he met, on Dr. Acland's invitation, at the Workmen's Reading Rooms. He said that his object was not to give labouring men the chance of becoming masters of other labouring men, and to help the few at the expense of the many, but to lead them to those sources of pleasure, and power over their own minds and hands, that more educated people possess. He did not sympathise with the socialism that had been creeping into vogue since 1848. He thought existing social arrangements good, and he agreed with his friends the Carlyles, who had found that it was only the incapable who could not get work. But it was the fault of the wealthy and educated that working people were not better trained ; it was not the working-men's fault, at bottom. The modern architect used his workman as a mere tool ; while the Gothic spirit set him free as an original designer, to gain —not more wages and higher social rank, but pleasure and instruction, the true happiness that lies in good work well done.

That was his view in those times. The Oxford Museum prospered, and Dr. Acland and he together wrote a small book, reporting its aims and progress in 1858 and 1859, illustrated with an engraving of one of the workmen's capitals. It was no secret, then, that the Museum was an experiment ; and, like all experiments, it left much to be desired ; but it paved the way, on the one hand, to the general adoption of Gothic for domestic purposes, and on the other, to the recognition of a new class of men—the art-craftsmen.

Parallel with this movement for educating the " working-class " there was the scheme for the improvement of middle-class education, which was then going on at Oxford—the beginning of University Extension—supported by the Rev. F. Temple (now Bishop of London), and Mr. (afterwards Sir) Thomas Dyke Acland. Mr. Ruskin was heartily for them ; and in a letter on the subject, he tried to show how the teaching of Art might be made to work in with the scheme. He did not think that in this plan, any more than at the Working Men's College, there need be an attempt to teach drawing with a view to forming artists ; but there were three objects they might hold in view : the first, to give every student the advantage of the happiness and knowledge which the study of Art conveys ; the next, to enforce some knowledge of Art amongst those who were likely to become patrons or critics ; and the last, *to leave no Giotto lost among hill shepherds.* The study of art-history he considered unnecessary to ordinary education, and too wide a subject to be treated in the usual curriculum of schools ; but the practice of drawing might go hand in hand with natural history, and the habit of looking at things with an artist's eye would be invaluable. He proposed a plan of studies, interweaving the art-lessons with every other department, instead of relegating them to a poor hour a week of idling or insubordination under a master who ranked with the drill-sergeant.   Something has been done, both by the delegates for local examinations (whom this movement created), and by the schools themselves, to improve the teaching of drawing ; but nothing like Mr. Ruskin's proposal has been attempted —simply because it would involve the employment of schoolmasters who could draw ; and the introduction of the object-lesson system into the higher forms.

This intercourse with Oxford and willingness to help, even at the lower end of the ladder, is a pleasant episode in the life of a man struggling in the wider world against Academicism and the various fallacies of traditional creeds and cultures.   There was nothing of the Byronic in Mr. Ruskin's attitude, nor did he try to advertise his individuality by a childish petulance toward poor old Alma Mater.

CHAPTER X.

"MODERN PAINTERS" CONCLUDED.

(1858—1860.)

> " So the dreams depart,
>   So the fading phantoms flee,
>   And the sharp reality
>   Now must act its part."
>
> WESTWOOD'S " Beads from a Rosary."

OXFORD and old friends did not monopolise Mr. Ruskin's attention : he was soon seen at Cambridge —on the same platform with Mr. Richard Redgrave, R.A., the representative of Academicism and officialism—at the opening of the School of Art for workmen on October 29th, 1858. His Inaugural Address struck a deeper note, a wider chord, than previous essays ; it was the forecast of the last volume of *Modern Painters*, and it sketched the train of thought into which he had been led during his tour abroad, that summer.

Mr. Ruskin is morally Conservative, intellectually Radical. His instincts cling to the past, his intelligence leads him ahead of his time. The battles between faith and criticism, between the historical and the scientific attitudes, which had been going on in his mind, were taking a new form. At the outset, we saw, the naturalist overpowered respect

216

for tradition,—in the first volume of *Modern Painters* ; then the historical tendency won the day, in the second volume. Since that time, the critical side had been gathering strength, by his alliance with progressist movements and by his gradual detachment from associations that held him to the older order of thought.   And just as in his lonely journey of 1845 he first took independent ground upon questions of religion and social life, so in 1858, once more travelling alone, he was led by his meditations,—freed from the restraining presence of his parents,—to conclusions which he had been all these years evading, yet finding at last inevitable.

He went abroad for a third attempt to write and illustrate his History of Swiss Towns.   The drawings of the year were still in the style of fine pen-etching combined with broadly gradated and harmonious tints of colour ; or, when they were simply pen or pencil outlines, they were much more refined than those of ten years earlier.   He spent May on the Upper Rhine between Basle and Schaffhausen, June in the neighbourhood of the Swiss Baden, July at Bellinzona.   In reflecting over the sources of Swiss character, as connected with the question of the nature and origin of art in morality, he was struck with the fact that all the virtues of the Swiss did not make them artistic.   Compared with most nations they were as children in painting, music and poetry.   And, indeed, they ranked with the early phases of many great nations— the period of pristine simplicity " uncorrupted by the arts."

From Bellinzona he went to Turin on his way to the Vaudois Valleys, where he meant to compare the Waldensian Protestants with the Swiss.   Accidentally he saw

Paul Veronese's "Queen of Sheba" and other Venetian pictures; and so fell to comparing a period of fully ripened art with one of artlessness; discovering that the mature art, while it appeared at the same time with decay in morals, did not spring from that decay, but was rooted in the virtues of the earlier age. He grasped a clue to the puzzle, in the generalisation that Art is the product of human happiness; it is contrary to asceticism; it is the expression of pleasure. But when the turning point of national progress is once reached, and art is regarded as the laborious incitement to pleasure,—no longer the spontaneous blossom and fruit of it,—the decay sets in for art as well as for morality. Art, in short, is created *by* pleasure, not *for* pleasure.

And so both the ascetics who refuse art are wrong, and the Epicureans who make it a means of pleasure-seeking: the latter obviously and culpably, because in their hands it becomes rapidly degraded into a mere sensational or sensual stimulus, and loses its own finest qualities—technically as well as morally. But the ascetics are wrong, too; because we cannot place ourselves at the fountain head again, and resume the pristine simplicity of nascent society. Such was the claim of the Modern Vaudois whom he had gone forth to bless, as descendants of those "slaughtered saints whose bones lay scattered on the Alpine mountains cold." He found them keeping but the relics and grave-clothes of a pure faith; * and that at

---

* I think I owe it to some who will be pained by this paragraph to say here, once for all, that I am trying to give them Mr. Ruskin's Life and Work, not my opinions. And, consequently, I write as if the reader had no personal feelings. It is surely possible to admire a great man, though one differs from him (as I do from Mr. Ruskin) in everything

the cost of abstention from all service to the struggling Italy of their time,—at the cost, too, of a flat refusal to reverence the best achievements of the past. No doubt there were exemplary persons among them; but the standard of thought, the attitude of mind of the Waldensians, Mr. Ruskin now perceived to be quite impossible for himself. He could not look upon every one outside their fold as heathens and publicans; he could not believe that the pictures of Paul Veronese were works of iniquity, nor that the motives of great deeds in earlier ages were lying superstitions. He took courage to own to himself and others that it was no longer any use trying to identify his point of view with that of Protestantism. He saw both Protestants and Roman Catholics, in the perspective of history, converging into a primitive, far distant, ideal unity of Christianity, in which he still believed; but he could take neither side, after this.

The first statement of the new point of view was, as we said, the Inaugural Lecture of the Cambridge School of Art. The next important utterance was at Manchester, Feb. 22nd, 1859, where he spoke on the *Unity of Art*, by which he meant—not the fraternity of handicrafts with painting, as the term is used nowadays—but that, in whatever branch of Art, the spirit of Truth or Sincerity is the same. In this lecture there is a very important passage showing how he had at last got upon firm ground in the question of art and morality :—" *I do* NOT *say in the least that in order to be a good painter you must be a good man ; but I do say that in order to be a good natural painter*

that goes to make prejudice; in nationality, to begin with, and in all the associations of religion, politics, and art. I can only ask the reader to take the same standpoint,—and to read on to the end.

there must be strong elements of good in the mind, however warped by other parts of the character." So emphatic
a statement deserves more attention than it has received
from readers and writers who assume to judge Mr. Ruskin's
views after a slight acquaintance with his earlier works. He
was well aware himself that his mind had been gradually
enlarging, and his thoughts changing; and he soon saw as
great a difference between himself at forty and at twenty-
five, as he had formerly seen between the Boy poet and the
Art critic. He became as anxious to forget his earlier
great books, as he had been to forget his verse-writing;
and when he came to collect his " Works," these lectures,
under the title of *The Two Paths*, were the earliest admitted
into the library.

In 1859 the last Academy Notes, for the time being,
were published. The Pre-Raphaelite cause had been fully
successful, and the new school of naturalist landscape was
rapidly asserting itself. Old friends were failing, such as
Stanfield, Lewis, and Roberts : but new men were growing
up, among whom Mr. Ruskin welcomed G. D. Leslie,
F. Goodall, J. C. Hook,—who had come out of his " Pre-
Raphaelite measles" into the healthy naturalism of " Luff
Boy ! "—Clarence Whaite, Henry Holiday, and above all
John Brett, who showed the " Val d'Aosta." Mr. Millais'
" Vale of Rest" was the picture which attracted most
notice : something of the old rancour against the school
was revived in the *Morning Herald*, which called his works
"impertinences," " contemptible," "indelible disgrace," and
so on. It was the beginning of a transition from · the
delicacy of the Pre-Raphaelite Millais to his later style ;
and as such the preacher of " All great art is delicate "
could not entirely defend it. But the serious strength of

the imagination and the power of the execution he praised with unexpected warmth.

He then started on the last tour abroad with his parents. He had been asked, rather pointedly, by the National Gallery Commission, whether he had seen the great German museums, and had been obliged to reply that he had not. Perhaps it occurred to him or to his father that he ought to see the pictures at Berlin and Dresden and Munich, even though he heartily disliked the Germans, with their art and their language and everything that belonged to them,—except Holbein and Dürer. By the end of July the travellers were in North Switzerland ; and they spent September in Savoy, returning home by October 7th.

Old Mr. Ruskin was now in his seventy-fifth year ; and his desire was to see the great work finished before he died. There had been some attempt to write this last volume of *Modern Painters* in the previous winter, but it had been put off until after the visit to Germany had completed Mr. Ruskin's study of the great Venetian painters—especially Titian and Veronese. Now at last, in the autumn of 1859, he finally set to work on the writing.

He had to do for Vegetation, Clouds, and Water, what Vol. IV. had done for Mountains ; and also to treat of the laws of Composition. To do this on a scale corresponding with his foregoing work, would have needed four or five more volumes. As it was, the author dropped the section on Water, with promises of a book which he never wrote, and the rest was only sketched—somewhat ampler in detail than corresponding parts of the *Elements of Drawing*, but still inadequately and half-heartedly, as an artist would complete a work when the patron who commissioned it had died.

The whole book had been simply the assertion of Turner's genius—plucky and necessary in the young man of 1843, but superfluous in 1860, when his main thesis was admitted, and his own interests, as well as the needs of a totally different period, had drifted far away from the original subject. Turner was long since dead, his fame thoroughly vindicated ; his bequest to the nation dealt with, so far as possible. The Early Christian Art was recognised—almost beyond its claims ; for Angelico and his circle, great as they were in their age, had begun to lead modern religious painters into affectation. The Pre-Raphaelites and naturalistic landscapists no longer needed the hand which *Modern Painters* had held out to them by the way. Of the great triad of Venice, Tintoret had been expounded, Veronese and Titian were now taken up and treated with tardy, but ample. recognition.

And now, after twenty years of labour, Mr. Ruskin had established himself as the recognised leader of criticism and the exponent of painting and architecture. He had created a department of literature all his own, and adorned it with works of which the like had never been seen. He had enriched the art of England with examples of a new and beautiful draughtsmanship, and the language with passages of poetic description and eloquent declamation, quite, in their way, unrivalled. As a philosopher, he had built up a theory of art, as yet uncontested, and treated both its abstract nature and its relations to human conduct and policy. As a historian, he had thrown new light on the Middle Ages and Renaissance, illustrating, in a way then novel, their chronicles by their remains. He had beaten down all opposition, risen above all detraction, and won the prize of honour—only to realise, as he received it, that

the fight had been but a pastime tournament, after all ;
and to hear, through the applause, the enemy's trumpet
sounding to battle.   For now, without the camp, there were
realities to face ; as to Art—"the best in this kind are but
shadows."

APPENDIX.

APPENDIX TO VOL. I.

CHRONOLOGY.

(1819—1860.)

1819.—Feb. 8. John Ruskin born: 54, Hunter St., Brunswick Sq. ... ... London.

1822.—To Scotland, Perth. Portrait by North-
Age 3. cote ... ... —

1823.—Summer tour in S.W. of England. Removed
Age 4. to (No. 28) ... ... Herne Hill.

1824.—Tour to the Lakes. Stayed at Keswick and
Age 5. Perth ... ... —

1825, age 6.—To Paris, Brussels, Waterloo ... ... —

1826.—In January wrote first poem, "The Needless
Age 7. Alarm." Visited Hastings ... ... —

  „ Summer tour to the Lakes and Perth. Began
        Latin grammar at ... ... —

1827.—Summer at Perth; fever at Dunkeld; autumn
Age 8. wrote "Papa, how pretty those icicles are!" —

1828.—Summer in West of England. Mary Richard-
Age 9. son adopted by his parents ... ... —

1829.—Summer in Kent. Wrote dramatic poem on
Age 10. "Waterloo" ... ... —

1830.—Tour to the Lakes. "Iteriad." Began Greek.
Age 11. Copied Cruikshank ... ... —

1831.—First drawing lessons from Runciman. First
Age 12. sketching from nature ... ... —

  „ Summer tour in Wales. Began mathematics
        under Rowbotham ... ... —

1832.—Summer tour in Kent. Wrote "Mourn, Miz-
Age 13. raim, mourn" ... ... —

227

1833.—Wrote "I weary for the torrent."   First Turner
Age 14.   study in Rogers' "Italy"   ...   .   Herne Hill.
  „   Introduced by Pringle to Hogg and Rogers   ...   —
  „   May 11—Sept. 21.—Tour to the Rhine and   ...   Switzerland.
  „   Copied Rembrandt   ...   .   Paris.
  „   Wrote poetical journal of tour.   Went to
            school to Rev. T. Dale while living at   ...   Herne Hill.
1834.—First study of Alpine geology in Saussure.
Age 15.   First published writings   ...   .   —
  „   Summer tour to West of England.   Returned
            to school   ...   .   —
1835.—Left school owing to attack of pleurisy in the
Age 16.   spring ...   .   —
  „   June 2—Dec. 10.—Tour to Switzerland and   Italy.
  „   First Published Poems.   Wrote the "Don
            Juan" Journal, etc. ...   .   Herne Hill.
1836.—Visit of the Domecqs.   First Love-poems, and
Age 17.   study of Shelley   ...   .   —
  „   Lessons from Copley Fielding.   Attended
            Lectures at King's College, London   ...   —
  „   July at Richmond.   Wrote "Marcolini" and
            Defence of Turner ...   .   —
  „   Tour to the South Coast, after matriculating at
            Christ Church...   ...   .   Oxford.
1837.—Jan. 14.   Went into residence at Oxford: wrote
Age 18.   "The Gipsies"   ...   .   —
  „   Summer tour to the Lakes and Yorkshire:
            began "Poetry of Architecture"   ...   ...   Herne Hill.
  „   Began papers on "The Convergence of Per-
            pendiculars"   ...   .   Oxford.
1838.—Jan., to Oxford; returned (June 28) to   ...   Herne Hill.
Age 19. Wrote Essay, "Comparative Advantages of
            Music and Painting"   ...   .   —
  „   July 3—Sept. 3.—Tour with parents to the
            Lakes and   ...   .   Scotland.
  „   Oct. — Dec., Oxford.   Dec., visit of the
            Domecqs   ...   .   Herne Hill.
1839.—Jan. to Oxford.   Recited "Newdigate" at
Age 20.   Commemoration   ...   .   Oxford.
  „   Tour with parents: Cheddar, Devon, and   ...   Cornwall.
  „   Sept., read with Osborne Gordon.   Wrote
            "Farewell"   ...   .   Herne Hill.
  „   Kept Michaelmas Term at   ...   .   Oxford.

1840.—Jan., to Oxford. Threatened with consump- Oxford.
Age 21.   tion (May) ...   .   —
    „   Sept. 25. Travelled with parents by the
            Loire and Riviera to (Nov. 28) ...   ...   Rome.
1841.—Jan. 9—March 17, at Naples; March 22—
Age 22.   April 18, at ...   .   —
    „   May 1, Bologna; May 6—17, Venice; June 5, at   Geneva.
    „   June 12, Basle; returning by Laon and Calais
            to (June 29) ...   .   Herne Hill.
    „   Aug., Wales. Sept. 2—Oct. 21, under Dr.
            Jephson at ...   .   Leamington.
    „   Reading with O. Gordon; drawing lessons
            from Harding   ...   .   Herne Hill.
1842.—May, passed final examination, and took B.A.
Age 23.   degree at   ...   .   Oxford.
    „   Saw Turner's Swiss sketches: study of Ivy   Herne Hill.
    „   May 24—Aug. 19, tour with parents: France,
            Switzerland ...   .   Germany.
    „   Wrote "Modern Painters," vol. i., during
            winter at   ...   .   Herne Hill.
1843.—Removed from Herne Hill to (No. 163)   ...   Denmark Hill.
Age 24.   Oct. 28, took M.A. degree ...   .   Oxford.
1844.—May 14, tour with parents; June, with Couttet,
Age 25.   Chamouni; July 16, met Forbes at Simplon;
            July 19, with Gordon at Zermatt ...   ...   Switzerland.
    „   Aug. 17, 18, studying old masters at the Louvre   Paris.
    „   Aug. 24, to Denmark Hill. Dec. 12 to   ...   Hastings.
1845.—Jan. 10 to   ...   .   Denmark Hill.
Age 26. April, first tour alone; June 9, to Pisa; last
            poems; first study of Christian art, Lucca
            and Florence; July, Macugnaga and St. Got-
            hard; end of August, Italian Lakes; with
            J. D. Harding at Verona, and studying
            Tintoret at Venice ...   .   Italy.
    „   During the winter wrote "Modern Painters,"
            vol. ii.   ...   .   Denmark Hill.
1846.—April 2, with parents through France and the
Age 27.   Jura to Geneva; April 27, Mont Cenis;
            May 4, Vercelli; May 10, to Verona; May   Italy.
            14, to Venice; June 3, to Bologna; June 7,
            to Florence; Aug. 15, Geneva; Aug. 23,
            Chamouni; Aug. 31, to the Oberland   ...
    „   Oct. 6 returned to   ...   .   Denmark Hill.

1847.—June, at Oxford, and Ambleside; July at ... Leamington.
Age 28. Aug., tour in Scotland; Sept. at ... ... Crossmount.
  ,,   Nov., Folkestone; Dec. at ... ... Denmark Hill.
1848.—April 10, married at Perth; thence to ... Keswick.
Age 29. Summer, attempted pilgrimage to English
       cathedrals ... ... Salisbury.
  ,,   Aug.—Oct., tour to Amiens, Paris, and ... Normandy.
  ,,   Winter, writing "Seven Lamps" at 31, Park St., London.
1849.—April 18, tour with parents through France
Age 30.   and Jura; June 1, Vevey; June at Cha-
       mouni; July, St. Martin's and Zermatt ... Switzerland.
  ,,   Nov., settled for the winter at ... ... Venice.
1850.—Studying architecture till end of Feb. at ... —
Age 31. Began the study of missals; wrote " Stones
       of Venice," vol. i. ... ... Park St.
1851.—" Notes on Sheepfolds;" acquaintance with
Age 32.   Carlyle and Maurice ... ... —
  ,,   May, First defence of the Pre-Raphaelites ... —
  ,,   Aug. 4, with Mr. Moore through France;
       Aug. 11, met Mr. Newton, Les Rousses;
       Aug. 14, Chamouni; 19, Geneva; 22, Great
       St. Bernard; Sept. 1, settled for winter at Venice.
  ,,   (Dec. 19, J. M. W. Turner died.)
1852.—Until the end of June studying architecture —
Age 33. During autumn and winter writing " Stones
       of Venice," vols. ii. and iii., at (No. 29) ... Herne Hill.
1853.—Aug., with Dr. Acland and Mr. Millais at ... Glenfinlas.
Age 34. Nov. 1—18, " Lectures on Architecture and
       Painting" ... ... Edinburgh.
1854.—June 4, with parents at ... ... Geneva.
Age 35. June, drawing for proposed work on Swiss
       Towns, at ... ... Thun.
  ,,   July 2, Lucerne, Chamouni; Aug. ... ... Mont Cenis.
  ,,   Oct. 30, Working Men's College inaugurated Denmark Hill.
  ,,   Nov. 18—Dec. 9, Lectures to Decorative
       Workmen ... ... —
1855.—May, Academy Notes begun ... ... —
Age 36. July and Aug., Tunbridge Wells; and study-
       ing shipping at ... ... Deal.
  ,,   During this year writing "Modern Painters,"
       vols. iii. and iv. ... ... Denmark Hill.
1856.—April 15. Address to workmen of the
Age 37. Museum ... ... Oxford.

1856.—May 14, tour with parents: Amiens, Basle;
Age 37. June 10—23, Interlaken; July 29, with
Messrs. Norton, Simon & Trench, Cha-
mouni; Aug., drawing for Swiss Towns at
Fribourg ... ... Switzerland.
" Winter, writing "Elements of Drawing" at Denmark Hill.
1857.—Jan. 23, Lect. to Archit. Assoc.: "Imagi-
Age 38. nation in Architecture" ... ... —
" April 3, Address, St. Martin's School of Art ... —
" April 6, Evidence before National Gallery
Site Commission ... ... —
" May 6, Address on Thomas Seddon (at
Society of Arts) ... ... —
" July 10, 13, Lectures, "Political Economy
of Art" ... ... Manchester.
" Aug. and Sept., tour with parents in ... ... Scotland.
" Oct., address to Working Men's College on
"France" ... ... Denmark Hill.
" During the winter arranging Turners at
Nat. Gall. ... ... —
1858.—Jan. 13, Lect. "Conventional Art," S. Ken-
Age 39. sington Mus. ... ... —
" Feb. 16, Lect. "Work of Iron" (Sussex
Hotel) ... ... Tunbridge Wells.
" March 27, Official Report on Turner Bequest Denmark Hill.
" April 16, Address, "Study of Art" (St.
Martin's School) ... ... Denmark Hill.
" May 13, tour alone to draw for "Swiss
Towns"; May 18, ... Rheinfelden.
" June 9, Bremgarten, Baden; July to Aug. 1, Bellinzona.
" Aug., studying Paul Veronese at ... ... Turin.
" Sept. 1, Mont Cenis, returning to ... ... Denmark Hill.
" Oct. 29, Inaugural address to School of
Art ... ... Cambridge.
1859.—Feb. 22, Lect. "Unity of Art" (Royal In-
Age 40. stitution) ... ... Manchester.
" March 1, Lect. "Modern Manufacture and
Design" ... ... Bradford.
" May 2, Address, "Switzerland" (Work.
Men's Coll.) ... ... Denmark Hill.
" May 14, last tour with parents: Düsseldorf
and Berlin; June, Dresden, Nuremberg;
July, Munich ... ... Germany.

1859.—Aug. 1, Schaffhausen; Aug. 18, Thun; Sept. 4,
Age 40.   Bonneville; Sept. 10, Lausanne; ten days
               or a fortnight at St. Michael, Mont Cenis Switzerland.
   ,   Oct. 7   ...   . Denmark Hill.
   ,,   Nov. 1, Winnington; winter, writing
               "Modern Painters," vol. v.   ...   ...   —
1860.—March 8, Address, "Religious Art" (Work.
Age 41.   Men's Coll.) ...   .   —
   ,,   March 26, Evidence before Committee on
               Public Institutions ...   .   —
   ,,   "Modern Painters" finished ...   .   —

BIBLIOGRAPHY.

(1834—1866.)

THE Book-lover and collector of Editions will consult "A Bibliography of the Writings in Prose and Verse of John Ruskin, LL.D., edited by Thomas J. Wise, London. Printed for subscribers only, 1889—1892"; an elaborate work, of which Vol. I. and five parts of Vol. II. (329 + 161 pages) have appeared up to September 1892. The general reader will be content with short notices, briefly recording Mr. Ruskin's literary activity. With permission from Mr. Wise and his co-editor, Mr. James P. Smart, Jun., to avail myself of their work, I have rearranged the titles of Mr. Ruskin's writings, whether issued separately or in periodicals, under the dates of their first appearance in print; and I have omitted several mere compilations not actually edited by him, and reports of lectures not furnished by him, as well as minor letters given in "Arrows of the Chace" and "Ruskiniana," or mentioned in the great Bibliography as uncollected.

The publisher's name is given in brackets after each work: English editions only are named. Works without name of magazine or publisher were printed for private circulation.

1834.—"Enquiries on the Causes of the Colour of the Water of the Rhine"; "Note on the Perforation of a Leaden Pipe by Rats": and "Facts and Considerations on the Strata of Mont Blanc,"etc. (Loudon's "Mag. of Nat. Hist." for Sept., Nov., and Dec.), reprinted in "On the Old Road."

1835.—*Saltzburg*, and *Fragments from a Metrical Journal* ("Friendship's Offering," Smith, Elder and Co.).*

1836.—"The Induration of Sandstone"; "Observations on the Causes which occasion the Variation of Temperature between Spring and River Water" (Loudon's "Mag. Nat. Hist." for Sept. and Oct.), reprinted in "On the Old Road."

---

* All the poems—their titles are given in italics—were reprinted in "The Poems of John Ruskin" 1891; and all except those of 1835 in "Poems—J. R.," 1850.

1836.—*The Months* (" Friendship's Offering ").

1837.—*The Last Smile* (" Friendship's Offering ").

1837.—"Leoni," a legend of Italy (" Friendship's Offering "), reprinted separately with preface in 1868.

1837-8.—"The Poetry of Architecture"; a series of articles (" Loudon's Architectural Magazine "), reprinted 1892 (George Allen).

1838.—" The Convergence of Perpendiculars," five articles; and " The Planting of Churchyards " (Loudon's " Arch. Mag ").

1838.—*The Scythian Grave, Remembrance,* and *Christ Church, Oxford* (" Friendship's Offering ").

1839.—" Whether Works of Art may, with Propriety, be combined with the Sublimity of Nature; and what would be the most appropriate Situation for the Proposed Monument to the Memory of Sir Walter Scott, in Edinburgh " (Loudon's " Arch. Mag." for January).

1839.—Song—*We care not what Skies:* song—*Though thou hast not a Feeling*: Horace—*Iter ad Brundusium* (" London Monthly Miscellany " for January).

1839.—*Memory,* and *The Name* (" London Monthly Misc." for Feb.).

1839.—Canzonet—*The Winter's Chill: Fragments from a Meteorological Journal:* canzonet—*There's a Change:* and *The Mirror* (" London Monthly Misc." for March).

1839.—*Song of the Tyrolese* (" London Monthly Misc." for April).

1839.—*Salsette and Elephanta* (Newdigate prize poem), printed separately and in " Oxford Prize Poems " (J. Vincent), new edition, 1879 (Allen).

1839.—" Remarks on the Present State of Meteorological Science " (Trans. Met. Soc.), reprinted in " Monthly Met. Mag." for April 1870; and in " On the Old Road."

1839.—*Scythian Banquet Song* (" Friendship's Offering ").

1840.—*The Scythian Guest* (" Friendship's Offering "), reprinted with preface, 1849.

1840-43.—*The Broken Chain* (" Friendship's Offering ").

1840.—*To [Adèle]* (" Friendship's Offering ").

1841.—*The Tears of Psammenitus: The Two Paths: The Old Water-wheel: Farewell: The Departed Light;* and *Agonia* (" Friendship's Offering ").

1842.—*The Last Song of Arion,* and *The Hills of Carrara* (" Friendship's Offering ").

1843.—" Modern Painters, Vol. I." Seven editions of this volume were published separately up to 1867 (Smith, Elder & Co.) For subsequent editions see under 1860.

1844.—*The Battle of Montenotte,* and *A Walk in Chamouni* (" Friendship's Offering ").

1845.—*La Madonna dell'Acqua* (Heath's "Book of Beauty").

1845.—*The Old Seaman;* and *The Alps, seen from Marengo* ("Keepsake").

1846.—"Modern Painters, Vol. II." Five editions of this volume were published separately up to 1869 (Smith, Elder). Also rearranged edition in 2 vols., of which there have been four issues (Allen). For other editions see under 1860.

1846.—*Mont Blanc;* and *The Arve at Cluse* ("Keepsake").

1846.—*Lines written among the Basses Alpes;* and *The Glacier* (Heath's "Book of Beauty").

1847.—Lord Lindsay's "Christian Art" ("Quarterly Review" for June), reprinted in "On the Old Road."

1848.—Eastlake's "History of Oil Painting" ("Quarterly Review" for March), reprinted in "On the Old Road."

1849.—"Samuel Prout" ("Art Journal" for March), reprinted separately 1870, and in "On the Old Road."

1849.—"The Seven Lamps of Architecture," two editions (Smith, Elder), and four subsequent issues (Allen).

1850.—"Poems—J. R."; containing the above-mentioned, with additions.

1851.—"The King of the Golden River" (written 1841), seven editions (Smith, Elder), and three subsequent editions (Allen).

1851.—"The Stones of Venice," Vol. I., two editions of this volume published separately (Smith, Elder), for other editions see under 1853.

1851.—"Examples of the Architecture of Venice" (Smith, Elder, & Co., and Colnaghi), reissued 1887 (Allen).

1851.—"Notes on the Construction of Sheepfolds": two editions (Smith, Elder), and two subsequent reissues (Allen), also reprinted in "On the Old Road." With this may be named:—

"Two letters concerning Notes, etc.," addressed to the Rev. F. D. Maurice, 1851: printed by Dr. F. J. Furnivall, 1889.

1851.—"Pre-Raphaelitism," two editions (Smith, Elder), reprinted in "On the Old Road."

1852.—"The National Gallery" (letters to "The Times"), printed separately; also in "Arrows of the Chace."

1853.—"The Stones of Venice," Vols. II. and III., two editions of each published separately (Smith, Elder). The three vols. were published together in 1874, the so-called "Autograph" edition (Smith, Elder), and reprinted 1886 (Allen). In 1879 appeared the Travellers' edition, abridged; four issues (Allen). With this may be named:—"On the Nature of Gothic, etc." (from "Stones of Venice"), printed by F. J. Furnivall, 1854; two issues (Smith, Elder), and reprinted in antique form by William Morris, 1892 (Allen).

1853-60.—"Giotto and his Works in Padua" in three parts; collected into one vol. 1877 (Arundel Society).

1854.—"Lectures on Architecture and Painting" (Edinburgh, Nov. 1853); two editions (Smith, Elder), new edition, 1891 (Allen).

1854.—"Letters to the *Times* on the Principal Pre-Raphaelite Pictures in the Exhibition": printed separately, reprinted 1876, also in "Arrows of the Chace."

1854.—"The Opening of the Crystal Palace," etc. (Smith, Elder); reprinted in "On the Old Road."

1855.—"Notes on some of the Principal Pictures in . . . the Royal Academy"; three editions (Smith, Elder).

1856.—"Notes on . . . the Royal Academy, etc.," No. II., six editions (Smith, Elder).

1856.—"Modern Painters," Vols. III. and IV.: two editions of each (Smith, Elder); for subsequent issues see under 1860.

1856.—"The Harbours of England," two editions (E. Gambart & Co.); edition 3 (Day & Son); edition 4 (T. J. Allman); edition 5 dated 1877, (Smith; Elder).

1857.—"Notes on . . . the Royal Academy, etc.," No. III., two editions (Smith, Elder).

1857.—"Notes on the Turner Gallery at Marlborough House"; five editions variously revised (Smith, Elder).

1857.—"Catalogue of the Turner Sketches in the National Gallery," Part I.; also enlarged edition, 1857.

1857.—"Catalogue of the Sketches and Drawings by J. M. W. Turner, R.A., exhibited at Marlborough House," 1857-8; also enlarged edition, 1858.

1857.—"The Elements of Drawing": eight "thousands" (Smith, Elder); new edition, 1892 (Allen); partly reprinted in "Our Sketching Club" by the Rev. R. St. J. Tyrwhitt; four editions (Macmillan).

1857.—"The Political Economy of Art," three editions (Smith, Elder); reprinted in "A Joy for Ever (and its Price in the Market)," three editions (Allen): which includes the following pamphlets:—

"Education in Art," 1858 (Trans. Nat. Assoc. for the Promotion of Social Science); "Remarks addressed to the Mansfield Art Night Class," 1873; and "Social Policy," etc. (a paper for the Metaphysical Society), 1875.

1858.—Notice respecting some artificial sections illustrating the Geology of Chamouni (Proc. Royal Soc. of Edinburgh).

1858.—"Notes on . . . the Royal Academy," etc., No. IV. (Smith, Elder).

1858.—"Inaugural Address at the Cambridge School of Art" (Deighton, Bell, & Co., and Bell & Daldy); another edition printed for the

Committee of the School; republished separately, 1879 (Allen), and reprinted in "On the Old Road."

1859.—"The Oxford Museum," by Henry W. Acland, M.D., etc., and John Ruskin; various issues forming four editions (Parker, and Smith, Elder.) Mr. Ruskin's contributions were reprinted in "Arrows of the Chace."

1859.—"Notes on . . . the Royal Academy," etc., No. V. (Smith, Elder).

1859.—"The Two Paths" (Smith, Elder) and three subsequent editions (Allen). The work includes :—"The Unity of Art" (lecture at Manchester, Feb. 22, 1859), privately printed.

1859.—"The Elements of Perspective" (Smith, Elder).

1860.—"Sir Joshua and Holbein" ("Cornhill Mag." for March); reprinted in "On the Old Road."

1860.—"Modern Painters," Vol. V. (Smith, Elder). The five volumes of "Modern Painters" were published together in the issue known as the autograph edition in 1873 (Smith, Elder). They were reprinted with additions and index in 1888, and again in 1892 (Allen). With these may be named :—"Frondes Agrestes" (selections from "Modern Painters" by Miss Susanna Beever), edited by Mr. Ruskin, 1875; of which ten issues, totalling 18,000, copies, have been published (Allen). "In Montibus Sanctis, Studies of Mountain Form and its Visible Causes, collected and completed out of Modern Painters": two parts only appeared, 1884-5 (Allen); and "Cœli Enarrant, Studies of Cloud Form, etc.," 1885 (Allen).

The well-known "Selections from the Writings [above-named] of John Ruskin" were published in 1861 (Smith, Elder). .

CATALOGUE OF DRAWINGS BY MR. RUSKIN.

(1829—1859.)

THIS list contains only the more important and dated drawings. A full *catalogue raisonné* would be almost as elaborate a work as the great Bibliography; but the following entries will serve to show Mr. Ruskin's industry in practical art, and the development of his style of draughtsmanship.

1829.—Maps, of which a specimen was shown at the Fine Art Society's Galleries, 1878 ... ... Brantwood.

1830.—Copies from Cruikshank's "Grimm" ... ... —

1831.—Canterbury Cathedral (first architectural study), and Battle Abbey ... ... Miss Gale.
Sevenoaks; Rocks at Tunbridge Wells; Canterbury; Battle Abbey ... ... Brantwood.
First study of clouds (pen and pencil): Dover ... —

1832.—Tunbridge Castle (pencil, "drawing master's style") —

1833.—[First Swiss tour; vignettes on grey paper worked up in pen from sketches] Mont Blanc; Aiguilles; Wetterhorn and Bernese Alps;· Jungfrau, etc., Sempach; Rhine, Sargans and Coire; Pissevache and Bex; Lille; Splügen; Domo d'Ossola; between Novi and Genoa; Mediterranean; Dijon Church; and other vignettes. Watch-tower at Andernach (*Poems*, 1891). In pencil: Cassel, Hôtel de Ville; a Façade; a Tree ... ... —

1834.—Twenty-eight original vignettes on white paper in imitation of Turner's vignettes in Rogers' Poems; of which "The Jungfrau," published in *Poems*, 1891, is a specimen; with others from Prout and Turner —
St. Mary's, Bristol (dated 1833), Proutesque ... G. Holt, Esq.

1835.—[Second Swiss tour; pencil drawings in Prout's style] Dover; Calais; Rouen (*Poems*, 1891); Rouen,

façade, Arc de l'Horloge and street; Rouen, Butter-
tower ("Mag. of Art," Jan. 1888); Sens; Nancy
(*Poems*, 1891); Tête Noir; Bex; La Halle, Neu-
chatel; Baden, Switzerland; a Turret; Zug
("Poetry of Architecture," 1892); St. Gothard;
Amsteg; Meyringen; Rosenlaui; St. Gall   ...   Brantwood.
Main street of Innsbrück   ...   .   Dr. Pocock.
Zirl; Stelvio; St. Anastasia, Verona; Vicenza (?);
St. Mark's; Ulm ("Poetry of Architecture," 1892)   Brantwood.
Strasburg; Château, Thun   ...   .   Oxford.
[The following are in pen] Rouen, Cathedral Spire;
Montreuil; Bonneville; Mont Velan (*Poems*, 1891);
Fortress in Val d'Aosta (*Poems*, 1891); Ancienne
Maison (*Poems*); Hospital, Pass of St. Gothard
(*Poems*); Grimsel   ...   .   Brantwood.
1836.—Richmond   ...   .   —
1837.—[Still in the Proutesque style, but more advanced;
quarto imperial size] Brougham Castle; Furness
Abbey; Ruin near Ambleside (*Poems*); R. Brathay;
Rydal (*Poems*); Choir of Bolton Abbey   ...   ...   —
West end of Bolton Abbey; High Tor, Matlock   ...   Mrs. Talbot.
Rocks above Strid; Matlock; Ashby; Peterborough;
Lichfield Cathedral; Dorchester, and niche   ...   Brantwood.
Cottage in Troutbeck (line and wash)   ...   ...   G. Holt, Esq.
Also drawings for "Poetry of Architecture," as the
"Cottage near Aosta" (re-engraved 1892) ...   —
1838.—[Same style and size.] Lodgings at Oxford   ...   Brantwood.
Stirling; Stirling from Cambuskenneth Abbey   ...   Mrs. Talbot.
Palace of Stirling; Edinburgh from Castle Rock;
Roslin; Prentice's pillar; Haddon Hall (*Poems*) ...   Brantwood.
1839.—St. Michael's, Cornwall (pencil and white)   ...   —
1840-41.—[New style based on David Roberts, pencil and
tint, half imperial size; of these fine drawings the
chief are]: Château de Blois; St. Pierre, Avignon;
Nice ("Poetry of Architecture)"; Pisa, Spina chapel
Pisa, Spina Chapel (another) at St. George's Museum   Sheffield.
Ponte. Vecchio, Florence; Palazzo Vecchio, Florence;
Piazza S. M. del Pianto, Rome ("Amateur's Portfolio," 1844); Quattro Fontane, Rome; Fountain
at Rome; the Aventine; Street of Trinita di Monte;
Aqueducts of Campagna; La Riccia (see "Modern
Painters," vol. i., p. 153); Naples, Gate; Castel
del Uovo; Street Architecture; Windows, Street,

and Bay ("Poetry of Architecture," 1892) ; Castel
Vecchio and other drawings. Pompeii ; Castle of
Itri (see "Præterita," ii., p. 91) ; Bologna ; Fountain
at Verona ; Piazza d'Erbe, Verona ; and Giant's
Staircase, Venice (Verona Exhibition, 1870) ; Venice,
Ca' Contarini Fasan ...   .   Brantwood.
Also several water-colour sketches in style of Copley
Fielding   ...   .   —
[On returning to England, autumn 1841, produced
coloured drawings in imitation of Turner's vig-
nettes ; Wendlebury Church (given to the Rev.
Walter Brown) ; and Amboise ; Coast of Genoa ;
and Glacier des Bois (*Poems*).]
1842.—[After lessons from Harding: first naturalistic
study, the sketch of Ivy, and Aspen at Fontaine-
bleau (now lost ?) ; and last Proutesque drawings.]
Tree at Dulwich (*Poems*) ; Calais : Town-hall,
Belfry and Lighthouse   ...   .   —
Study at Chamouni (pencil, wash and white, quarto
imperial)   ...   .   Sir J. Simon.
Great square at Cologne (given to Miss Pritchard) ;
St. Quentin ; Antwerp ; Bruges   ...   .   —
Perhaps this year, Falls of Schaffhausen (12 × 7½)—
the study Turner liked—and sketch of same sub-
ject ; Sketch-book (6½ × 8½ in.) with journal of
tour ; and the two first studies of early sacred art :
St. Peter, attributed to Cimabue ; and Virgin, attributed to Duccio, Christ Church, Oxford   ...   Prof. C. E. Norton.
1844.—[First diagrammatic sketching, giving up the attempt
to make pictures ; studies of geology and botany
for "Modern Painters" at Chamouni.]
Panorama of Simplon and Bernese Alps   ...   Sheffield Museum.
Fletschhorn and Weisshorn, at Simplon ...   ...
Some drawings at Chamouni, Aiguille Verte   ...   Brantwood.
1845.—[After study of Turner's "Liber Studiorum," using
strong outline in pen or pencil, and wash in full
colour or chiaroscuro.]
Towers at Montbard   ...   .   Herne Hill.
Lucca : San Michele   ...   .   Oxford.
Pisa : Duomo ; Baptistery ; studies in Campo Santo   Brantwood.
Pisa : Sta. Maria della Spina ...   .   Sheffield Museum.
Florence : San Miniato (6¾ × 3¼ in.) ...   .   Prof. Norton.
Florence : Garden of San Miniato ; Avenue of Porta

Romana; View of Arno and Town; Fiesole; Copy
of Angelico's Annunciation ("Modern Painters");
Vogogna.   Milan : Eve and the Serpent ("Seven
Lamps ")   ...   .   Brantwood.
Study of Tree (Aug. 4th)   ...   .   Oxford.
Torrent in Val Anzasca (half imp., colour) ...   ...   Brantwood.
Studies on St. Gothard
           Some at Brantwood, one owned by Prof. Norton.
Baveno : Mill and Sunset (*Poems*, 1891). Brescia :
Twilight (copied for "Storm Cloud" lecture, 1884);
Verona ; Vicenza, windows and interior (pencil);
Venice, Ca d'Oro ; Ca' Foscari ; copies, etc.   ...   Brantwood.
Capitals at Venice, sketch on brown paper (8¼ × 6 in.)   Prof. Norton.
Perhaps this year, two sketches of Ponte Vecchio,
Florence   ...   .   F. W. Hilliard, Esq.
1846.—[Bold and clear tinting with full brush over outline.]
Calais Belfry ; the Cathedral before Restoration,
and other drawings at Sens ...   .   Brantwood.
Perhaps this year, "Mountain Gloom at St. Jean de
Maurienne"   ...   .   Sir J. Simon.
Porch of Duomo, Verona ; St. Mark's after rain, Venice   Oxford.
Griffin at Verona ("Modern Painters"); Window,
Ca' Foscari, Balcony and Capital ("Seven Lamps");
Cottage Gallery, Pistoja (?) (" Poetry of Architec-
ture"); Lauterbrunnen Cliffs   ...   .   Brantwood.
St. Urbain, Troyes; Ferrara Cathedral ("Seven
Lamps ")   ...   .   Sir J. Simon.
Perhaps this year, Folkstone from the Pavilion Hotel
(sepia, quarto)   ...   .   —
1848.—Caen, main street; St. Lo, Cathedral (both half
imperial)   ...   .   Prof. Norton.
Caudebec, flamboyant sculpture   ...   ...   Harvard College.
Also drawings and sketches for "Seven Lamps"   ...   Brantwood.
1849.—Annecy, houses and bridge (pen and tint, 6¾ × 4¾ in.) Prof. Norton.
Mountains from Vevey; several drawings of the
Matterhorn   ...   .   Brantwood.
Matterhorn, for "Modern Painters" (colour, quarto
imperial); perhaps this year "Woodland, Rock, and
Cloud, in the byway to the Chapeau, Chamouni"
(sepia, 10 × 15 in.); and Church tower, Courmayeur
(colour, 10 × 6 in.).   ...   .   Sir J. Simon.
Camera lucida drawing of Chamouni ; detail of Doge's
Palace, and other drawings for "Stones of Venice"   Brantwood.

1851-2.—Further drawings for "Stones of Venice" ... Brantwood.
　　Also (Feb. 24th, 1852) Vicenza (colour, 10 × 5 in.);
　　　　and perhaps Capitals of St. Mark's (colour, 6 × 4 in.) Sir J. Simon.
　　Sketch of Tintoret's Annunciation (3½ × 4½ in.) ... Prof. Norton.
　　Sarcophagus of Can Mastino II.; and detail of Ducal
　　　　Palace ... ... Verona Ex., 1870.

1853.—Gneiss rock in Glenfinlas—lampblack (Cook's
　　"Studies in Ruskin") ... ... Oxford.
　　Perhaps this year, Granite boulder (colour, 12 × 18½ in.) Prof. Norton.

1854.—Outlines of Turner's two Nottinghams and other
　　drawings for " Modern Painters," III. and IV. ... —
　　Jib of Calais boat ("Præterita") ... ... Brantwood.
　　Perhaps this year: Lake of Brientz (9½ × 6¾ in.); and
　　"Old Hall in Worcestershire or Herefordshire"
　　(quarto) ... ... Prof. Norton.
　　Perhaps this year: Towers of Fribourg and copy of
　　Turner's " St. Gothard" ("Modern Painters " IV.)
　　　　　　　　　　　　　　　　　Mrs. W. H. Churchill.
　　Also Pine forest at St. Michel; and Glacier des
　　Bossons, Chamouni (Cook's " Studies in Ruskin ") Oxford.

1855.—Deer's head engraved on bone (British Museum) Prof. Norton.

1856.—Amiens Porch (" Bible of Amiens ") ... ... Oxford.
　　Thun, for " Swiss Towns," (13 × 18 in.) or in 1854;
　　Fribourg, drawings for " Swiss Towns" ... ... Brantwood.
　　Fribourg (Cook's " Studies in Ruskin ") ... ... Oxford.
　　Perhaps this year the following coloured drawings :
　　Old Houses at Geneva on the Rhone Island
　　(15 × 13 in.); At the Foot of the Mole, near Bonne-
　　ville (14 × 12 in.); Rocks and Lichen below Les
　　Montets, Chamouni (14 × 11 in.); Cascade de la
　　Folie, Chamouni (12 × 9 in.); Head of the Lake of
　　Geneva (14 × 6 in.); Wayside near Bonneville
　　(14 × 9 in.) ... ... Sir J. Simon.

1857.—About this time, Bird drawn at the Working Men's
　　College ... ... Mr. W. H. Hooper.
　　Drawings of leaves (Cook's " Studies in Ruskin ")
　　and others ... ... Oxford.

1858.—Enlargements from St. Louis' Psalter, and others;
　　Hotel Dessin, Calais ... ... Brantwood.
　　Basle ; Rheinfelden ; Hapsburg (Cook's " Studies ") Oxford.
　　Several studies at Baden, Hapsburg, Bellinzona,
　　Turin; Storm clouds on Mt. Cenis, and other sketches Brantwood.

Rheinfelden, pen sketch ; Head of Veronese's Solo-
   mon (11 × 14½ in.) ...   . Prof. Norton.
Perhaps this year, Lauffenburg (body colour on gray,
   10 × 8 in.)   ...   . Sir J. Simon.
1859.—Kempten Tower, two sketches ; Field of corn,
   Munich ; Lauterbrunnen ; Dawn at Neuchatel
   (perhaps this year)   ...   . Prof. Norton.
Kempten, pen outline   ...   . Harvard Coll.
Nuremberg, Dormers, and Street ; sketch at Munich   Brantwood.
   Nuremberg, Moat ("Modern Painters")   ...   ...   —
Copy from Vandyck at Munich   ...   . Herne Hill.
Lauffenburg ; Bridge of Constance   ...   . Brantwood.

END OF VOL. I.

A LIST OF NEW BOOKS AND ANNOUNCEMENTS OF METHUEN AND COMPANY PUBLISHERS : LONDON
18 BURY STREET
W.C.

CONTENTS

OCTOBER 1892

MESSRS. METHUEN'S
AUTUMN ANNOUNCEMENTS

GENERAL LITERATURE

Rudyard Kipling. BARRACK-ROOM BALLADS; And Other Verses. By RUDYARD KIPLING. *Extra Post 8vo, pp.* 208. *Laid paper, rough edges, buckram, gilt top.* 6s.

A special Presentation Edition, *bound in white buckram, with extra gilt ornament.* 7s. 6d.

The First Edition was sold on publication, and two further large Editions have been exhausted. The Fourth Edition is Now Ready.

Gladstone. THE SPEECHES AND PUBLIC ADDRESSES OF THE RT. HON. W. E. GLADSTONE, M.P. With Notes. Edited by A. W. HUTTON, M.A. (Librarian of the Gladstone Library), and H. J. COHEN, M.A. With Portraits. *8vo. Vol. IX.* 12s. 6d.

Messrs. METHUEN beg to announce that they are about to issue, in ten volumes 8vo, an authorised collection of Mr. Gladstone's Speeches, the work being undertaken with his sanction and under his superintendence. Notes and Introductions will be added.

In view of the interest in the Home Rule Question, it is proposed to issue Vols. IX. and X., which will include the speeches of the last seven or eight years, immediately, and then to proceed with the earlier volumes. Volume X. is already published.

Collingwood. JOHN RUSKIN: His Life and Work. By W. G. COLLINGWOOD, M.A., late Scholar of University College, Oxford, Author of the 'Art Teaching of John Ruskin,' Editor of Mr. Ruskin's Poems. *2 vols. 8vo.* 32s.

Also a limited edition on hand-made paper, with the Illustrations on India paper. £3, 3s. *net.*

Also a small edition on Japanese paper. £5, 5s. *net.*

This important work is written by Mr. Collingwood, who has been for some years Mr. Ruskin's private secretary, and who has had unique advantages in obtaining materials for this book from Mr. Ruskin himself and from his friends. It will contain a large amount of new matter, and of letters which have never been published, and will be, in fact, as near as is possible at present, a full and authoritative biography of Mr. Ruskin. The book will contain numerous portraits of Mr. Ruskin, including a coloured one from a water-colour portait by himself, and also 13 sketches, never before published, by Mr. Ruskin and Mr. Arthur Severn. A bibliography will be added.

Baring Gould. THE TRAGEDY OF THE CAESARS: The Emperors of the Julian and Claudian Lines. With numerous Illustrations from Busts, Gems, Cameos, etc. By S. BARING GOULD, Author of 'Mehalah,' etc. *2 vols. Royal 8vo. 30s.*

This book is the only one in English which deals with the personal history of the Caesars, and Mr. Baring Gould has found a subject which, for picturesque detail and sombre interest, is not rivalled by any work of fiction. The volumes are copiously illustrated.

Baring Gould. SURVIVALS AND SUPERSTITIONS. With Illustrations. By S. BARING GOULD. *Crown 8vo. 7s. 6d.*

A book on such subjects as Foundations, Gables, Holes, Gallows, Raising the Hat, Old Ballads, etc. etc. It traces in a most interesting manner their origin and history.

Perrens. THE HISTORY OF FLORENCE FROM THE TIME OF THE MEDICIS TO THE FALL OF THE REPUBLIC. By F. T. PERRENS. Translated by HANNAH LYNCH. In three volumes. Vol. I. *8vo. 12s. 6d.*

This is a translation from the French of the best history of Florence in existence. This volume covers a period of profound interest—political and literary—and is written with great vivacity.

Henley & Whibley. A BOOK OF ENGLISH PROSE. Collected by W. E. HENLEY and CHARLES WHIBLEY. *Crown 8vo. 6s.*

Also small limited editions on Dutch and Japanese paper. *21s.* and *42s.*

A companion book to Mr. Henley's well-known *Lyra Heroica.*

"Q." GREEN BAYS: A Book of Verses. By "Q.," Author of 'Dead Man's Rock' &c. *Fcap. 8vo. 3s. 6d.*

Also a limited edition on large Dutch paper.

A small volume of Oxford Verses by the well-known author of 'I Saw Three Ships,' etc.

Wells. OXFORD AND OXFORD LIFE. By Members of the University. Edited by J. WELLS, M.A., Fellow and Tutor of Wadham College. *Crown 8vo. 3s. 6d.*

This work will be of great interest and value to all who are in any way connected with the University. It will contain an account of life at Oxford—intellectual, social, and religious—a careful estimate of necessary expenses, a review of recent changes, a statement of the present position of the University, and chapters on Women's Education, aids to study, and University Extension.

Driver. SERMONS ON SUBJECTS CONNECTED WITH THE OLD TESTAMENT. By S. R. DRIVER, D.D., Canon of Christ Church, Regius Professor of Hebrew in the University of Oxford. *Crown 8vo. 6s.*

An important volume of sermons on Old Testament Criticism preached before the University by the author of 'An Introduction to the Literature of the Old Testament.'

Prior. CAMBRIDGE SERMONS. Edited by C. H. PRIOR, M.A., Fellow and Tutor of Pembroke College. *Crown 8vo. 6s.*

A volume of sermons preached before the University of Cambridge by various preachers, including the Archbishop of Canterbury and Bishop Westcott.

Kaufmann. CHARLES KINGSLEY. By M. KAUFMANN, M.A. *Crown 8vo. 5s.*

A biography of Kingsley, especially dealing with his achievements in social reform.

Lock. THE LIFE OF JOHN KEBLE. By WALTER LOCK, M.A., Fellow of Magdalen College, Oxford. With Portrait. *Crown 8vo. 5s.*

Hutton. CARDINAL MANNING : A Biography. By A. W. HUTTON, M.A. With Portrait. *New and Cheaper Edition. Crown 8vo. 2s. 6d.*

Sells. THE MECHANICS OF DAILY LIFE. By V. P. SELLS, M.A. Illustrated. *Crown 8vo. 2s. 6d.*

Kimmins. THE CHEMISTRY OF LIFE AND HEALTH. By C. W. KIMMINS, Downing College, Cambridge. Illustrated. *Crown 8vo. 2s. 6d.*

Potter. AGRICULTURAL BOTANY. By M. C. POTTER, Lecturer at Newcastle College of Science. Illustrated. *Crown 8vo. 2s. 6d.*

The above are new volumes of the " University Extension Series."

Cox. LAND NATIONALISATION. By HAROLD COX, M.A. *Crown 8vo. 2s. 6d.*

Hadfield & Gibbins. A SHORTER WORKING DAY. By R. A. HADFIELD and H. de B. GIBBINS, M.A. *Crown 8vo. 2s. 6d.*

The above are new volumes of " Social Questions of To-day " Series.

FICTION.

Norris. HIS GRACE. By W. E. NORRIS, Author of ' Mdle. de Mersac,' ' Marcia,' etc. *Crown 8vo. 2 vols. 21s.*

Pryce. TIME AND THE WOMAN. By RICHARD PRYCE, Author of ' Miss Maxwell's Affections,' ' The Quiet Mrs. Fleming,' etc. *Crown 8vo. 2 vols. 21s.*

Parker. PIERRE AND HIS PEOPLE. By GILBERT PARKER. *Crown 8vo. Buckram. 6s.*

Marriott Watson. DIOGENES OF LONDON and other Sketches. By H. B. MARRIOTT WATSON, Author of 'The Web of the Spider.' *Crown 8vo. Buckram.* 6s.

Baring Gould. IN THE ROAR OF THE SEA. By S. BARING GOULD, Author of 'Mehalah,' 'Urith,' etc. Cheaper Edition. *Crown 8vo.* 6s.

Clark Russell. MY DANISH SWEETHEART. By W. CLARK RUSSELL, Author of 'The Wreck of the Grosvenor,' 'A Marriage at Sea,' etc. With 6 Illustrations by W. H. OVEREND. *Crown 8vo.* 6s.

Mabel Robinson. HOVENDEN, V. C. By F. MABEL ROBINSON, Author of 'Disenchantment,' etc. Cheaper Edition. *Crown 8vo.* 3s. 6d.

Meade. OUT OF THE FASHION. By L. T. MEADE, Author of 'A Girl of the People,' etc. With 6 Illustrations by W. PAGET. *Crown 8vo.* 6s.

Cuthell. ONLY A GUARDROOM DOG. By Mrs. CUTHELL. With 16 Illustrations by W. PARKINSON. *Square Crown 8vo.* 6s.

Collingwood. THE DOCTOR OF THE JULIET. By HARRY COLLINGWOOD, Author of 'The Pirate Island,' etc. Illustrated by GORDON BROWNE. *Crown 8vo.* 6s.

Bliss. A MODERN ROMANCE. By LAURENCE BLISS. *Crown 8vo. Buckram.* 3s. 6d. *Paper.* 2s. 6d.

CHEAPER EDITIONS.

Baring Gould. OLD COUNTRY LIFE. By S. BARING GOULD, Author of 'Mehalah,' etc. With 67 Illustrations. *Crown 8vo.* 6s.

Clark. THE COLLEGES OF OXFORD. Edited by A. CLARK, M.A., Fellow and Tutor of Lincoln College. *8vo.* 12s. 6d.

Russell. THE LIFE OF ADMIRAL LORD COLLINGWOOD. By W. CLARK RUSSELL, Author of 'The Wreck of the Grosvenor.' With Illustrations by F. BRANGWYN. *8vo.* 10s. 6d.

Author of 'Mdle. Mori.' THE SECRET OF MADAME DE Monluc. By the Author of 'The Atelier du Lys,' 'Mdle. Mori.' *Crown 8vo.* 3s. 6d.

'An exquisite literary cameo.'—*World.*

𝔑𝔢𝔴 𝔞𝔫𝔡 𝔑𝔢𝔠𝔢𝔫𝔱 𝔅𝔬𝔬𝔨𝔰

Poetry

Rudyard Kipling. BARRACK-ROOM BALLADS; And Other Verses. By RUDYARD KIPLING. *Fourth Edition. Crown 8vo. 6s.*

'Mr. Kipling's verse is strong, vivid, full of character. . . . Unmistakable genius rings in every line.'—*Times.*

'The disreputable lingo of Cockayne is henceforth justified before the world; for a man of genius has taken it in hand, and has shown, beyond all cavilling, that in its way it also is a medium for literature. You are grateful, and you say to yourself, half in envy and half in admiration: " Here is a *book*; here, or one is a Dutchman, is one of the books of the year." '—*National Observer.*

' "Barrack-Room Ballads" contains some of the best work that Mr. Kipling has ever done, which is saying a good deal. "Fuzzy-Wuzzy," "Gunga Din," and "Tommy," are, in our opinion, altogether superior to anything of the kind that English literature has hitherto produced.'—*Athenæum.*

'These ballads are as wonderful in their descriptive power as they are vigorous in their dramatic force. There are few ballads in the English language more stirring than "The Ballad of East and West," worthy to stand by the Border ballads of Scott.'—*Spectator.*

'The ballads teem with imagination, they palpitate with emotion. We read them with laughter and tears; the metres throb in our pulses, the cunningly ordered words tingle with life; and if this be not poetry, what is?'—*Pall Mall Gazette.*

Ibsen. BRAND. A Drama by HENRIK IBSEN. Translated by WILLIAM WILSON. *Crown 8vo. 5s.*

'The greatest world-poem of the nineteenth century next to "Faust." "Brand" will have an astonishing interest for Englishmen. It is in the same set with "Agamemnon," with "Lear," with the literature that we now instinctively regard as high and holy.'—*Daily Chronicle.*

Henley. LYRA HEROICA: An Anthology selected from the best English Verse of the 16th, 17th, 18th, and 19th Centuries. By WILLIAM ERNEST HENLEY, Author of 'A Book of Verse,' 'Views and Reviews,' etc. *Crown 8vo. Stamped gilt buckram, gilt top, edges uncut. 6s.*

'Mr. Henley has brought to the task of selection an instinct alike for poetry and for chivalry which seems to us quite wonderfully, and even unerringly, right.'—*Guardian.*

Tomson. A SUMMER NIGHT, AND OTHER POEMS. By GRAHAM R. TOMSON. With Frontispiece by A. TOMSON. *Fcap. 8vo. 3s. 6d.*

Also an edition on handmade paper, limited to 50 copies. *Large crown 8vo. 10s. 6d. net.*

'Mrs. Tomson holds perhaps the very highest rank among poetesses of English birth. This selection will help her reputation.'—*Black and White.*

Langbridge. A CRACKED FIDDLE. Being Selections from the Poems of FREDERIC LANGBRIDGE. With Portrait. *Crown 8vo.* 5s.

Langbridge. BALLADS OF THE BRAVE: Poems of Chivalry, Enterprise, Courage, and Constancy, from the Earliest Times to the Present Day. Edited, with Notes, by Rev. F. LANGBRIDGE. *Crown 8vo.*

Presentation Edition, 3s. 6d. School Edition, 2s. 6d.

'A very happy conception happily carried out. These "Ballads of the Brave" are intended to suit the real tastes of boys, and will suit the taste of the great majority. —*Spectator.* 'The book is full of splendid things.'—*World.*

History and Biography

Gladstone. THE SPEECHES AND PUBLIC ADDRESSES OF THE RT. HON. W. E. GLADSTONE, M.P. With Notes and Introductions. Edited by A. W. HUTTON, M.A. (Librarian of the Gladstone Library), and H. J. COHEN, M.A. With Portraits. *8vo. Vol. X.* 12s. 6d.

Russell. THE LIFE OF ADMIRAL LORD COLLING-WOOD. By W. CLARK RUSSELL, Author of 'The Wreck of the Grosvenor.' With Illustrations by F. BRANGWYN. *8vo.* 10s. 6d.

'A really good book.'—*Saturday Review.*
'A most excellent and wholesome book, which we should like to see in the hands of every boy in the country.'—*St. James's Gazette.*

Clark. THE COLLEGES OF OXFORD: Their History and their Traditions. By Members of the University. Edited by A. CLARK, M.A., Fellow and Tutor of Lincoln College. *8vo.* 12s. 6d.

'Whether the reader approaches the book as a patriotic member of a college, as an antiquary, or as a student of the organic growth of college foundation, it will amply reward his attention.'—*Times.*
'A delightful book, learned and lively.'—*Academy.*
'A work which will certainly be appealed to for many years as the standard book on the Colleges of Oxford.'—*Athenæum.*

Hulton. RIXAE OXONIENSES: An Account of the Battles of the Nations, The Struggle between Town and Gown, etc. By S. F. HULTON, M.A. *Crown 8vo.* 5s.

James. CURIOSITIES OF CHRISTIAN HISTORY PRIOR TO THE REFORMATION. By CROAKE JAMES, Author of 'Curiosities of Law and Lawyers.' *Crown 8vo.* 7s. 6d.

Clifford. THE DESCENT OF CHARLOTTE COMPTON
(BARONESS FERRERS DE CHARTLEY). By her Great-Granddaughter,
ISABELLA G. C. CLIFFORD. *Small 4to.* 10s. 6d. *net.*

General Literature

Bowden. THE IMITATION OF BUDDHA : Being Quotations from Buddhist Literature for each Day in the Year. Compiled
by E. M. BOWDEN. With Preface by Sir EDWIN ARNOLD. *Second
Edition.* 16mo. 2s. 6d.

Ditchfield. OUR ENGLISH VILLAGES : Their Story and
their Antiquities. By P. H. DITCHFIELD, M.A., F.R.H.S., Rector
of Barkham, Berks. *Post 8vo.* 2s. 6d. Illustrated.

'An extremely amusing and interesting little book, which should find a place in
every parochial library.'—*Guardian.*

Ditchfield. OLD ENGLISH SPORTS. By P. H. DITCH-
FIELD, M.A. *Crown 8vo.* 2s. 6d. Illustrated.

'A charming account of old English Sports.'—*Morning Post.*

Burne. PARSON AND PEASANT : Chapters of their
Natural History. By J. B. BURNE, M.A., Rector of Wasing.
Crown 8vo. 5s.

'"Parson and Peasant" is a book not only to be interested in, but to learn something
from—a book which may prove a help to many a clergyman, and broaden the
hearts and ripen the charity of laymen."'—*Derby Mercury.*

Massee. A MONOGRAPH OF THE MYXOGASTRES. By
G. MASSEE. *8vo.* 18s. *net.*

Cunningham. THE PATH TOWARDS KNOWLEDGE :
Essays on Questions of the Day. By W. CUNNINGHAM, D.D.,
Fellow of Trinity College, Cambridge, Professor of Economics at
King's College, London. *Crown 8vo.* 4s. 6d.

Essays on Marriage and Population, Socialism, Money, Education, Positivism, etc.

Anderson Graham. NATURE IN BOOKS : Studies in Literary
Biography. By P. ANDERSON GRAHAM. *Crown 8vo.* 6s.

The chapters are entitled : I. 'The Magic of the Fields' (Jefferies). II. 'Art and
Nature' (Tennyson). III. 'The Doctrine of Idleness' (Thoreau). IV. 'The
Romance of Life' (Scott). V. 'The Poetry of Toil' (Burns). VI. 'The Divinity
of Nature' (Wordsworth).

Works by S. Baring Gould.

Author of ' Mehalah,' etc.

OLD COUNTRY LIFE. With Sixty-seven Illustrations by W. PARKINSON, F. D. BEDFORD, and F. MASEY. *Large Crown 8vo, cloth super extra, top edge gilt*, 10s. 6d. *Fourth and Cheaper Edition.* 6s. [*Ready.*

' "Old Country Life," as healthy wholesome reading, full of breezy life and movement, full of quaint stories vigorously told, will not be excelled by any book to be published throughout the year. Sound, hearty, and English to the core.'—*World.*

HISTORIC ODDITIES AND STRANGE EVENTS. *Third Edition, Crown 8vo.* 6s.

' A collection of exciting and entertaining chapters. The whole volume is delightful reading.'—*Times.*

FREAKS OF FANATICISM. (First published as Historic Oddities, Second Series.) *Third Edition. Crown 8vo.* 6s.

' Mr. Baring Gould has a keen eye for colour and effect, and the subjects he has chosen give ample scope to his descriptive and analytic faculties. A perfectly fascinating book.—*Scottish Leader.*

SONGS OF THE WEST : Traditional Ballads and Songs of the West of England, with their Traditional Melodies. Collected by S. BARING GOULD, M.A., and H. FLEETWOOD SHEPPARD, M.A. Arranged for Voice and Piano. In 4 Parts (containing 25 Songs each), *Parts I., II., III.,* 3s. *each.* Part IV., 5s. *In one Vol., roan,* 15s.

' A rich and varied collection of humour, pathos, grace, and poetic fancy.'—*Saturday Review.*

YORKSHIRE ODDITIES AND STRANGE EVENTS. *Fourth Edition. Crown 8vo.* 6s.

SURVIVALS AND SUPERSTITIONS. *Crown 8vo.* Illustrated. [*In the press.*

JACQUETTA, and other Stories. *Crown 8vo.* 3s. 6d. *Boards,* 2s.

ARMINELL : A Social Romance. *New Edition. Crown 8vo.* 3s. 6d. *Boards,* 2s.

' To say that a book is by the author of "Mehalah" is to imply that it contains a story cast on strong lines, containing dramatic possibilities, vivid and sympathetic descriptions of Nature, and a wealth of ingenious imagery. All these expectations are justified by "Arminell." —*Speaker.*

URITH: A Story of Dartmoor. *Third Edition. Crown 8vo.* 3s. 6d.
'The author is at his best.'—*Times.*
'He has nearly reached the high water-mark of "Mehalah."'—*National Observer.*

MARGERY OF QUETHER, and other Stories. *Crown 8vo.* 3s. 6d.

IN THE ROAR OF THE SEA: A Tale of the Cornish Coast. *New Edition.* 6s.

Fiction

Author of 'Indian Idylls.' IN TENT AND BUNGALOW: Stories of Indian Sport and Society. By the Author of 'Indian Idylls.' *Crown 8vo.* 3s. 6d.

Fenn. A DOUBLE KNOT. By G. MANVILLE FENN, Author of 'The Vicar's People,' etc. *Crown 8vo.* 3s. 6d.

Pryce. THE QUIET MRS. FLEMING. By RICHARD PRYCE, Author of 'Miss Maxwell's Affections,' etc. *Crown 8vo.* 3s. 6d. *Picture Boards,* 2s.

Gray. ELSA. A Novel. By E. M'QUEEN GRAY. *Crown 8vo.* 6s.
'A charming novel. The characters are not only powerful sketches, but minutely and carefully finished portraits.'—*Guardian.*

Gray. MY STEWARDSHIP. By E. M'QUEEN GRAY. *Crown 8vo.* 3s. 6d.

Cobban. A REVEREND GENTLEMAN. By J. MACLAREN COBBAN, Author of 'Master of his Fate,' etc. *Crown 8vo.* 4s. 6d.
'The best work Mr. Cobban has yet achieved. The Rev. W. Merrydew is a brilliant creation.'—*National Observer.*
'One of the subtlest studies of character outside Meredith.'—*Star.*

Lyall. DERRICK VAUGHAN, NOVELIST. By EDNA LYALL, Author of 'Donovan.' *Crown 8vo.* 31st *Thousand.* 3s. 6d. ; *paper,* 1s.

Linton. THE TRUE HISTORY OF JOSHUA DAVIDSON, Christian and Communist. By E. LYNN LINTON. Eleventh and Cheaper Edition. *Post 8vo.* 1s.

Grey. THE STORY OF CHRIS. By ROWLAND GREY, Author of 'Lindenblumen,' etc. *Crown 8vo.* 5s.

Dicker. A CAVALIER'S LADYE. By CONSTANCE DICKER. *With Illustrations. Crown 8vo.* 3s. 6d.

Dickinson. A VICAR'S WIFE. By EVELYN DICKINSON.
Crown 8vo. *6s.*

Prowse. THE POISON OF ASPS. By R. ORTON PROWSE.
Crown 8vo. *6s.*

Taylor. THE KING'S FAVOURITE. By UNA TAYLOR.
Crown 8vo. *6s.*

Novel Series

MESSRS. METHUEN will issue from time to time a Series
of copyright Novels, by well-known Authors, handsomely
bound, at the above popular price of three shillings and six-
pence. The first volumes (ready) are :—

$3/6$

1. THE PLAN OF CAMPAIGN. By F. MABEL ROBINSON.

2. JACQUETTA. By S. BARING GOULD, Author of ' Mehalah,
etc.

3. MY LAND OF BEULAH. By Mrs. LEITH ADAMS (Mrs.
De Courcy Laffan).

4. ELI'S CHILDREN. By G. MANVILLE FENN.

5. ARMINELL : A Social Romance. By S. BARING GOULD,
Author of ' Mehalah,' etc.

6. DERRICK VAUGHAN, NOVELIST. With Portrait of
Author. By EDNA LYALL, Author of ' Donovan,' etc.

7. DISENCHANTMENT. By F. MABEL ROBINSON.

8. DISARMED. By M. BETHAM EDWARDS.

9. JACK'S FATHER. By W. E. NORRIS.

10. MARGERY OF QUETHER. By S. BARING GOULD.

11. A LOST ILLUSION. By LESLIE KEITH.

12. A MARRIAGE AT SEA. By W. CLARK RUSSELL.

13. MR. BUTLER'S WARD. By F. MABEL ROBINSON.

14. URITH. By S. BARING GOULD.

15. HOVENDEN, V.C. By F. MABEL ROBINSON.

Other Volumes will be announced in due course.

NEW TWO-SHILLINQ EDITIONS
Crown 8vo, Ornamental Boards.

2/-

ARMINELL. By the Author of 'Mehalah.'

ELI'S CHILDREN. By G. MANVILLE FENN.

DISENCHANTMENT. By F. MABEL ROBINSON.

THE PLAN OF CAMPAIGN. By F. MABEL ROBINSON.

JACQUETTA. By the Author of 'Mehalah.'

Picture Boards.

A DOUBLE KNOT. By G. MANVILLE FENN.

THE QUIET MRS. FLEMING. By RICHARD PRYCE.

JACK'S FATHER. By W. E. NORRIS.

A LOST ILLUSION. By LESLIE KEITH.

Books for Boys and Girls

Walford. A PINCH OF EXPERIENCE. By L. B. WAL-
FORD, Author of 'Mr. Smith.' With Illustrations by GORDON
BROWNE. *Crown 8vo.* 6s.

'The clever authoress steers clear of namby-pamby, and invests her moral with a
fresh and striking dress. There is terseness and vivacity of style, and the illustrations are admirable.'—*Anti-Jacobin.*

Molesworth. THE RED GRANGE. By Mrs. MOLESWORTH,
Author of 'Carrots.' With Illustrations by GORDON BROWNE.
Crown 8vo. 6s.

'A volume in which girls will delight, and beautifully illustrated.'—*Pall Mall
Gazette.*

Clark Russell. MASTER ROCKAFELLAR'S VOYAGE. By
W. CLARK RUSSELL, Author of 'The Wreck of the Grosvenor,' etc.
Illustrated by GORDON BROWNE. *Crown 8vo.* 3s. 6d.

'Mr. Clark Russell's story of "Master Rockafellar's Voyage" will be among the
favourites of the Christmas books. There is a rattle and "go" all through it, and
its illustrations are charming in themselves, and very much above the average in
the way in which they are produced.—*Guardian.*

Author of 'Mdle. Mori.' THE SECRET OF MADAME DE
Monluc. By the Author of 'The Atelier du Lys,' 'Mdle. Mori.'
Crown 8vo. 3s. 6d.

'An exquisite literary cameo.'—*World.*

Manville Fenn. SYD BELTON : Or, The Boy who would not go to Sea. By G. MANVILLE FENN, Author of 'In the King's Name,' etc. Illustrated by GORDON BROWNE. *Crown 8vo.* 3s. 6d.

'Who among the young story-reading public will not rejoice at the sight of the old combination, so often proved admirable—a story by Manville Fenn, illustrated by Gordon Browne ! The story, too, is one of the good old sort, full of life and vigour, breeziness and fun. —*Journal of Education.*

Parr. DUMPS. By Mrs. PARR, Author of 'Adam and Eve,' 'Dorothy Fox,' etc. Illustrated by W. PARKINSON. *Crown 8vo.* 3s. 6d.

'One of the prettiest stories which even this clever writer has given the world for a long time.'—*World.*

Meade. A GIRL OF THE PEOPLE. By L. T. MEADE, Author of 'Scamp and I,' etc. Illustrated by R. BARNES. *Crown 8vo.* 3s. 6d.

'An excellent story. Vivid portraiture of character, and broad and wholesome lessons about life.'—*Spectator.*
'One of Mrs. Meade's most fascinating books.'—*Daily News.*

Meade. HEPSY GIPSY. By L. T. MEADE. Illustrated by EVERARD HOPKINS. *Crown 8vo,* 2s. 6d.

'Mrs. Meade has not often done better work than this.'—*Spectator.*

Meade. THE HONOURABLE MISS : A Tale of a Country Town. By L. T. MEADE, Author of 'Scamp and I,' 'A Girl of the People,' etc. With Illustrations by EVERARD HOPKINS. *Crown 8vo,* 3s. 6d.

Adams. MY LAND OF BEULAH. By MRS. LEITH ADAMS. With a Frontispiece by GORDON BROWNE. *Crown 8vo,* 3s. 6d.

English Leaders of Religion

Edited by A. M. M. STEDMAN, M.A. *With Portrait, crown 8vo,* 2s. 6d.

A series of short biographies, free from party bias, of the most prominent leaders of religious life and thought in this and the last century.

2/6

The following are already arranged—

CARDINAL NEWMAN. By R. H. HUTTON.   [*Ready.*

'Few who read this book will fail to be struck by the wonderful insight it displays into the nature of the Cardinal's genius and the spirit of his life.'—WILFRID WARD, in the *Tablet.*
'Full of knowledge, excellent in method, and intelligent in criticism. We regard it as wholly admirable.'—*Academy.*

JOHN WESLEY. By J. H. OVERTON, M.A.   [*Ready.*
'It is well done : the story is clearly told, proportion is duly observed, and there is no lack either of discrimination or of sympathy.'—*Manchester Guardian.*

BISHOP WILBERFORCE. By G. W. DANIEL, M.A. [*Ready.*

CHARLES SIMEON. By H. C. G. MOULE, M.A.   [*Ready.*

JOHN KEBLE. By W. LOCK, M.A.   [*Nov.*

F. D. MAURICE. By COLONEL F. MAURICE, R.E.

THOMAS CHALMERS. By Mrs. OLIPHANT.

CARDINAL MANNING. By A. W. HUTTON, M.A. [*Ready.*

Other volumes will be announced in due course.

University Extension Series

A series of books on historical, literary, and scientific subjects, suitable for extension students and home reading circles. Each volume will be complete in itself, and the subjects will be treated by competent writers in a broad and philosophic spirit.

Edited by J. E. SYMES, M.A.,
Principal of University College, Nottingham.

Crown 8vo.   2s. 6d.

2|6

The following volumes are ready :—

THE INDUSTRIAL HISTORY OF ENGLAND. By H. DE B. GIBBINS, M.A., late Scholar of Wadham College, Oxon., Cobden Prizeman. *Second Edition.* With Maps and Plans.   [*Ready.*
'A compact and clear story of our industrial development. A study of this concise but luminous book cannot fail to give the reader a clear insight into the principal phenomena of our industrial history. The editor and publishers are to be congratulated on this first volume of their venture, and we shall look with expectant interest for the succeeding volumes of the series.'—*University Extension Journal.*

A HISTORY OF ENGLISH POLITICAL ECONOMY. By L. L. PRICE, M.A., Fellow of Oriel College, Oxon.

PROBLEMS OF POVERTY: An Inquiry into the Industrial Conditions of the Poor. By J. A. HOBSON, M.A.

VICTORIAN POETS. By A. SHARP.

THE FRENCH REVOLUTION. By J. E. SYMES, M.A.

PSYCHOLOGY. By F. S. GRANGER, M.A., Lecturer in Philosophy at University College, Nottingham.

THE EVOLUTION OF PLANT LIFE: Lower Forms. By G. MASSEE, Kew Gardens. With Illustrations.

AIR AND WATER. Professor V. B. LEWES, M.A. Illustrated.

THE CHEMISTRY OF LIFE AND HEALTH. By C. W. KIMMINS, M.A. Camb. Illustrated.

THE MECHANICS OF DAILY LIFE. By V. P. SELLS, M.A. Illustrated.

ENGLISH SOCIAL REFORMERS. H. DE B. GIBBINS, M.A.

ENGLISH TRADE AND FINANCE IN THE SEVENTEENTH CENTURY. By W. A. S. HEWINS, B.A.

The following volumes are in preparation :—

NAPOLEON. By E. L. S. HORSBURGH, M.A. Camb., U. E. Lecturer in History.

ENGLISH POLITICAL HISTORY. By T. J. LAWRENCE, M.A., late Fellow and Tutor of Downing College, Cambridge, U. E. Lecturer in History.

AN INTRODUCTION TO PHILOSOPHY. By J. SOLOMON, M.A. Oxon., 'ate Lecturer in Philosophy at University College, Nottingham.

THE EARTH : An Introduction to Physiography. By E. W. SMALL, M.A.

Social Questions of To-day

Edited by H. DE B. GIBBINS, M.A.

Crown 8vo, 2s. 6d.   2/6

A series of volumes upon those topics of social, economic, and industrial interest that are at the present moment foremost in the public mind. Each volume of the series will be written by an author who is an acknowledged authority upon the subject with which he deals.

The following Volumes of the Series are ready :—

TRADE UNIONISM—NEW AND OLD. By G. HOWELL, M.P., Author of ' The Conflicts of Capital and Labour.'

THE CO-OPERATIVE MOVEMENT TO-DAY. By G. J. HOLYOAKE, Author of 'The History of Co-operation.'

MUTUAL THRIFT. By Rev. J. FROME WILKINSON, M.A., Author of 'The Friendly Society Movement.'

PROBLEMS OF POVERTY : An Inquiry into the Industrial Conditions of the Poor. By J. A. HOBSON, M.A.

THE COMMERCE OF NATIONS. By C. F. BASTABLE, M.A., Professor of Economics at Trinity College, Dublin.

THE ALIEN INVASION. By W. H. WILKINS, B.A., Secretary to the Society for Preventing the Immigration of Destitute Aliens.

THE RURAL EXODUS. By P. ANDERSON GRAHAM.

LAND NATIONALIZATION. By HAROLD COX, B.A.

A SHORTER WORKING DAY. By H. DE B. GIBBINS (Editor), and R. A. HADFIELD, of the Hecla Works, Sheffield.

The following Volumes are in preparation :—

ENGLISH SOCIALISM OF TO-DAY. By HUBERT BLAND one of the Authors of 'Fabian Essays.'

POVERTY AND PAUPERISM. By Rev. L. R. PHELPS, M.A., Fellow of Oriel College, Oxford.

ENGLISH LAND AND ENGLISH MEN. By Rev. C. W. STUBBS, M.A., Author of 'The Labourers and the Land.'

CHRISTIAN SOCIALISM IN ENGLAND. By Rev. J CARTER, M.A., of Pusey House, Oxford.

THE EDUCATION OF THE PEOPLE. By J. R. DIGGLE, M.A., Chairman of the London School Board.

WOMEN'S WORK. By LADY DILKE, MISS BEILLEY, and MISS ABRAHAM.

RAILWAY PROBLEMS PRESENT AND FUTURE. By R. W. BARNETT, M.A., Editor of the 'Railway Times.'

Printed by T. and A. CONSTABLE, Printers to Her Majesty, at the Edinburgh University Press.

www.ingramcontent.com/pod-product-compliance
Lightning Source LLC
Chambersburg PA
CBHW021037030726
47496CB00006B/1583